## HER OWN RULES

"Clever . . . a satisfying fary tale, with a '90s twist."
—*People*

"Barbra Taylor Bradford can always be relied on to tell a good story, and she does just that in *Her Own Rules*."
—*The Chattanooga Times*

## LOVE IN ANOTHER TOWN

"Well written and tells a good story . . . A true Barbra Taylor Bradford novel."
—*Brimingham Post-Herald*

"A touching, moving and dramatic page turner."
—*Times* (Milford, NE)

## DANGEROUS TO KNOW

"Has all the earmarks that made Bradford an icon of the contemporary novel."
—*News-Progress* (Chase City, VA)

"A wonderful book of mystery, ingrigue and love."
—*Times* (Valdosta, GA)

road, where Constable O'Shea could be found when he was on his beat.

Letting go of her mother's hand, Mari headed upstairs. She went to the bathroom, washed her face and hands, cleaned her teeth, and got dressed in the cotton shorts and top she had worn the day before. After buckling on her sandals, she returned to the kitchen.

Mari stood over Kate, staring down at her for a moment or two, her alarm and concern flaring up in her more than ever. And then, turning on her heel, decisively, she hurried outside into the sunny morning air.

Mari raced down the garden path and out onto the tree-lined lane, her feet flying as she ran all the way to the main road. It was there that the police box was located. Painted dark blue and large enough to accommodate two policemen if necessary, the box was a great convenience for the bobby on the beat. Fitted out with a telephone, running water, and a gas burner, it was there that a policeman could make a cup of tea, eat a sandwich, write up a report, and phone the main police station when he had to report in or request help. These police boxes were strategically placed in cities and towns all over England, and were indispensable to the bobbies on the beat, especially when they were on night duty and when the weather was bad.

By the time Mari reached the police box she was panting and out of breath. But much to her relief Constable O'Shea was there. He'll help me, I know not at first glance. But as she peered around the room, she suddenly saw her mother on the floor near the stove.

"Mam! Mam!" she shouted, ran around the table, and came to a standstill in front of her mother. Kate was lying in a crumpled heap; her eyes were closed and her face was deathly white.

Mari saw that there was blood on her mother's nightgown, and she was so frightened she could not move for a moment. Then she hunkered down and took hold of her mother's hand. It was cold. Cold as ice.

"Mam, Mam," she wailed in a tremulous voice, the fear intensifying. "What's the matter, Mam?" Kate did not answer; she simply lay there.

Mari touched her cheek. It was as cold as her hand.

The child remained with her mother for a few minutes, patting her hand, touching her face, endeavoring to rouse her, but to no avail. Tears welled in Mari's eyes and rolled down her cheeks. A mixture of panic and worry assailed her; she did not know what to do.

Eventually it came to her. She remembered what her mother had always told her: "If there's ever anything wrong, an emergency, and I'm not here, go and find Constable O'Shea. He'll know what's to be done. He'll help you."

Reluctant though she was to leave her mother, Mari now realized that this was exactly what she must do. She must go to the police box on the main

"A vibrantly characterized leading lady and a glimpse at the dazzling world of the rich and powerful. . . . [A] richly woven tale."

—*Working Woman*

"It is easy to want every item Bradford catalogues, easy to imagine wearing it, eating and drinking it, driving it, smelling like it. . . . The geography of *Voice of the Heart* takes a reader to all the right places."

—*Los Angeles Times*

"Meant to be read in a peignoir on a chaise lounge whilst nibbling scented chocolates."

—*Cosmopolitan*

"A captivating work filled with glamour, intrigue and ironic reversal . . . Richly textured, highly entertaining."

—*Booklist*

"Engrossing . . . Stunning."

—*Pittsburgh Press*

"A rich tapestry of love and romance . . . The surprise ending is both poignant and fitting."

—*San Diego Union*

"If you like Victorian splendor [and] long sweet pasages of simple love . . . this one's for you."

—*Oklahoman* (Oklohoma City, OK)

"Moving and unforgettable."

—*Romantic Times*

Books by Barbara Taylor Bradford

*A Secret Affair\**

*Her Own Rules\**

*Love in Another Town\**

*Dangerous to Know\**

*Everything to Gain\**

*A Woman of Substance\**

*Voice of the Heart\**

*Hold the Dream\**

*Act of Will\**

*To Be the Best\**

*The Women in His Life*

*Remember*

*Angel*

\*Available from HarperCollins*Publishers*

# Barbara
# Taylor
# Bradford

---

## *HER OWN RULES*

---

📚 HarperPaperbacks
*A Division of HarperCollinsPublishers*

■ HarperPaperbacks
*A Division of* HarperCollins*Publishers*
10 East 53rd Street, New York, N.Y. 10022-5299

This is a work of fiction. The characters, incidents, and
dialogues are products of the author's imagination and are not to
be construed as real. Any resemblance to actual events or
persons, living or dead, is entirely coincidental.

ISBN 0-06-109586-9

HarperCollins®, ■®, and HarperPaperbacks™
are trademarks of HarperCollins*Publishers* Inc.

Cover photography by Adam Smith/Westlight;
Hallinan/FPG International.

A hardcover edition of this book was published in 1996 by
HarperCollins*Publishers*.

First HarperPaperbacks printing: June 1997

Printed in the United States of America

Visit HarperPaperbacks on the World Wide Web at
http://www.harpercollins.com/paperbacks

❖ 10 9 8 7 6 5 4 3 2 1

*For Bob, with love*

# CONTENTS

| | | |
|---|---|---|
| Prologue | TIME PAST | 1 |
| Part One | TIME PRESENT | 17 |
| Part Two | TIME PRESENT, TIME PAST | 181 |
| Epilogue | TIME FUTURE | 329 |

# Prologue

## *TIME PAST*

The child sat on a rock perched high up on the river's bank. Elbows on knees, chin cupped in hands, she sat perfectly still, her eyes trained on the family of ducks circling around on the surface of the dark water.

Her eyes were large, set wide apart, grayish-green in color and solemn, and her small face was serious. But from time to time a smile would tug at her mouth as she watched the antics of the ducklings.

It was a bright day in August.

The sky was a piercingly blue arc unblemished by cloud, the golden sun a perfect sphere, and on this balmy summer's afternoon nothing stirred. Not a blade of grass or a leaf moved; the only sounds were the faint buzzing of a bee hovering above roses rambling along a crumbling brick wall, the splash of water rushing down the dappled stones of the river's bed.

The child remained fascinated by the wildlife on the river, and so intent was she in her concentration, she barely moved. It was only when she heard her name being called that she bestirred herself and glanced quickly over her shoulder.

Instantly she scrambled to her feet, waving at the young woman who stood near the door of the cottage set back from the river.

"Mari! Come on! Come in!" the woman called, beckoning to the child as she spoke.

It took Mari only a moment to open the iron gate in the brick wall, and then she was racing along the dirt path, her plump little legs running as fast as they could.

"Mam! Mam! You're back!" she cried, rushing straight into the woman's outstretched arms, almost staggering in her haste to get to her.

The young woman caught her daughter, held her close, and nuzzled her neck. She murmured, "I've a special treat for tea," and then she looked down into the child's bright young face, her own suddenly serious. "I thought I told you not to go down to the river alone, Mari, it's dangerous," she chastised the girl, but she did so softly and her expression was as loving as it always was.

"I only sit on the rock, Mam, I don't go near the edge," Mari answered, lifting her eyes to her mother's. "Eunice said I could go and watch the baby ducks."

The woman sighed under her breath. Straightening, she took hold of the child's hand and led her into the cottage. Once they were inside, she addressed the girl who was sitting in a chair at the far end of the kitchen, reading a book.

"Eunice, I don't want Mari going to the river alone, she might easily slip and fall in, and then where would you be? Why, you wouldn't even know it had happened. And I've told you this so many times before. Eunice, are you listening to me?"

"Yes, Mrs. Sanderson. And I'm sorry, I won't let her go there by herself again."

"You'd better not," Kate Sanderson said evenly, but despite her neutral tone there was no doubt from the look in her eyes that she was annoyed.

Turning away abruptly, Kate went and filled the teakettle, put it on the gas stove, and struck a match.

The girl slapped her book shut and rose. "I'll get off then, Mrs. Sanderson, now that you're home."

Kate nodded. "Thanks for baby-sitting."

"Shall I come tomorrow?" the teenager asked in a surly voice as she crossed the kitchen floor. "Or can you manage?"

"I think so. But please come on Friday morning for a few hours. That would help me."

"I'll be here. Is nine all right?"

"That's fine," Kate responded, and forced a smile despite her lingering irritation with the teenager.

"Ta'rar, Mari," Eunice said, grinning at the child.

"Ta'rar, Eunice," Mari answered, and fluttered her small, chubby fingers in a wave.

When they were alone, Kate said to her five-year-old daughter, "Go and wash your hands, Mari, that's a good girl, and then we'll have our tea."

The child did as she was bidden, and went upstairs to the bathroom, where she washed her hands and dried them. A few seconds later, she returned to the kitchen; this was the hub of the house and the room they used the most. It was good sized and rustic. There was a big stone fireplace with an old-fashioned oven built next to it, lattice windows over the sink, wooden beams on the ceiling and brightly colored rag rugs covered the stone floor.

Aside from being warm and welcoming, even cozy, it was a neat and tidy room. Everything was in its proper place; pots and pans gleamed, and the two windows behind the freshly laundered lace curtains sparkled in the late afternoon sunshine. Kate took pride in her home, and this showed in the care and attention she gave it.

Mari ran across to the table in the center of the floor, which her mother had covered with a white tablecloth and set for tea, and scrambled up onto one of the straight wooden chairs.

She sat waiting patiently, watching Kate moving with swiftness, bringing plates of sandwiches and scones to the table, turning off the whistling kettle, pouring hot water onto the tea leaves in the brown teapot, which Kate always said made the tea taste all that much better.

The child loved her mother, and this adoration shone on her face as her eyes followed Kate everywhere. She was content now that her mother had come home. Kate had been out for most of the day. Mari missed her when she was gone, even if this was for only a short while. Her mother was her entire world. To the five-year-old, Kate was the perfect being, with her gentle face, her shimmering red-gold hair, clear blue eyes and loving nature. They were always together, inseparable really, for the feeling was mutual. Kate loved her child to the exclusion of all else.

Kate moved between the gas oven and the countertop next to the sink, bringing things to the table, and when finally she sat down opposite Mari, she said, "I bought your favorite sausage rolls at the bakery in town, Mari. Eat one now, lovey, while it's still warm from the oven."

Mari beamed at her. "Oooh, Mam, I do love 'em."

"Them," Kate corrected her softly. "Always say them, Mari, not 'em."

The child nodded her understanding and reached for a sausage roll, eating it slowly but with great relish. Once she had finished, she eyed the plates of sandwiches hungrily. There were various kinds— cucumber, polony, tomato, and egg salad. Mari's mouth watered, but because her mother had taught her manners, had told her never to grab for food greedily, she waited for a second or two, sipped the glass of milk her mother had placed next to her plate.

Presently, when she thought enough time had elapsed, she reached for a cucumber sandwich and bit into it, savoring its moist crispiness.

Mother and child exchanged a few desultory words as they munched on the small tea sandwiches Kate had made, but mostly they ate in silence, enjoying the food thoroughly. Both of them were ravenous.

Mari had not had a proper lunch that day because Eunice had ruined the cottage pie her mother had left for them, and which had needed only to be reheated. The baby-sitter had left it in the oven far too long, and it had burned to a crisp. They had had to make do with bread and jam and an apple each.

Kate was starving because she had skipped lunch altogether. She had been tramping the streets of the nearby town, trying to find a job, and she had not had the time or the inclination to stop at one of the local cafes for a snack.

Kate's hopes had been raised at her last interview earlier that afternoon just before she had returned home. There was a strong possibility that she would get a job at the town's most fashionable dress shop, Paris Modes. There was a vacancy for a salesperson and the manager had seemed to like her, had told her to come back on Friday morning to meet the owner of the shop. This she fully intended to do. Until then she was keeping her fingers crossed, praying that her luck was finally about to change for the better.

Once Kate had assuaged her hunger, she got up and went to the pantry. The thought of the job filled her with newfound hope and her step was lighter than usual as she brought out the bowl of strawberries and jug of cream.

Carrying them back to the table, she smiled with pleasure when she saw the look of delight on her child's face.

"Oh Mam, *strawberries,*" Mari said, and her eyes shone.

"I told you I had a treat for you!" Kate exclaimed, giving Mari a generous portion of the berries, adding a dollop of cream and then serving herself.

"But we have treats only on special days, Mam. Is today special?" the child asked.

"It might turn out to be," Kate said enigmatically. And then seeing the look of puzzlement on Mari's face, she added, "Anyway, it's nice to have a treat on days that aren't particularly special. That way, the treat's a bigger surprise, isn't it?"

Mari laughed and nodded.

As so often happens in England, the warm August afternoon turned into a chilly evening.

A fine rain had been falling steadily since six o'clock and there was a dank mist on the river; this had slowly crept across the low-lying meadows and fields surrounding the cottage, obscuring almost everything. Trees and bushes had taken on strange new shapes, looked like inchoate monsters and illusory beings out there beyond the windows of the cottage.

For once Mari was glad to be tucked up in her bed. "Tell me a story, Mam," she begged, slipping farther down under the warm covers.

Kate sat on the bed and straightened the top of the sheet, saying as she did, "What about a poem instead? You're always telling me you like poetry."

"Tell me the one about the magic wizard."

Kate smoothed a strand of light brown hair away from Mari's face. "You mean *The Miraculous Stall*, don't you, angel?"

"That's it," the child answered eagerly, her glowing eyes riveted on her mother's pretty face.

Slowly Kate began to recite the poem in her soft, mellifluous voice.

> *A wizard sells magical things at this stall,*
> *Astonishing gifts you can see if you call.*
> *He can give you a river's bend*
> *And moonbeam light,*
> *Every kind of let's pretend,*
> *A piece of night.*
> *Half a mile,*
> *A leaf's quiver,*
> *An elephant's smile,*
> *A snake's slither.*
> *A forgotten dream,*
> *A frog's croaks,*
> *Firefly gleam,*
> *A stone that floats.*
> *Crystal snowflakes,*
> *Dew from flowers,*
> *Lamb's tail shakes,*
> *The clock's hours.*
> *But—surprise!*

> *Not needle eyes.*
> *Those he does not sell at all,*
> *At his most miraculous stall.*

Kate smiled at her daughter when she finished, loving her so much. Yet again she smoothed the tumbling hair away from Mari's face and kissed the tip of her nose.

Mari said, "It's my best favorite, Mam."

"Mmmmm, I know it is, and you've had a lot of your favorite things today, little girl. But now it's time for you to go to sleep. It's getting late, so come on, snuggle down in bed . . . have you said your prayers?"

The child shook her head.

"You must always remember to say them, Mari. I do. Every night. And I have since I was small as you are now."

Mari clasped her hands together and closed her eyes.

Carefully she said: "Matthew, Mark, Luke, and John, bless this bed that I lay on. Four corners to my bed, four angels round my head. One to watch and one to pray and two to keep me safe all day. May the grace of Our Lord Jesus Christ, the love of God and the fellowship of the Holy Spirit be with us all now and forevermore. Amen. God bless Mam and keep her safe. God bless me and keep me safe. And make me a good girl."

Opening her eyes, Mari looked at Kate intently. "I am a good girl, aren't I, Mam?"

"Of course you are, darling," Kate answered.

"The best girl I know. My girl." Leaning forward, Kate put her arms around her small daughter and hugged her close.

Mari's arms went around Kate's neck and the two of them clung together. But after a moment or two of this intimacy and closeness, Kate released her grip and settled Mari down against the pillows.

Bending over the child, she kissed her cheek and murmured, "God bless. Sweet dreams. I love you, Mari."

"I love you, Mam."

Wide rafts of sunlight slanted through the window, filling the small bedroom with radiance. The constant sunshine flooding across Mari's face awakened her. Opening her eyes, blinking and adjusting herself to the morning light, she sat up.

Mari had recently learned to tell the time, and so she glanced over at the clock on the bedside stand. It was nearly nine. This surprised the child; her mother was usually up and about long before this time every morning, calling her to come down for breakfast well before eight o'clock.

Slipping out of bed, thinking that her mother had overslept, Mari trotted across the upstairs hall to her mother's bedroom. The bed was empty. Holding on to the banister, the way she had been taught, she went down the stairs carefully.

Much to Mari's further surprise, her mother was nowhere to be seen in the kitchen either. At least,

he will, she thought as she came to a stop in front of him.

The policeman was standing in the doorway of the box, smoking a cigarette. He threw it down and stubbed his toe on it when he saw Mari.

Taking a closer look at the panting child, Patrick O'Shea immediately detected the fear in her eyes and saw that she was in a state of great agitation. Recognizing at once that something was terribly wrong, he bent over her, took hold of her hand, and looked into her small, tear-stained face. "What's the matter, Mari love?" he asked gently.

"It's me mam," Mari cried, her voice rising shrilly. "She's lying on the kitchen floor. I can't make her wake up." Mari began to cry even though she was trying hard to be brave. "There's blood. On her nightgown."

Constable O'Shea had known Mari all of her young life, and he was well aware that she was a good little girl, well brought up and certainly not one for playing tricks or prone to exaggeration. And in any case her spiraling anxiety was enough to convince him that something had gone wrong at Hawthorne Cottage.

"Just give me a minute, Mari," he said, stepping inside the police box. "Then we'll go home and see what's to be done." He phoned the police station, asked for an ambulance to be sent to Hawthorne Cottage at once, closed the door, and locked it behind him.

Reaching down, he swung the child up into his

arms, making soothing noises and hushing sounds as he did so.

"Now then, love, let's be on our way back to your house to see how your mam is, and I'm sure we can soon put everything right."

"But she's dead," Mari sobbed. "Me mam's dead."

# PART ONE

---

# *TIME PRESENT*

---

# CHAPTER ONE

Meredith Stratton stood at the large plate-glass window in her private office which looked downtown, marveling at the gleaming spires rising up in front of her. The panoramic vista of the Manhattan skyline was always eye-catching, but tonight it looked more spectacular than ever.

It was a January evening at the beginning of 1995, and the sky was ink black and clear, littered with stars. There was even a full moon. Not even a Hollywood set designer could have done it better, Meredith thought, there's no improving on nature. And then she had to admit that it was the soaring skyscrapers and the overall architecture of the city that stunned the eye.

The Empire State Building still wore its gaudy Christmas colors of vivid red and green; to one side of it, slightly to the left, was the more sedate

Chrysler Building with its slender art deco spire illuminated with pure white lights.

Those two famous landmarks dominated the scene, as they always did, but that evening the entire skyline seemed to have acquired more glittering aspects than ever, seemed more pristinely etched against the dark night sky.

"There's nowhere in the world quite like New York," Meredith said out loud.

"I agree."

Meredith swung around to see her assistant, Amy Brandt, standing in the doorway of her office.

"You gave me a start, creeping in on me like that," Meredith exclaimed with a grin, and then turned back to the window. "Amy, come and look. The city takes my breath away."

Amy closed the door behind her and walked across the room. She was petite and dark-haired in contrast to Meredith, who was tall and blonde. Amy felt slightly dwarfed by her boss, who stood five feet seven in her stocking feet. But since Meredith always wore high heels, she generally towered over most people, and this gave Amy some consolation, made her feel less like a munchkin.

Gazing out of the window, Amy said, "You're right, Meredith, Manhattan's looking sensational, almost unreal."

"There's a certain clarity about the sky tonight, even though it's dark," Meredith pointed out. "There're no clouds at all, and the lights of the city are creating a wonderful glow. . . . "

The two women stood looking out the window for a few seconds longer, and then, turning away, moving toward her desk, Meredith said, "I just need to go over a couple of things with you, Amy, and then you can go." She glanced at her watch. "It's seven already. Sorry to have kept you so late."

"It's not a problem. And you'll be away for a week, so I'll be able to take it easy while you're gone."

Meredith laughed and raised a perfectly shaped blonde brow. "You taking it easy would be the miracle of the century. You're a workaholic."

"Oh no, not me, that's you, lady boss. You take first prize in that category."

Meredith's deep green eyes crinkled at the corners as she laughed again, and then, pulling a pile of manila files toward her, she opened the top one, glanced down at the sheet of figures, and studied them for a split second.

Finally, she looked up and said, "I'll be gone for longer than a week, Amy. I think it will be two at least. I've quite a lot to do in London and Paris. Agnes is very set on buying that old manor house in Montfort-L'Amaury, and you know she's like a dog with a bone when she gets her teeth into something. However, I'm going to have to work very closely with her on this one."

"From the photographs she sent it looks like a beautiful property, and it's perfect for us," Amy volunteered, and then asked, "You're not suddenly against it, are you?"

"No, I'm not. And what you say is true, it is ideal

for Havens. My only worry is how much do we have to spend in order to turn that old house into a comfortable inn with all the modern conveniences required by the seasoned, indeed pampered, traveler? That's the key question. Agnes gets rather vague when it comes to money, you know that. The cost of new plumbing is not something that concerns her particularly, or even interests her. I'm afraid practicalities have always eluded Agnes."

"She's very creative, though, especially when it comes to marketing the inns."

"True. And I'm usually stuck with the plumbing."

"And the decorating. Let's not forget that, Meredith. You know you love designing the inns, putting your own personal stamp on them, not to mention everything in them."

"I do enjoy that part of it, yes. On the other hand, I must consider the costs, and more than ever, this time around. Agnes can't put up any more of her own money, so she won't be involved in the purchase of the manor or the cost of its remodeling. And the same applies to Patsy in England, she can't offer any financial help either. I have to raise the money myself. And I will. Agnes and Patsy are somewhat relieved that I'll be taking care of the financing, but, more so than ever, I will have to keep a tight rein on the two of them when it comes to the remodeling."

"Are you sure you want to go ahead with the new inns in Europe?" Amy asked. Until that moment she had not realized that Meredith would be doing all the financing, and she detected a degree of worry in her voice.

"Oh yes, I do want to buy them. We have to acquire additional inns in order to expand properly. Not that I want the company to become too big. I think six hotels is enough, Amy, certainly that number's just about right for me, easy to manage, as long as Agnes is running the French end and Patsy the English."

"Six," Amy repeated, eyeing Meredith quizzically. "Are you trying to tell me something?"

Meredith looked baffled. "I'm not following you."

"You said six inns are easy to manage, but with the two new ones in Europe you'll actually own seven, if you count the three here. Are you thinking of selling off one of the American hostelries?"

"I have been toying with the idea," Meredith admitted.

"Silver Lake Inn would bring in the most money," Amy remarked. "After all, it's the most successful of the three."

Meredith stared at Amy.

Suddenly she felt the same tight pain in her chest that she had the week before, when Henry Raphaelson, her friendly private banker, had uttered the same words over lunch at '21'.

"I could never sell Silver Lake," Meredith answered at last, repeating what she had said to Henry.

"I know what you mean."

No, you don't, Meredith thought, but she remained silent. She simply inclined her head, lowered her eyes, stared at the financial breakdown, the costs of remodeling the manor in Montfort-L'Amaury, but not really concentrating on the figures.

She was thinking of Silver Lake Inn. No one really knew what it meant to her, not even her daughter and her son, who had both been born there. Silver Lake had always been her haven, the first safe haven she had known, and the first real home she had ever had. And Jack and Amelia Silver, the owners, had been the first people who had ever shown her any kindness in her entire life. They had loved and cherished her like a younger sister, nurtured her, brought out her potential—encouraged her talent, helped her to hone her business acumen, applauded her style. And from them she had learned about decency and kindness, dignity and courage.

*Jack and Amelia.* The only family she had ever had. For a moment she saw them both very clearly in her mind's eye. They were the first human beings she had ever loved. There had been no one to love before them. Except Spin, the little dog, and even she had been taken away from her just when they had become attached to each other.

Silver Lake was part of her very being, part of her soul. She knew she could never, would never, sell it whatever the circumstances.

Meredith took a deep breath and eventually the pain in her chest began to subside. Lifting her eyes, focusing on Amy, she remarked almost casually, "I might have a buyer for Hilltops. That's why I've decided to go up to Connecticut tonight."

Amy was surprised, but she merely nodded. "What about Fern Spindle? Don't you think you'd get more for the Vermont inn than for Hilltops?"

"It's certainly a much more valuable property, Amy, that's true, valued in the many millions. But someone has to want it, has to want to buy. Only then does it become viable to me."

Amy nodded.

Meredith went on. "Blanche knows I'm coming up tonight. I'm staying at Silver Lake, there's no point in having her open up the house for one night. Jonas will stay over and drive me up to Sharon tomorrow morning, to meet the potential buyers. After the meeting at Hilltops I'll come straight back to the city, and I'll leave for London on Saturday as planned."

Meredith picked up a manila folder and handed it to Amy. "Here're my letters, all signed, and a bunch of checks for Lois." Leaning back in her chair, she finished with, "Well, I guess that's it."

"No . . . you have e-mail, Meredith."

Meredith swung around to face her computer on the narrow table behind her chair, peered at the screen.

```
Thurs. Jan 5 1995
Hi Mom:


Thanks for check. Helps. Have a fab
trip. Go get 'em. Bring back the
bacon. Luv ya loads.

JON
```

"Well, well, doesn't he have a way with words," Meredith said pithily, shaking her head. But she was smiling inwardly, thinking of her twenty-one-year-old son, Jonathan, who had always had the ability to amuse her. He had turned out well. Just as his sister had. She was lucky in that respect.

Left alone in her office, Meredith studied the figures from her French partner. She thought they seemed a bit on the high side, and reminded herself that Agnes was not always as practical as she should be when it came to refurbishing. It might be possible to shave them a bit, she decided.

Agnes D'Auberville and she had been involved in business together for the past eight years, and their partnership had been a successful one. They got on well and balanced each other, and Agnes's flair for marketing had helped to put the inns on the map. With her long scarves and trailing skirts she was bohemian but stylish.

Agnes ran the Paris office of Havens Incorporated and oversaw the management of the château-hotel they jointly owned in the Loire Valley. She was unable to participate financially in the acquisition of the manor house in Montfort-L'Amaury, although she was eager that they buy it. "You won't regret it, Meredith, it's a good investment for the company," Agnes had said to her during their phone conversation earlier that day.

Meredith knew that this was true. She also knew that a charming inn, situated only forty-eight kilometers from Paris, and within easy striking distance of

Versailles and the forest of Rambouillet was bound to be a moneymaker, especially if it had a good restaurant.

According to Agnes, she had already lined up a well-known chef, as well as a distinguished architect who would properly redesign the manor house, help to turn it into a comfortable inn.

As for Patsy Canton, her English partner who had come on board ten years earlier, the story was a little different in one respect. Patsy had fallen upon two existing inns for sale and quite by accident. She believed them to be real finds.

One was in Keswick, the famous beauty spot in the Lake District in Cumbria; the other was in the Yorkshire dales near the cathedral towns of York and Ripon. Both were popular places with foreign visitors. Again, such an inn, with its good reputation already established, would more than earn its keep.

Unfortunately, Patsy had the same dilemma as Agnes. She was unable to put up any more money. She had already invested everything she had in Havens Incorporated; her inheritance from her parents had gone into Haddon Fields, the country inn Havens owned in the Cotswolds.

In much the same way Agnes did in Paris, Patsy oversaw the management of Haddon Fields, and ran the small London office of Havens. Her strong suits were management and public relations.

Meredith let out a small sigh, thinking about the problems she was facing. On the other hand, they weren't really unsurmountable problems, and, in the long run, the two new inns in Europe were going to be extremely beneficial to the company.

Expansion had been her idea, and hers alone, and she was determined to see it through; after all, she was the majority stockholder of Havens and the chief executive officer. In essence it was her company, and she was responsible for all of its operations.

Henry Raphaelson had told her at the beginning of the week that the bank would lend her the money she needed for her new acquisitions. The inns Havens already owned would be used as collateral for the loan. But Silver Lake Inn was not included. Henry had agreed to this stipulation of hers, if somewhat reluctantly, because she had convinced him Hilltops would be sold quickly. And hopefully she was right. With a little luck Elizabeth and Philip Morrison would commit to it the next day. Of course they will, she told herself, always the eternal optimist.

Pushing back her chair, Meredith rose and crossed to the lacquered console against the long wall, where she had put her briefcase earlier.

Tall though she was, she had a shapely, feminine figure and long legs. She moved with lithesome grace and swiftness; in fact, she was generally quick in everything she did, and she was full of drive and energy.

At forty-four Meredith Stratton looked younger than her years. This had a great deal to do with her vitality and effervescent personality as well as her youthful face and pale blonde hair worn in a girlish pageboy. This framed her rather angular, well-defined features and arresting green eyes.

Good-looking though she was, it was her pleasant demeanor and a winning natural charm that captivated most people. She had a way about her that was unique, and she left a lasting impression on all who met her.

Meredith carried her briefcase back to the desk, a glass tabletop mounted on steel sawhorses, and filled it with the manila folders and other papers she had been working on all day. After closing it and placing it on the floor, she picked up the phone and dialed her daughter's number.

"It's me," Meredith said when Catherine answered.

"Hi, Mom!" Catherine exclaimed, sounding genuinely pleased to hear her mother's voice. "How're things?"

"Pretty good. I'm off to London and Paris on Saturday."

"Lucky thing! Can I come with you?"

"Of course! I'd love it. You know that, darling."

"I can't, Mom, much as I'd enjoy playing hookey in Paris with you, having a good time. I have to finish the illustrations for Madeleine McGrath's new children's book, and I've several book jackets lined up. Oh but I can dream, can't I?"

"Yes, you can, and I'm so glad things are going well for you with your work. But if you suddenly decided you can get away, call Amy. She'll book your flight and get you a ticket before you can even say Jack Robinson."

Catherine began to laugh. "I haven't heard you use that expression for years, not since I was a kid.

You told me once where it came from, but now I can't remember. It's such an odd expression."

"Yes, it is, and it's something I learnt when I was growing up in Australia. I think it originated in England and was brought over by the Pommies. Australians started to use it, and I guess it became part of our idiomatic speech. Sort of slang, really."

"Now I remember, and you told us that it meant *in a jiffy.*"

"Less than a jiffy, actually," Meredith said, laughing with her daughter. "Anyway, think about coming to Paris or London. You know how much I enjoy traveling with you. How's Keith?"

Catherine let out a long sigh. "He's fantastic . . . yummy."

"You sound happy, Cat."

"Oh I am, Mom, I am. I'm crazy about him."

"Is it getting serious?"

"*Very.*" Catherine cleared her throat. "Mom, I think he's going to propose soon."

For a split second Meredith was taken aback and she was silent at the other end of the phone.

"Mom, are you still there?"

"Yes, darling."

"You do approve . . . don't you?"

"Of course I do. I like Keith a lot, and I was just surprised for a moment, that's all. It seems to have progressed very quickly . . . what I mean is, you haven't known him all that long."

"Six months. That's enough time, isn't it?"

"I suppose so."

Catherine said, "Actually, Keith and I fell in love with each other the moment we met. It was a *coup de foudre*, as the French are wont to say."

Meredith smiled to herself. "Ah yes, struck by lightning . . . I know what you mean."

"Is that how it was with my father?"

Meredith hesitated. "Not really, Cat . . . Well, in a way, yes. Except we didn't admit that to each other for a long time."

"Well, you couldn't, could you. I mean, given the peculiar circumstances. It must've been hell for you."

"No, it wasn't, strangely enough. Anyway, that's an old, *old* story, and now's not the time to start going into it again."

"Was it a *coup de foudre* when you met David?"

"No," Meredith said, and thought of Jonathan's father for the first time in several years. "We loved each other, but it wasn't a . . . crazy love."

"I always knew that, I guess. It's a crazy love between me and Keith, and when he asks me, I'm obviously going to say yes. You really *do* approve, don't you, Mom?" she asked again.

"Very much so, darling, and if he pops the question while I'm in London or Paris, you will let me know at once, won't you?"

"I sure will. And I bet we make you a grandmother before you can say . . . Jack Robinson." Catherine giggled.

Meredith said, "You're not pregnant, are you?"

"Don't be silly, Mom, of course I'm not. But I can't wait to have a baby. Before I get too old."

Meredith burst out laughing. "Don't be so ridiculous, you're only twenty-five."

"I know, but I want to have children while I'm young, the way you did."

"You always were a regular old mother hen, even when you were little. But listen, honey, I'm going to have to go. Jonas is driving me up to Silver Lake Inn tonight. I have a meeting at Hilltops tomorrow. I'll be back in New York tomorrow evening, if you need me. Good night, Cat. I love you."

"I love you too, Mom. Say hello to Blanche and Pete, give them my love. And listen, take care."

"I will. Talk to you tomorrow, and God bless."

After hanging up the phone, Meredith sat at her desk for a moment or two, her thoughts with her daughter. Of course Keith Pearson would propose, and very soon, Meredith was quite certain of that. There was going to be a wedding this year. Her face lit up at the thought of it. Catherine was going to be a beautiful bride, and she would give her daughter a memorable wedding.

Meredith rose, walked over to the window, and stood staring out at the Manhattan skyline. New York City, she murmured to herself, the place I've made my home. Such a long way from Sydney, Australia . . . how far I've come and in so many different ways. I took my terrible life and turned it around. I made a new life for myself. I took the pain and heartbreak and I built on them . . . I used them as pilings upon which to build *my* strong citadel in much the same way the Venetians built theirs on pilings driven into the sandbanks. And I did it all by myself . . . no, not entirely by myself. Jack and Amelia helped me.

Meredith's eyes swept around the elegant room decorated in various shades of pale gray, lavender, and amethyst. They took in the rich silks and velvets used to upholster the sofas and chairs, the sleek gray lacquer finishes on the modern furniture, the French and American modern impressionist paintings by Taurelle, Epko, and Guy Wiggins.

And she saw it as if for the first time, through newly objective eyes, and she could not help wondering what Jack and Amelia would think of it . . . what they would think of all that she had accomplished.

Her throat tightened with a rush of sudden emotion, and she stepped back to the desk and sat down, her eyes now lingering on the two photographs in their silver frames that she always kept there in front of her.

One photograph was of Catherine and Jonathan taken when they were children; Cat had been twelve, Jon eight, and what beauties they had been. Free spirits and so finely wrought.

The other picture was of Amelia and Jack and her. How young she looked. Tanned and blonde and so unsophisticated. She had been just twenty-one years old when the picture was taken at Silver Lake.

Jack and Amelia would be proud of me, she thought. After all, they helped to make me what I am, and in a sense I am their creation. And they are the best part of me.

# Chapter Two

Whenever she came back to Silver Lake, Meredith experienced a feeling of excitement. No matter how long she had been absent, be it months on end, a week, or merely a few days, she returned with a sense of joyousness welling inside, the knowledge that she was coming home.

Tonight was no exception.

Her anticipation started the moment Jonas pulled off Route 45 North near Cornwall, and nosed the car through the big iron gates that marked the entrance to the vast Silver Lake property.

Jonas drove slowly down the road that led to the lake, the inn, and the small compound of buildings on its shores. It was a good road, well illuminated by the old-fashioned street lamps Meredith had installed some years before.

Peering out of the car windows, she could see that Pete had had some of the workers busy with the bulldozer earlier in the day. The road was clear, the snow banked high like giant white hedges, and in the woods that traversed the road on either side there were huge drifts blown by the wind into weird sand-dune shapes.

The branches of the trees were heavy with snow, many of them dripping icicles, and in the moonlight the pristine white landscape appeared to shimmer as if sprinkled with a fine coating of silver dust.

Meredith could not help thinking how beautiful the woods were in their winter garb. But then, this land was always glorious, no matter what the season of the year, and it was so special to her, no other place in the world could compare to it.

The first time she had set eyes on Silver Lake she had been awed by its majestic beauty—the great lake shining in the spring sunlight, a smooth sheet of glass, surrounded by lush meadows and orchards, the whole set in a natural basin created by the soaring wooded hills that rose up to encircle the entire property.

She had fallen in love with it instantly and had gone on loving it with a growing passion ever since.

Twenty-six years ago this year, she thought, I was only eighteen. So long ago, more than half her life ago. And yet it might have been only yesterday, so clear and fresh was the memory in her mind.

She had come to Silver Lake Inn to apply for the job of receptionist, which she had seen advertised in the local paper. The Paulsons, the American family who had brought her with them from Australia as an au pair, were moving to South Africa because of Mr. Paulson's job. She did not want to go there. Nor did she wish to return to her native Australia. Instead, she preferred to stay in America, in Connecticut, to be precise.

It had been the middle of May, not long after her birthday, and she had arrived on a borrowed bicycle, looking a bit windswept, to say the least.

Casting her mind back now, she pictured herself as she had been then—tall, skinny, all arms and legs like a young colt. Yet pretty enough in a fresh young way. She had been full of life and vitality, eager to be helpful, eager to please. That was her basic nature and she was a born peacemaker.

Jack and Amelia Silver had taken to her at once, as she had to them. But they had been concerned about her staying in America without the Paulsons, had inquired about her family in Sydney, and what they would think. Once she explained that her parents were dead, they had been sympathetic, sorry that she had lost them so young. And they had understood then that she had no real reason to go back to the Antipodes.

After they had talked on the phone to Mrs. Paulson, they had hired her on the spot.

And so it had begun, an extraordinary relationship that had changed her life.

Meredith straightened in her seat as the inn came into view. Lights blazed in many of the windows, and this was a welcoming sight. She could hardly wait to be inside, to be with Blanche and Pete, surrounded by so many familiar things in that well-loved place.

Within seconds Jonas was pulling up in front of the inn. He had barely braked when the front door flew open and bright light flooded out onto the wide porch.

A moment later Blanche and Pete O'Brien were at the top of the steps, and as Meredith opened the car door, Pete was already halfway down, exclaiming, "Welcome, Meredith, you've certainly made it in good time despite the snow."

"Hello, Pete," she said as he enveloped her in a hug. She added, as they drew apart, "There's nobody like Jonas when it comes to driving. He's the best."

"That he is. Hi, Jonas, good to see you," Pete said, nodding to the driver, smiling at him. "I'll help you with Mrs. Stratton's bags."

"Evening, Mr. O'Brien, but I can manage. There's nothing much to carry."

Meredith left the two men to deal with the bags, and ran up the steps.

"It's good to be back here, Blanche!"

The two women embraced and then Blanche, smiling up at Meredith, led her inside. "And it's good to have you back, Meredith, if only for one night."

"I wish I could stay longer, but as I explained on the phone, I've got to get back to the city after the meeting at Hilltops tomorrow."

Blanche nodded. "I think you're going to make a deal with the Morrisons. They're awfully eager to buy an inn, get away from New York, lead a different kind of life."

"I'm keeping my fingers crossed," Meredith said, shrugging out of her heavy gray wool cape, throwing it down on a bench.

"I know you'll like them, they're a lovely couple, very sincere, straight as a dye, and quite aside from wanting to start a new business, they love this part of Connecticut."

"And why not, it's God's own country," Meredith murmured. She glanced around the entrance hall. "Everything looks wonderful, Blanche, so warm, welcoming."

Blanche beamed at her. "Thanks, Meredith, you know I love this old place as much as you do. Anyway, you must be starving. I didn't think you'd want a full dinner at this late hour, so I made some smoked salmon sandwiches, and there's fruit and cheese. Oh and I have a hunter's soup bubbling on the stove."

"The soup sounds great. You make the best, and they're usually a meal in themselves. I'm sure Jonas is hungry after the long drive, so perhaps you'd offer him the soup too, and some sandwiches."

"I will."

Pete came in with Meredith's overnight bag and briefcase. "Jonas has gone to park the car," he explained. "I'll take these upstairs."

"Thanks, Pete," Meredith said.

"I've put you in the toile de Jouy suite," Blanche told her, "because I know how much you like it. Now, do you want a tray up there? Or shall I bring it to the bar parlor?"

"I'll have it down here in the parlor, thanks, Blanche," Meredith said, peering into the room that opened off the inn's large entrance hall. "I see you have a fire going . . . that's nice. I think I'll make myself a drink. Would you like one, Blanche?"

"Why not. I'll join you in a vodka and tonic. But first let me go and fix a tray for Jonas, I'll be back in a few minutes." She hurried off in the direction of the kitchen.

Meredith went into the bar parlor, glancing around as she strolled over to the huge stone hearth at the far end of the room. The fire burning brightly, the red carpet, the red velvet sofas and tub chairs covered in red and cream linen, gave the parlor a warm, rosy feeling. This was further enhanced by the red brocade curtains at the leaded windows, the polished mahogany paneled walls, and the red shades on the wall sconces. It was a slightly masculine room in feeling and rather English in overtone; there was a mellowness about it that Meredith had always liked.

The carved mahogany bar was to the left of the fireplace, facing the leaded windows. Meredith went behind it, took two glasses, added ice, and poured a good measure of Stolichnaya Cristal into each one. She smiled to herself when she noticed the small plate of lime wedges next to the ice bucket. Blanche had second-guessed her very accurately. Her old friend had known she would have her drink in here. The bar parlor had always been a favorite spot of hers in the inn, as it was with everyone, because it was so intimate and cozy. And conducive to drinking. Jack had been smart when he had created the bar parlor.

Once she had made the drinks, Meredith went over to the fireplace. She stood with her back to it, enjoying the warmth, sipping her vodka, relaxing as she waited for Blanche, whom she thought had never looked better. If there was a tiny fleck of silver in her bright red hair, she was, nonetheless, as slim as she had been as a girl, and the merry dark-brown eyes were as lively as ever. She's wearing well, Meredith thought, very well indeed.

The two women, who were the same age, had been friends for twenty-four years. Blanche had come to Silver Lake Inn two years after Meredith had taken the job as the receptionist. She had started as a pastry chef in the kitchens, had soon been promoted to chef, since she was an inspired cook. Blanche had enjoyed working in the kitchens until she married Pete, who had always managed the estate for the Silvers, and became pregnant with Billy.

By then Meredith was running the inn, and she offered Blanche the job of assistant manager. Blanche had been delighted to accept the offer at once, glad to be out of the heat, relieved not to lift heavy pots and pans, and thrilled to be able to continue working at the inn.

These days she and Pete ran Silver Lake Inn together and were responsible for its overall management as well as the upkeep of the entire estate. She's
been good for this place, Meredith mused. She's as
passionate about it as I am, and it shows everywhere, and in everything she does.

Blanche interrupted her musings, walking
rapidly into the bar parlor, saying, "By the way,
you're not going to believe this, but we're rather
busy this coming weekend. All the rooms are taken.
And several suites. Unusual for January, I must say,
but I'm not complaining."

"I'm delighted, and in some ways it's not that surprising. A lot of people do like being in the country
in the snowy weather, and this place has such a great
reputation. Thanks, in no uncertain terms, to you
and Pete. I do appreciate all you both do, Blanche."

"We love the inn, you know that."

"By the way, Catherine sends her love to you and
Pete."

Blanche smiled. "And give her ours. How is she,
Meredith?"

"As wonderful as always, and doing so well with
her work; she's turned out to be a fine illustrator.
And, of course, she's madly in love."

"With Keith Pearson?"

Meredith nodded. "She told you?"

"Yes, when you were all here at Thanksgiving."

"I think it's become rather serious."

"Are we looking forward to a wedding?" Blanche
asked, staring at Meredith quizzically.

"I think so . . . I'm pretty sure."

"You will have it here, won't you?"

"Where else, Blanche? Cat was born here, grew up here, and so I'm certain she'll want to be married here. And it is the perfect setting."

"Oh I can't wait to start planning it!" Blanche cried, taking a sip of her drink. "Cheers. And here's to Cat and the wedding."

"The wedding," Meredith said, and lifted her glass as Blanche was doing. She wondered if it was bad luck to drink to something so prematurely.

"*Marquees*. We'll have to have marquees," Blanche said, gazing into space, obviously already envisioning the reception.

"But they'll no doubt get married in the summer," Meredith pointed out.

"Yes, I know. June probably, every girl wants to be a June bride. But it *can* rain up here at that time of year, you know that as well as I do, and it's best to be safe. Oh it'll be great, though. We'll do wonderful flowers and table settings. And a special menu. Oh it's going to be fabulous. Leave it all to me."

Meredith laughed. "I'm happy to, my darling Blanche."

"Good." Blanche sipped her drink, and then suddenly she looked across at Meredith and said, "Do you ever hear from David?"

"David Layton?" Meredith asked, slightly surprised.

"Yes."

"Rarely. Why do you ask?"

"I thought of him just now . . . have you forgotten that you married him here and that I did the entire wedding?"

"No, I hadn't," Meredith said slowly, and began to shake her head. "Funny, isn't it, how someone's name is rarely, if ever, mentioned, and then it comes up twice in one day."

"Who else mentioned David?"

"Catherine. When we were talking on the phone earlier this evening. She asked me if I'd been crazy in love with him, or words to that effect."

"And what did you say?"

"I told her the truth. I said that I hadn't."

"Of course not. You were only crazily in love once, and that was with her father."

Meredith was silent.

"Have you ever wondered what your life would have been like if he hadn't—"

"I really don't want to discuss it," Meredith snapped, cutting in peremptorily. Then she bit her lip, looking chagrined. "I'm sorry, Blanche, I didn't mean to bite your head off like that, it's just that I prefer to leave that particular subject matter alone tonight. It's been a long day and I don't really feel like delving into the tragedies of the past."

Blanche smiled gently. "It's my fault. I brought it up and I shouldn't have . . . now you're looking sad . . . I've upset you."

"No, you haven't, I promise you, Blanche."

Deeming it wiser to change the subject, Blanche

put down her drink and said, "By the way, we're going to have to order new carpet for the toile de Jouy suite, and the blue room. There's been some leaks this winter, and the carpets are damaged. I hate to tell you this, but there's also been a leak in your bedroom in the house. I'll show you tomorrow. I'm afraid you'll have to replace the carpet there as well."

"These things happen, Blanche, we know that from years of experience. And even after we put in new roofs last year. I'll call Gary at Stark tomorrow, before I go to London. He's got everything on the computer, so it won't be a problem." Meredith frowned. "The carpets were from the standard lines, weren't they?"

"Yes, I'm sure," Blanche said, and then began to walk toward the door. "It's getting late. I'm going to the kitchen to bring you that bowl of soup."

Meredith put down her glass and followed her. "I'll eat in the kitchen, Blanche, it's much easier."

# Chapter Three

Hilltops, the inn Meredith owned near Sharon, was built on top of a hill, as its name suggested. The site was the highest point above Lake Wononpakook, and the views from the inn's windows were spectacular: endless miles of lake and sky and wooded hills, with hardly another structure in evidence on the expansive land.

The inn started out as a mansion, the summer retreat of one of America's great tycoons, who built it in the late 1930s, sparing no expense. He and his family spent summers there until his death in the mid sixties, when it was sold.

When Meredith bought it in 1981 it had been an inn for almost twenty years, and it was already well established. But it was her stylish refurbishing and the two new restaurants she created that gave it a certain cachet and put it on the map.

Hilltops evoked images of Switzerland in her mind, and turning to Paul Ince, who was the manager of the inn, she said, "I feel as if I'm looking down on Lake Geneva this morning, Paul."

He laughed and answered, "I know what you mean, I always get the sensation of being in the Swiss Alps myself, especially in winter."

Meredith had arrived at Hilltops fifteen minutes earlier, and the two of them stood together in the inn's lovely old pine-paneled library, waiting for the Morrisons to arrive for the meeting.

Glancing out of the window again, Meredith murmured, "All this snow. It really came down this year, but it doesn't seem to have affected business, does it?"

"No, not at all, Meredith. Well, I shouldn't say that. As you know, we did have a few problems last week, and had to close the restaurants for a few days. But we soon got rid of the snow, once the bulldozer was up on the main road here. When it was shifted we were fine." He paused, turned to her. "And we are fine," he reassured her.

"What are your bookings like for the weekend?" she asked.

"Pretty good, twelve out of the fifteen rooms are taken. And both restaurants are almost full. Local trade as well as the hotel guests."

Paul cleared his throat, briefly hesitating, and then said, "I know you'll be able to sell this place, Meredith. Whether it's to the Morrisons or someone else, because it's such a good buy. And I just wanted to say this now . . . I'm really going to miss working with you. You've always been great, such a wonderful boss."

"That's nice of you to say so, Paul, thank you. And I've enjoyed working with *you* all these years. And I couldn't have done it without you. You're definitely a big part of the inn's success, you've put so much of yourself into it, built up the business so well. And as I told you earlier, if the Morrisons do end up taking it over, I'm sure they'll want you to stay on. If *you* want to, that is."

"I do, and when they were over here last weekend they indicated they felt the same way."

"What're your feelings about them? About their intentions, Paul?"

"They're more than interested, Meredith. I'd say they are extremely eager to get their hands on Hilltops, as I told Blanche the other day. It's apparently what they've wanted for the last few years . . . a country inn in Connecticut, far away from the hectic pace of New York City and the rat race of Wall Street and Madison Avenue. New careers for them both. New lifestyles for them and their kids."

"I didn't know they had children," Meredith said, frowning. "Does that mean they'd want to live in the cottage? Your cottage?"

Paul shook his head. "No, Mrs. Morrison's indicated that they're going to keep their house in Lakeville. But if they did want the cottage, Anne and I could always move into the inn until that apartment over the garage was made livable."

Meredith nodded her understanding; she walked over to the fireplace, where she sat down, poured herself another cup of coffee. "Do you want a second cup, Paul?"

"Yes, please." Paul joined her by the fireside.

They sat in silence for a few minutes, drinking their coffee, lost in their own thoughts. It was Meredith who spoke first, when she said, "As you know, the asking price for the inn is four million dollars, and so far I've not budged from that figure. Between us, I would come down a bit, just to make the sale. What's your assessment of them regarding the price?"

"It's hard to say," Paul replied, looking thoughtful. After a moment or two's reflection, he went on. "I'd stick to your guns for a bit and see what happens. But just be mentally prepared to accept three million."

She shook her head. "No way, Paul, I've got to get three and a half million, at least. Anyway, the inn's worth that . . . in fact, it's worth four. My real estate people actually valued it at four and a half."

"But you've always said to me that someone's got to want to buy a property to make it a viable holding, an asset."

"I know, I know, but I really do need three and a half million dollars for my expansion program," Meredith said, putting her cup down with a clatter. "The two inns in Europe are going to cost money, and I'd like to have something left over from this sale for operating costs and to plow back into Havens."

"Look, Meredith, I'm sure the Morrisons are quite well placed. He's worked on Wall Street for years, and she's been one of the partners in an ad agency on Madison Avenue. In any case, when you meet them, talk to them, you'll be able to judge for yourself what the freight can bear."

"Too true . . . why try to second guess?"

There was a knock on the door, and as Paul called, "Come in!" it opened.

The receptionist looked in and said, "Mr. and Mrs. Morrison have arrived."

Paul nodded. "Show them in, Doris, please."

Several seconds later Paul was introducing Elizabeth and Philip Morrison to Meredith. Once the handshakes were over, they all sat down in the chairs near the fire.

Meredith said, "Can I offer you something? Coffee, tea, a soda, perhaps?"

"No, thank you," Mrs. Morrison said.

Her husband shook his head and murmured something about just having had breakfast. Then he began to speak to Paul about the weather, the snow on the roads, and the drive over from Lakeville, where they owned a weekend home.

Mrs. Morrison looked across at Meredith and said, "I love the way you've decorated Hilltops . . . it's so charming and intimate. It reminds me of an English country house."

"Thank you," Meredith said, smiling at the other woman. "I like decorating, creating a look, an ambiance. And lots of comfort for the guests, of course. I think an inn should be a haven, that's why I called my company Havens Incorporated."

Elizabeth Morrison nodded. "Very apt, very apt indeed. And I think all of your little touches are wonderful. The hot water bottles in silk cases, the special reading lights by the bed, the afghans on the chaises, little luxuries like that make all the difference."

"That's what I believe," Meredith murmured, "and that's my policy in all of the inns we own."

"We've always wanted to run an inn like this," Mrs. Morrison confided. "And now's the time to do it, when we're both still young. Also, we want to get out of the city, bring up our three children in the country. The city's become so violent, hard to take in general."

"I understand. I raised two children in Connecticut, and I've always felt lucky that I was able to do so. As you know, since you've been residents up here for a few years, there are plenty of good schools. Yes, it's a great spot for a family."

Elizabeth Morrison was about to say something else, when she caught her husband's warning look; she simply cleared her throat and sat back in her chair, having suddenly become a mere spectator at this meeting.

Meredith, who missed nothing, noticed this infinitesimal exchange. She understood immediately that Philip Morrison did not want his wife saying any more. Nor did he wish her to sound too enthusiastic about the inn. He wanted her to play it cool.

As he had been doing all along. He was obviously ready to deal.

Not giving him an opportunity to start the ball rolling, Meredith jumped in with both feet.

Staring directly at him, fixing him with an appraising eye, she said, "I know you've been back to look at Hilltops many times now, and that you both like it. The question is, do you really want to buy it?"

"Yes," Philip Morrison said. "At the right price. For us, that is."

"The price is four million dollars, Mr. Morrison. I think my real estate lawyer in the city has already told you that."

"He did. But as I told Mr. Melinger, it's a bit steep for me."

"Actually, the inn *is* worth four million dollars, even more if the truth be known," Meredith pointed out. "As a matter of fact, it's true value is four and a half million dollars. You can check that with the real estate people both here and in the city. It just so happens that I'm willing to take less because I'm expanding my company. Otherwise, I'd hold out for the *proper* price, I can assure you."

"I'll give you three million," Philip Morrison said, glanced at his wife, and added, "That's all we can pay, isn't it, Liz?"

Momentarily startled to suddenly be drawn into this exchange, she looked nonplussed. Then she said quickly, emphatically, "We're selling our Manhattan co-op and hoping to get a mortgage on the Lakeville house, and by cashing in some of our other assets, we can raise three million. But that's it."

Meredith gave her a long and thoughtful look but made no comment. Leaning forward, she picked up her cup of coffee and took a sip.

Morrison said, "What do you say, Mrs. Stratton? Will you accept three million?"

"No," Meredith said, looking him right in the eye. "I can't. As I told you, when I first decided to sell Hilltops, my original price was four and a half million dollars, because that *is* its *true value*. It's in perfect condition. New roof, new plumbing, and new wiring in the last few years, among many other major improvements. And there's a great deal of land attached to the inn. I came down in price only because it was suggested I do so by my advisers, in order to sell now. But I must stick at four million."

"Three million and a quarter," Morrison countered.

Meredith pursed her lips and shook her head. "Four."

"Three and a quarter," he offered again.

Meredith let out a small sigh and gave the Morrisons a slow, resigned smile, glancing from one to the other. "I tell you what, I'll take three million seven hundred and fifty thousand."

"I just can't do it," Philip Morrison said.

"But it's a bargain," Meredith stated quietly. "If you consider that the proper price is really four and a half million, I've just come down by three quarters of a million dollars."

Philip Morrison smiled wryly. "But we've always been talking *four* million, not *four and a half,* Mrs. Stratton, let's not forget that, shall we?"

Meredith made no response.

She rose and walked across to the bank of windows overlooking the lake, and stood there staring out at the view for a few moments.

Finally, when she swung around, she said, "You want the inn. I want to sell it. So I'll tell you what I'll do, *I'll* compromise. I'll sell it to you for three point five million."

The Morrisons exchanged pointed glances.

At last Philip Morrison said, "I'd like to do it, but I just don't think I can. I can't raise any more."

"You could go to your bank," Meredith suggested, "and get a loan, or, better still, a mortgage on the inn."

Philip Morrison stared at her. But he remained silent.

"I can introduce you to the right bank," Meredith volunteered, wanting to conclude the deal.

"Do you think they would give me a mortgage on the inn?" he asked, taking the bait.

"I'm pretty certain, yes. There's something else I'll do. I'll have my real estate lawyer structure a reasonable payment schedule, one that won't cripple you."

Elizabeth Morrison said, "That's very decent of you."

Meredith answered, "I want to make the deal and I don't want to gouge you. You want to make the deal and I'm sure you don't want to cheat me."

"Never! We're not people like that!" the other woman exclaimed indignantly.

"I must say, you're making it very tempting," Morrison muttered, directing his gaze at Meredith. "Making it hard to resist."

"Then don't resist, Mr. Morrison," Meredith said, walking back to the fireplace.

He got to his feet when she drew to a stop next to his chair.

Meredith thrust out her hand. "Come on, let's not haggle. Let's make the deal. It's good for us both, beneficial to us both."

He hesitated only fractionally. Then he took her hand and shook it. "All right, Mrs. Stratton, you've got a deal. Three and a half million dollars it is."

Meredith nodded and smiled at him.

He returned her smile.

Elizabeth Morrison came over and shook Meredith's hand.

Paul Ince, who had been on pins and needles throughout this negotiation, congratulated everyone, then said, "I think this calls for a toast. Let's go to the bar and I'll open a bottle of Dom Pérignon."

"What a great idea, Paul," Meredith said, leading the way out of the library.

On the drive back to New York City, Meredith gave only fleeting thought to Hilltops. She had accomplished what she had set out to do; she had sold the inn for the amount she wanted through her shrewdness, and she was well satisfied. Three and a half million dollars would meet her expansion needs more than adequately.

Before leaving the inn, she had settled everything. Arrangements had been made for the Morrisons to meet with her real estate lawyer, who would draw up the necessary documents next week. She had also set up an appointment for them to see Henry Raphaelson. The banker had sounded amenable during the phone call, had assured her he would endeavor to work things out with the Morrisons.

And so she turned her thoughts to other matters as Jonas drove back to Manhattan. Mostly she focused her attention on her trip to England, and on the purchase of an inn there. She was confident she would like one of the two Patsy Canton had found. With luck, she would be able to bring that bit of business to a conclusion fairly quickly, so that she could go to Paris to see Agnes D'Auberville.

Patsy had invited her to lunch on Sunday so that they could go over business matters and map out a plan, and in so doing save time. The general idea was that they would travel to the north of England on Monday, going first to Cumbria. After looking at the inn located in the Lake District, they would drive down to Yorkshire to see the one in the dales.

When she had asked Patsy which of the two inns she preferred, her partner had been somewhat evasive. "The one in Keswick needs much less done to it," she had said, and then clammed up.

When Meredith had pressed her further, Patsy had refused to make any more comments. "I want this to be your decision and yours alone," Patsy had murmured. "If I give you my opinion now, before you've seen either hotel, I'll be influencing you, setting you up in advance. So don't press me."

It had been Patsy's suggestion that if she had no reason to return to London, she should fly to Paris from the Leeds-Bradford Airport. "There're lots of flights to Paris from there and also from Manchester, which is nearby." Meredith had agreed that this was a great idea, since it would save so much time.

Leaning back against the car seat, she closed her eyes, thinking of the packing she still had to do, trying to decide what clothes to take. Unexpectedly, she thought of Reed Jamison and the dinner date she had made with him. The mere idea of seeing him filled her with dismay, but she knew she must keep the appointment if she were to break off with him.

It was never on, she thought, sitting up, glancing out of the window. Their relationship had never really lifted off the ground, although lately he seemed to believe otherwise. In an effort to make herself feel better, she adopted a positive attitude, assured herself that it was going to be easy. He would understand. After all, he was a grown man.

Deep down Meredith knew she was wrong in this assessment of him. Instinctively, she felt he was going to be difficult. Her dismay turned into apprehension.

# CHAPTER FOUR

"I know you thought I was being stubborn the other day," Patsy Canton said, "when I wouldn't discuss the inns with you, but—"

"More like evasive," Meredith interrupted.

"Not evasive, not stubborn either. Just cautious. I didn't want you to get any preconceived ideas, especially from me, before you saw the inns. But now I can give you a sort of—*preview,* shall we say. The owner of the inn near Lake Windermere in the Lakes sent us a batch of photographs. They arrived yesterday. Let me get them for you."

Patsy pushed herself out of the chair, walked across the small red sitting room of her house in London's Belgravia, where she and Meredith were having a drink before lunch on Sunday.

In her late thirties, she was an attractive woman, in a way more handsome than pretty, almost as tall

as Meredith and well built. Her hair was blonde, cut
short, and it curled all over her head; her gray eyes
were large and full of intelligence. But it was her
flawless English complexion that everyone commented on.

Pausing at the small Georgian desk, Patsy picked
up a large envelope and walked back to the sofa,
where she sat down next to Meredith.

"Ian Grainger, the owner of Heronside, is rather
proud of the pictures. He took them himself, last
spring and summer." So saying, she handed the envelope to Meredith, who pulled out the photographs eagerly.

After a few seconds spent looking at them, she
turned to Patsy and said, "I'm not surprised he's
proud of them. The pictures are beautiful. So is
Heronside, if these are anything to go by."

"Very much so, Meredith. In a way, the photographs don't really do the inn and the grounds
justice. There's such a sense of luxury in the rooms,
you feel pampered just walking into one of them.
The whole inn is very well done, lovely antiques
and fabrics, and I know you'll like the decorative
schemes, the overall ambiance. As for the grounds,
they're breathtaking, don't you think?"

Meredith nodded, shuffled through the pictures
again, and picked one of them out. It was a wood-
land setting. The ground was carpeted with irises
and rafts of sunlight slanted down through the leafy
green canopies of the trees. Just beyond were brilliant yellow daffodils growing on a slope, and, far

beyond this, a stretch of the lake could be seen—
vast, placid, silvery, glistening in the sun.

"Look, Patsy," Meredith said, and handed it to
her partner. "Isn't this gorgeous?"

"Yes, and most especially the slope covered in
daffodils. Doesn't it remind you of Wordsworth's
poem?"

Meredith stared at her.

"The one about the daffodils. Don't you know it?"

Meredith shook her head.

Patsy confided, "It's one of my favorites." Almost
involuntarily, she began to recite it.

> *I wandered lonely as a cloud*
> *That floats on high o'er vales and hills,*
> *When all at once I saw a crowd,*
> *A host, of golden daffodils;*
> *Beside the lake, beneath the trees,*
> *Fluttering and dancing in the breeze.*

"It's lovely," Meredith said.

"Didn't you learn it at school?"

"No," Meredith murmured.

Patsy went on. "I like the last verse best of all.
Would you care to hear it?"

"Please," Meredith replied. "You recite poetry extremely well."

Once more Patsy launched into the poem:

> *For oft, when on my couch I lie*
> *In vacant or in pensive mood,*

*They flash upon that inward eye*
*Which is the bliss of solitude;*
*And then my heart with pleasure fills,*
*And dances with the daffodils.*

"It's really beautiful," Meredith said, smiling at her. "It's very peaceful . . . serene."

"That's how I feel about it."

"I think I've heard that last verse before. *Somewhere.* But I'm not sure where," Meredith murmured. "Not at school, though." For a moment or two she racked her brain, but try though she did, she could not remember. And yet the poem had struck a chord in her memory, but she was unable to isolate it. The fleeting memory remained elusive.

Patsy remarked, "Unfortunately, I don't have any pictures of the inn near Ripon. The Millers, who own it, did have a few photos, and they were very good, too. Yet somehow they didn't quite capture the spirit of the place, its soul. So I decided not to take them. You'll have to judge it cold when we get to the site."

"That's no problem." Meredith looked at her closely. "But you *do* like Skell Garth, don't you?"

"Oh yes, Meredith, very much, otherwise I wouldn't be dragging you there," Patsy quickly reassured her partner. "The setting is superb, the surrounding landscape awe-inspiring, picturesque actually. And from the inn there's a most fabulous view of Fountains Abbey, one of the most beautiful ruins in all of England. Yes, Skell Garth is a unique place."

"Skell Garth," Meredith repeated. "You know, when you first mentioned it, I thought it was such an odd name."

"I suppose it is. Let me explain. The Skell is a river that flows through Ripon and through the land on which both the inn and the abbey stand. *Garth* is the ancient Yorkshire word for *field,* and many of the local farmers still refer to their fields as garths."

"So the name actually means *the field of the river Skell*. Am I correct?"

Patsy laughed, delighted with Meredith's astuteness. "You're absolutely correct! I'll make a Yorkshirewoman of you yet."

The two friends and partners sat talking about the inns for a while as they sipped their white wine, and then they moved on, became involved in a long and involved discussion about their business in general.

It was Patsy who brought this to a sudden halt when she jumped up, exclaiming, "Oh my God! I smell something awful. I hope that's not our lunch getting burnt to a cinder."

She flew out of the sitting room and ran downstairs to the kitchen.

Meredith charged after her.

Patsy was crouching in front of the oven, looking at the roast, poking around in the pan with a long-handled spoon.

"Is it spoiled?" Meredith asked in concern as she walked in.

"Fortunately not," Patsy said, straightening. She closed the oven door and swung to face Meredith, grinning. "A couple of potatoes are singed around the edges, but the lamb's okay. It's the onions that are a bit scorched. They're *black,* actually. Anyway, everything's ready, well, *almost.* I hope you're hungry, because I've cooked up a storm."

"I'm starving. But you didn't have to go to all this trouble, you know, I was quite happy to take you out to lunch. Or have you come to the hotel."

"I enjoy doing this occasionally," Patsy assured her. "It reminds me of my childhood growing up in Yorkshire. And anyway, Meredith, it's not often you get a traditional English Sunday lunch, now, is it?"

Meredith chuckled. "No, and I'm looking forward to it."

# CHAPTER FIVE

It was a windy afternoon.

A few stray leaves danced around her feet, and her full-length cream tweed cape billowed occasionally as she walked briskly through Green Park.

Meredith did not mind the wind. It was sunny, and this counteracted the sudden gusts, the nip in the air, and she was glad to stretch her legs after sitting so long over lunch with Patsy.

But it had been fun to visit with her old friend and partner, and to catch up on everything, both business and personal. Also, Meredith always enjoyed going to Patsy's little doll's house, which is the way she thought of it. Situated in a mews in Belgravia, the house had four floors; it was charmingly decorated, very much in the style they used in the inns. This was a lush country look, which was built around good antique wood pieces, a melange of interesting fabrics skillfully mixed and matched, vibrant colors carefully coordinated to each other plus a selection of unusual accessories.

As Meredith walked on, her thoughts settled on Patsy, of whom she was extremely fond. It was her New York banker, Henry Raphaelson, who had introduced them in 1984. Henry had known Patsy from her teenage days, since he had been for many years a close friend and business associate of her father's, until his death a merchant banker in the City.

Patsy and she had taken to each other at once, and, after several constructive meetings, they had decided to go into business together, opening a London office of Havens Incorporated.

In the ensuing years Patsy had been good for the company, a great asset. She was as solid as a rock, hardworking, dependable, devoted, and loyal. While she was not as visionary or as imaginative as Agnes D'Auberville, Patsy more than made up for these minor shortcomings because she was loaded with common sense. Also, her talent for public relations had worked well for Havens. There wasn't a hotel in England that received as much publicity and press attention as Haddon Fields in the Cotswolds, and all of it was positive. In fact, they had never had a negative write-up in the entire ten years the inn had been open.

When Meredith had expressed an interest in opening a hotel in France, Patsy had taken her to Paris to meet Agnes D'Auberville. The two young women had attended the Sorbonne at the same time, which was when they first met, and they had been good friends since those youthful days in Paris.

Agnes, like Patsy two years earlier, had been looking to invest inherited money in a business she could be involved in on a full-time basis. And so she had jumped at the chance to open a Paris branch of Havens Incorporated, and had plunged enthusiastically into the creation of the inn situated in the Loire Valley.

Meredith and Agnes had found the Château de Cormeron, which stood on the banks of the beautiful Indre River and was in the center of the Loire Valley. After purchasing the château, they had spent almost a year getting it into proper shape and turning it into an inn. Many of the rooms had needed new floors, some new ceilings; they had had to install central heating and air-conditioning; almost all the plumbing had to be replaced, as had the wiring. Once this had been done, they had set about decorating it in the appropriate style, mostly using French country furniture, wonderful old tapestries, luxurious traditional fabrics, and unique accessories culled from local antique shops.

They had put a tremendous amount of energy, effort, talent, and money into its remodeling and redecoration, but the transformation was so stunning, they both knew it had been well worth it.

And much to their gratification, it had proved to be a tremendous success as a small hotel. Château de Cormeron was close to many of the great châteaux of the Loire, such as Chinon, Chenonceaux, Azay-le-Rideau, Loches, and Mont-poupon, all open to the public and especially popular with foreign visitors.

Well-heeled tourists gravitated to their charming little Château de Cormeron, seeking its luxury, comfort, and superlative service, which was becoming renowned, its bucolic surroundings, and its proximity to so many famous châteaux. And the fact that the hotel boasted one of the finest restaurants in the Loire region did it no harm.

Agnes D'Auberville had become as good a friend as Patsy, as well as a most dependable business partner, and all three women enjoyed a good relationship.

Patsy, like Meredith, was divorced with two children, twin boys of ten who were away at boarding school. Agnes, who was thirty-eight, the same age as Patsy, was married to Alain D'Auberville, the well-known stage actor, and they had a small daughter, Chloe, who was six.

I've been lucky with them, Meredith thought as she completed her circle around Green Park and went out into Piccadilly. We all balance each other very well, and they've both done a great deal to make Havens work in Europe, been instrumental in its success.

Drawing alongside the Ritz Hotel, she stood at the curb, waiting for the lights to change. Once they did, she crossed Piccadilly and headed back to Claridge's on Brook Street.

Meredith had always liked walking around

London, and she was thoroughly enjoying her stroll, feeling invigorated by the brisk air and the exercise. Turning down Hay Hill, she went up into Berkeley Square. But as she traversed it, she couldn't help thinking that the little park in the center looked a bit bleak today, with its bare trees and patches of dirty snow on the shriveled brown grass.

On the other hand, she took great pleasure in looking at the lovely old buildings in Mayfair, which was the one area of London she knew best. She had been coming here for twenty-one years, ever since her marriage to David Layton in 1974. Twenty-three she had been at the time, and so young in a variety of ways; yet in others she had been rather grown up.

England had made a lasting impression on her. She felt comfortable on its shores, and she enjoyed the British people, their idiosyncracies as well as their good manners and civility, not to mention their great sense of humor.

David Layton had been a transplanted Englishman, living and working in Connecticut when she met him. After their wedding at Silver Lake, he had brought her to London to meet his sister Claire, her husband, and children.

Meredith had liked David, and she had loved him well enough to marry him, and she had felt regretful that their marriage had foundered. Their genuine attempts to make it work had come to nothing, and in the end divorce had seemed to be the best, the only, solution.

The one good thing that had come out of this
rather dubious and tenuous union was their son,
Jonathan. The sad thing was, David never saw his
son these days. He had moved to California in the
1980s and had never made any effort to come east
to see Jonathan. Nor had he ever invited Jonathan
to visit him on the West Coast.

David's loss, Meredith muttered under her
breath. She couldn't help wishing that things were
somewhat different, for her son's sake at least,
though Jon didn't seem to care that he was so ne-
glected by David. He never mentioned his father.

Being a single parent all those years had been a
strain on her at times, Meredith was the first to admit
it. But Jon had turned out well, as had her darling
Cat. And so it had been worth it in the end . . . the
hard work, the sacrifices, the endless compromises,
the cajoling, the bullying, and the unconditional loving. Being a good mother had taken its toll on her
life, but she was proud of the children. And of herself
in a funny way.

Those years of bringing up Cat and Jon alone,
plus creating and developing her business, had left
her little time to meet another man, let alone become involved with him. There *had* been a few
boyfriends over the years, but somehow her children and her work had intruded, got in the way.
Deep down, she had never really minded. Her children had been her whole world, still were.

Circumstances had been right when she had met
Brandon Leonard four years earlier. But he was a

married man. In no time at all, she had come to understand that not only was he *not* separated, as he claimed, but he had no intention of ever leaving his wife or getting a divorce. Simply put, Brandon wanted his wife. He also wanted a mistress. Since she was not a candidate for the latter role, she had terminated their friendship, and in no uncertain terms.

Then this past September, on a trip to London, Patsy had taken her to the fancy opening of an exhibition of sculpture at the posh Lardner Gallery in Bond Street.

And there, lurking among the Arps and the Brancusis, the Moores, the Hepworths, and the Giacomettis had been Reed Jamison. The owner of the gallery.

Tall, dark, good-looking, charismatic. The most attractive man she had met in a long time. And seemingly very available. "Beware," Patsy had warned. When she had asked her what she meant, Patsy had said, "Watch it. He's brilliant but difficult." Again she had pressed Patsy, asked her to elucidate further. Patsy then answered her enigmatically. "Save us all from the brooding Byronic hero. Oh dear, shades of Heathcliff."

Meredith had only partially understood, and then before she could blink, Reed Jamison, having taken one look at her, was in hot pursuit.

Drawn to him initially, she had fallen under his spell; but gradually, over the following months, she had begun to feel suddenly and unexpectedly ill at ease with him. And she had begun to pull away from the relationship within herself.

On his last visit to New York, in late November, she had been turned off. He had been morose, argumentative, and possessive. Furthermore, she had detected a bullying attitude in him, and this had alarmed her.

Tonight she was going to tell him that she could not see him again, that their relationship, such as it was, had come to an end. She wasn't looking forward to it, but she knew it must be done.

"Why bother?" Patsy had said over lunch earlier. "Have dinner with him tonight. Say nothing. Tomorrow we're going to the Lake District and Yorkshire. And then you're off to Paris. Don't make yourself sick over this. Avoid a troublesome confrontation."

"I have to tell him it's over," Meredith answered. "Don't you see, he'll be in my life, pestering me, circling me, until I make it clear I don't want him anywhere near me."

"What went wrong?" Patsy asked curiously.

"Reed went wrong. He's just too complex a man for me."

"I hate to say I told you so," Patsy murmured.

"It's all right, you can say it, Patsy. Because you did warn me, and you were right about him all along."

They had then gone on to talk about other things, but now Meredith could not help wondering if maybe Patsy was right. Might it not be infinitely easier simply to have dinner with Reed and say nothing?

Maybe I should do that, she thought as she turned into Brook Street.

"Good afternoon, madam," the uniformed doorman outside Claridge's said as she went up the steps.

"Good afternoon," she responded, smiling pleasantly, and pushed through the door that led into the hotel.

Martin, one of the concierges, greeted her as she crossed the lobby, making for the elevator.

"Meredith!"

She stopped in her tracks, freezing as she recognized the cultivated masculine voice.

Slowly turning, she pasted a smile on her face as she moved toward the man who had called her name. "Reed! Hello! But you're a bit early, aren't you?"

He smiled and leaned into her, put his arm around her waist, drawing her closer. He kissed her cheek. "I'm here having tea with friends." He jerked his head in the direction of the salon, which opened off the lobby, and indicated a group of people at one of the tables. Afternoon tea was being served and a string quartet played.

"Darling, it's lovely to see you," he went on, staring deeply into her eyes. "I've missed you, but then, I told you that on the phone this morning. I was actually just coming out to ring you up in your room, to invite you to come down and join us, when I saw you heading for the lift." He took hold of her arm firmly, and drew her toward the salon.

Meredith resisted and held her ground, shaking her head. "Reed, I can't. It's so nice of you to invite me, and thank you, but there are a number of things I must do before dinner." Peeking at her watch, she added. "It's almost five. We're still meeting at six-thirty, aren't we?"

"Of course. Unless you want to make it earlier. Look, do join us now," he pressed, and once more tried to draw her into the salon.

Meredith said softly, "Please, Reed, don't make a scene here. I just can't have tea. I've some phone calls, and I must change for dinner."

He let go of her arm abruptly and stepped away from her. "Very well," he said, sounding suddenly grudging. "Don't get frightfully dressed up. I'm taking you slumming tonight."

Giving him a fraudulent smile, she murmured, "I'll see you in a short while, Reed." Not giving him a chance to say another word, Meredith spun around on her heel and walked rapidly to the elevator.

Once she was inside her suite, she threw off her cape and unbuttoned the jacket of her cream pantsuit, then went through into the bedroom. Pulling open the wardrobe door, she looked at her clothes hanging there, settled on a black pantsuit for dinner, wishing deep down inside herself that she had never met Reed Jamison.

# CHAPTER SIX

At precisely six-thirty there was a knock on the door of the suite, and Meredith knew it was Reed Jamison.

Walking out of the bedroom into the sitting room, buttoning her jacket, she arranged a pleasant smile on her face before opening the door.

"Not too early, I hope," Reed said, kissing her on the cheek.

"Exactly on time," Meredith replied, and stood back in order to let him walk into the suite. "I'll just get my bag and coat and we can be off."

"Oh but it's far too early for the restaurant, darling. Why don't we have a drink here first." He put his overcoat on a chair and sauntered into the middle of the sitting room. After giving it a sweeping glance, he went to the fireplace, where he draped himself against the mantel, striking an elegant pose.

"All right," Meredith said, endeavoring to be gracious, although she couldn't help wishing he had not come up to the suite. She had fully expected him to phone her from the lobby. Pressing the bell for the floor waiter and clearing her throat, she asked, "What would you like?"

"Scotch and soda, please, my dear."

"Where are we going for dinner?" she asked, making small talk.

"Ah-ha, that's a surprise!" he exclaimed.

"You said we were going slumming."

"I'm taking you to a wonderful Chinese restaurant, rather off the beaten track. But you'll enjoy it. The place has tremendous local color, and the food is the best Chinese in London. Genuine, too, not the bastardized stuff served in fancy West End restaurants."

"I'm looking forward to it," she murmured and then moved out into the foyer of the suite as the waiter knocked and then let himself in. After ordering their drinks, she returned to the fireside and sat down.

Looking at her intently, shifting his stance slightly and leaning forward, Reed said, "I'm really rather put out with you, darling."

"*Oh?*" Meredith stared at him questioningly. "Because I didn't want to come down to tea and meet your friends?"

"No, no, of course not. That didn't matter. But I am somewhat surprised that you went to lunch with Patsy when I had invited you to come over to the house."

Meredith was taken aback. "But, Reed, Patsy and I had a lot of business to discuss. I told you last week, when I was still in New York, that I had many things to attend to on this trip, and—"

"Oh *really!*" he cut in with a sardonic laugh. "You could have dealt with Patsy on the phone, surely."

"No, I couldn't!" she shot back, her voice rising in exasperation. She was irritated with him; she realized, yet again, that he did not really take her work seriously. Suppressing a rush of impatience, she went on more calmly. "We had business to discuss, and I was anxious to see her."

"But not anxious to see me."

"Reed, don't be—"

There was a loud knock and the waiter entered with the tray of drinks. Meredith got up, thanked him, and handed him some of the coins she kept in the ashtray for tips. After giving Reed his drink, she picked up her own, and sat on the sofa.

"Cheers," Reed said, and took a swallow of his scotch and soda.

"Cheers." Meredith merely touched the glass to her lips, then put it on the coffee table. She had no desire to drink tonight.

Once again Reed looked at her; this time he was smiling.

She was relieved the awkward moment had passed. It struck her that he seemed less morose tonight, and certainly he was in a better mood than he had been earlier, when she had run into him in the lobby.

"Have you told Patsy you're planning to move to London within the next few months?" he asked.

Meredith gaped at him. "What makes you say that, Reed? I'm not moving anywhere."

"When I was in New York in November you certainly indicated that you intended to live in London."

"No, I didn't."

"Oh Meredith, how can you say such a thing! I practically proposed to you, and I told you it was hard for me to go on like this any longer, that we couldn't continue our affair if we were separated by the Atlantic Ocean. I made it quite clear I wanted you here with me. Very much so. And you certainly acquiesced."

"Reed, that's not true, I didn't!"

"You did!"

"You imagined it, Reed. Never in a million years would I lead you to believe such a thing."

He stared at her incredulously, sudden anger flaring in his dark eyes. "I distinctly remember telling you that I needed you here with me in London. And you agreed to come."

Meredith had no recollection of this at all and was about to say so when he came and sat down next to her on the sofa.

"What's wrong with you, darling? Why are you behaving like this?" he asked, moving closer, draping his arm along the back of the sofa. "Don't be difficult, my dear, you know how I feel about you. I need you, Meredith, and I need you *here*. Not in

New York, but living with me in London. I told you this when I was in the States, and I assumed you would get rid of the business and move as soon as you could. Settle here permanently with me."

"Reed, you've truly misunderstood. I don't know how that happened ... but it did, somehow. And I've no intention of giving up my business."

"Then don't, darling. If you want to work, you can, although it's really not necessary. I can support us extremely well, you know that. Forget the gallery, that's not important, merely my hobby. Just remember that I do have a very large private income from my trust. Monty might be inheriting the old man's title when he dies, after all he is the eldest son, but I've got Mummy's money."

Meredith sat gazing at him mutely. She was at a complete loss for words and filled with acute dismay.

Suddenly, unexpectedly, Reed pulled her into his arms. He was a tall man, well built and strong, and he caught hold of her hard, held her in a viselike grip, pressing his mouth on hers.

She struggled, managed to partially push him away, and pulled herself up on the sofa, straining to extricate herself from his arms.

Unexpectedly, Reed let go of her as abruptly as he had grabbed her. Giving her an odd look, he said in a quiet, icy voice, "Why did you pull away from me in such a violent manner as if I'm suddenly a leper? What's wrong?"

Meredith bit her lip, said nothing. Then she

sprang to her feet, hurried over to the window, and stood looking out.

A cold silence filled the room.

Meredith was shaking inside. She wanted to get this over. Be done with him. End the whole thing as gracefully as she could. But he was being difficult, and worse, imagining things that hadn't happened.

After a moment or two, when she was calmer, she turned to face him and said slowly, in her kindest voice, "Reed, listen to me . . . things are . . . well, not right between us anymore. They haven't been for weeks."

"How on earth can you say that! We had a wonderful time in New York. Only a month ago, unless I'm sadly mistaken."

Meredith shook her head, her dismay intensifying. She wanted to be considerate, to let him down lightly, yet she knew within herself that she must make her feelings absolutely clear to him. "It wasn't wonderful, Reed, at least not for me. I realized you and I were completely incompatible, and not suited to each other at all. I began to feel ill at ease with you, and I certainly knew our relationship was on the skids, that it couldn't possibly work."

"That's not so, and you know it. If you lived here and we weren't conducting our relationship long distance, everything would be entirely different. Please move to London to be with me, Meredith."

"Reed, I've just told you, as far as I'm concerned we don't have a future together. And anyway, I have such a huge commitment to my business."

"Oh don't go on so, Meredith. I can't believe for one moment that you're such a dyed-in-the-wool career woman as you claim to be. I couldn't love that kind of woman, and I do love you."

Meredith was silent.

He repeated, "I love you."

"Oh Reed, I'm so sorry . . . but I just don't feel the same way."

"That's not what you led me to believe," he said softly, his eyes narrowing.

"I admit I was infatuated with you last fall, that's true. But it *was* an *infatuation*, nothing stronger or more lasting. I can't make a commitment to you, I just can't."

"It's been so good between us, Meredith. Why are you saying these things?"

Taking a deep breath, Meredith plunged in. "I very quickly came to understand that you don't take my life seriously. Not my personal family life with my children, and certainly not my work. I will not negate my children's existence for you, or anyone else for that matter, and I will never give up my work. It's far too important to me. I've put too many years and too much effort into my business."

"You're not living up to my expectations of you, Meredith," he said, his voice suddenly grown cold and disparaging. "Not at all. I thought you were different. I thought you were an old-fashioned woman with old-fashioned values. What a miscalculation on my part. I can't believe my judgment was so flawed. Or perhaps you simply deceived me." He raised a dark brow.

Slowly, and in a cold tone, Meredith answered, "You know, you've just put a finger on something of vital importance, Reed. I *feel* the weight of your expectations, and I just can't handle that. I began to realize in November that you believe you come first in my life. I'm afraid you don't. The reason I wanted to see you tonight was to explain this, to tell you about my feelings and to bring our relationship to an end."

Reed Jamison was speechless. In all of his forty-one years he had never been discarded by a woman. He had always been the one to end affairs or start them, controlling, manipulating, pulling the puppet's strings and getting his own way.

He continued to stare at Meredith. She was the only woman who had ever bested him, and a terrible rage began to fulminate in him. He leapt to his feet, glaring at her. "I'm glad I found out what kind of woman you really are! Before I made the terrible mistake of marrying you!" he shouted.

Without another word Reed strode across the room, picked up his coat, and left, banging the door behind him with such ferocity the chandelier rattled and swayed on its chain.

Meredith ran to the door and locked it; she leaned against it for a few seconds. She was shaking. Calming herself, she walked over to the desk, sat down, and dialed Patsy's number. It rang and rang. She was just about to hang up, when she heard Patsy saying, "Hello?"

"Patsy, it's me. Reed was here, and I told him it

was over between us. He's gone . . . he marched out
in a fury."

"Well, that's a relief. That you told him, I mean.
And naturally he left in a high dudgeon. He's not
used to getting dumped unceremoniously. That's
part of his problem, you know. He's always been
spoilt by women, and he thinks he's God's gift to everything that walks in skirts."

"Yes, I know what you mean. He's also a male chau-
vinist pig, to use a very outdated phrase. However, it is
appropriate. That's something I guess I detected when
he was last in New York. He doesn't take my business
seriously, or my life. He's self-involved, and he just
can't imagine why I'm not rushing over here to set up
house with him. He said he wanted me to marry him."

"He proposed! Good God! Well, I must say, you
must've really gotten to him, Meredith my girl. Ever
since his divorce from Tina Longdon, he's been a
hit-and-run man."

"I'm not sure what that means."

"You know, the kind of chap who has an attitude
. . . *love me on my terms, darling. Thanks for everything. Farewell.* Hit-and-run chaps, that's what we
call them over here. I know several women who
have suffered at Reed's hands."

"Why didn't you tell me?"

"I did, Meredith, at least I tried to warn you as
best I could. I did say he was a difficult man."

"Actually, you said he was a brooding Byronic
hero, or words to that effect, and I never did *really*
understand what you meant by that."

"Oh that's only the role he's adopted for years. In essence, it's a pose. But I suppose it has been rather effective, got him a long way with women. Not that he needs a pose, actually. His looks aside, he's charming most of the time, despite that smoldering manner of his."

"All too true. But do you think women fall for that . . . for that brooding stance?"

"Oh yes, I think so. Let's face it, *many* do. The smoldering eyes, the soulful expression, the moody demeanor, can be appealing. There are a lot of women who go for the suffering, anguished Heathcliffs of this world. They want to change them, make them happy." Patsy paused, then said, "Wasn't that one of the things about him that attracted you?"

"No," Meredith answered quickly. "To tell you the truth, it was only this past November, in New York, that he turned morose and moody. It irritated me more than anything else."

Patsy laughed. "I bet it did! Anyway, the main thing is you don't sound any the worse for giving him the boot."

Meredith also laughed. "I'm not. Naturally, I'm not thrilled about hurting someone's feelings. But it had to be done; Reed had to be told. I needed that closure."

"I realize you did."

"I thought it only fair that Reed knew exactly how I felt. And immediately. It was much better to clear the air, cut it off before it dragged on any longer. These kinds of situations can end in such bitterness."

"Don't I know it!" Patsy exclaimed. "Tony's been bitter about our divorce for years. Blames me, of course. Listen, do you want to come over for supper? Or we could go out if you like, if you don't want to be alone . . ." Patsy's voice trailed off.

"That's sweet of you, but I want to stay in tonight. I'll order room service and pack. You did say you were picking me up at six tomorrow morning, didn't you?"

"Yes. Sorry about that, but we do have to leave early. We'll be about four hours on the road, three and a half if the traffic's light. We'll spend a couple of hours in Keswick and then head down to Ripon. We've a great deal to do in one day. In fact, we might have to spend the night in Ripon."

"No problem. And Patsy?"

"Yes?"

"I don't think I hurt his feelings too much, do you?"

"You may have. Don't underestimate the effect you had on him."

"I've probably damaged his ego, that's all."

"Oh definitely, Meredith, I'm certain of that. But I also believe that our Reed, the glamorous playboy, fell rather heavily for you. That's *always* been my opinion. Oh well, what can one do . . . so he finally met his Waterloo."

# CHAPTER SEVEN

Meredith found it hard to fall asleep.

For a long time she tossed and turned until finally, in exasperation, she got out of bed. After putting on a warm woolen dressing gown, she went and sat on the sofa in the sitting room. Her mind was racing.

She had not drawn the heavy velvet draperies earlier, and moonlight was filtering in through the muslin curtains that hung against the window-panes. Everything had a silvery sheen from this natural light, and the room was peaceful.

Meredith leaned back against the silk cushions of the sofa, thinking of Reed. How unpleasant their parting had been, and how foolish she had been to get involved with him in the first place. She was forty-four years old; she ought to have known better.

How unlucky she was with men. Always.

No, that was not quite true.

There had been one man. *Once.* A man who had been exactly right for her. He was dead. He had died too young. Such an untimely death ... that's what they had all said. And how truthfully they had spoken.

To die at the age of thirty-six was some terrible trick of God's, wasn't it?

Meredith had asked herself this question a thousand times. She had striven hard to find some special meaning in that awful, untimely death. She had found nothing. There was no meaning in it. None at all.

And all she had been left with was a void.

Of course there had been Cat, just a toddler, and Amelia, poor Amelia, and they had shared that void with her, and the grief. How they had mourned him ... endlessly ... she and Amelia. His women. The women who had loved him.

I'll always mourn him, Meredith thought, the old familiar sadness rising in her, filling her throat. Oh Jack, why did you die? How many times had she asked herself that in the silence of her mind. There was no answer. There had never been an answer. Not ever in twenty-two years.

And how many times had she asked herself when she would meet another man like Jack. She never would, she knew that now, because men who were like him were among the very few. And they were already spoken for. Jack had been spoken for early on in his life, when he was only twenty-two. And he had married that youthful love of his. *Amelia.* Then one terrible day she had been thrown by her horse. When she was only twenty-five and pregnant. And she had lost the baby and been crippled for life, a paraplegic trapped in a wheelchair. But he loved her; he would always love and cherish Amelia and she would always be his wife; he had told Meredith that and she had understood. And she had loved Amelia and Amelia had loved her and Jack; and Cat, she had loved her, too. Amelia had given them her blessing in her own silent, smiling way, full of approval, and gratitude for their love and kindness and loyalty.

*Jack.*

Blond, blue-eyed, tanned. So quick and sprightly and energetic. Full of good humor, tall tales, laughter, and life. No wonder she had fallen in love with him instantly, the first day she had set eyes on him. A *coup de foudre.*

So long ago now.

May of 1969.

She had been just eighteen.

Meredith closed her eyes. Behind her lids she could see his face. She remembered what had gone through her mind that day as she had stared back at him, held in the grip of his mesmeric gaze.

Such a beautiful face for a man, she had thought, such a sensitive mouth and those extraordinary eyes. Such a lovely blue. Bits of sky, she had thought then. His eyes are like bits of a summer sky.

Now, tonight, so many years later, Meredith saw herself as she had been on that May afternoon . . . the images of the three of them floated before her eyes. They were all so clear . . . so very vivid and alive . . . she and Jack and Amelia.

The decades fell away.

She tumbled backward in time . . . tumbled back into the past.

"Can I help you?" the young man asked politely, getting up off the steps where he had been sitting, pulling off his tortoiseshell sunglasses and peering intently at her.

Meredith stared back at him. "I'm looking for a Mr. Silver," she answered, jumping off her bike, almost falling in her haste and sudden confusion. Unexpectedly she was feeling self-conscious in front of this handsome man, so well groomed and well dressed, wearing gray pants and a dark-blue cashmere sweater over his lighter blue shirt.

The man walked over to her, thrusting out his hand. "Well, you've found him," he announced, "I'm Mr. Silver."

"Mr. *Jack* Silver?" she asked, shaking his hand.

He nodded. "That's right. And the only Mr. Silver who's alive and kicking. That I know of, anyway. The rest are over there." He indicated a plot of land behind him.

She followed the direction of his gaze and saw a small walled cemetery to the right of a copse of trees. "You have your own graveyard?" she asked, sounding awed.

He nodded, and there was a questioning expression on his face as he asked, "How can I help you?"

"I've come about the advertisement in the newspaper . . . for a receptionist."

"Oh yes, of course, and whom might I be speaking to?"

"I'm Meredith Stratton."

"Well, hello, Meredith Stratton. Pleased to meet you!" he exclaimed, thrusting out his hand once more. "Pleased to meet you indeed, Meredith Stratton!"

She took his hand and shook it for a second time.

He did not let go of it. Then he smiled at her, a wide, warm smile that showed his beautiful teeth. They were very white in his tanned face.

She smiled back at him, liking him.

He started to laugh for no apparent reason.

She laughed with him, instantly captivated by this man whom she had never seen before.

Still holding on to her hand, he led her and the bike she was clinging to over to the front steps, where he had been sitting. "Come inside. But I do think you'll have to leave your transportation out here," he said, and grinned.

Meredith nodded, her eyes dancing, and then she removed her hand from his and propped her bike against the porch railings.

"Nice bike you have."

"It's not mine. I borrowed it. That was the only way I could get here."

"Where did you come from?"

"New Preston. We've been living up above Lake Wara-maug." She glanced away, her eyes focusing on the lake at the bottom of the rolling lawns and flower gardens. "You've got a nice lake," she murmured.

"Silver Lake," he told her. "It used to have a Native American name a few years ago, a few *hundred* years ago, that is. Lake Wappaconaca. But an ancestor of mine bought this land and the local folk got into the habit of calling it Silver Lake, after him, and that name stuck. And this, of course, is Silver Lake Inn, built in 1832 by that same ancestor . . . a hundred and sixty-three years ago this year."

Meredith stood looking up at the inn. "It's a lovely old building."

"Come on, let's go inside. I want you to meet Amelia."

The moment she stepped through the doorway of the inn Meredith knew that it was a very special place. The walls were painted a cloudy mottled pink and they gave the entrance the warmest of rosy feelings. The floor was so highly polished it gleamed like a dark mirror; an old carved chest, two high-backed chairs and a small desk were obviously vintage antiques, and looked valuable even to her untrained eye.

Everywhere there were fresh flowers in tall crystal vases and bulbs growing in Chinese porcelain bowls; their mixed fragrances assailed her . . . the scent of mimosa, hyacinth, narcissi mingled with the smell of beeswax, lemons, and dried roses, ripe apples cooking on a stove somewhere.

As she took all of this in, looking around her wide-eyed, Meredith was awed. Yet she was filled with a curious kind of excitement and pleasure such as she had never known before. She crossed her fingers, praying she would get the job. Glancing at the small antique desk with its silk-shaded porcelain lamp and telephone, she could not help thinking how nice it would be to sit in this entrance hall, being a receptionist, greeting guests. It was certainly more appealing to her than working as an au pair, looking after children all day long, even though she loved children.

Jack ushered her down a short corridor and opened the door at the end. A woman sat behind a desk with her back to the door; she was gazing out of the window.

"Amelia," Jack said. "We have an applicant at last. For the job of receptionist."

The woman slowly turned, and Meredith realized immediately that she was sitting in a wheelchair. Her breath caught in her throat as she returned the woman's steady gaze. Meredith was startled by her beauty. Dark hair, parted in the middle, tumbled around a pale, heart-shaped face. Wonderful high cheekbones, a dimpled chin, and a sensual mouth were nothing in comparison to the amazing vivid green eyes below perfectly arched black brows. It's the woman from *Gone With the Wind*, she thought.

Amelia said, "You're looking rather strange. Are you feeling all right?"

Meredith realized she was staring and exclaimed, "Oh yes, I'm fine. *Sorry*. I'm so sorry to stare at you, it's very rude." The words tumbled out, and then because of her youth and ingenuousness, she rushed on unthinkingly. "You're so beautiful. You look like Vivien Leigh in *Gone With the Wind.* Doesn't everybody tell you that?"

"Not everyone. And thank you for your lovely compliment," Amelia answered with a smile and exchanged an amused look with Jack.

Jack cleared his throat and took charge. "Amelia darling, may I introduce Miss Meredith Stratton. Miss Stratton, this is my wife, Mrs. Amelia Silver."

Meredith walked across the polished wood floor and took the woman's slender hand in hers, then stepped back, still moved by such perfect beauty.

"Please, do sit down, Miss Stratton," Amelia murmured. "Make yourself comfortable."

"Thank you." Meredith lowered herself into a chair, straightening her cotton skirt as she did. "I'd feel better if you called me Meredith, Mrs. Silver. I'm not used to *Miss Stratton.*"

Again a small smile fluttered briefly on Amelia's pretty mouth. "I'd be happy to call you by your first name."

Jack, who was now sitting on the window seat to the right of his wife, remarked, "Meredith comes from New Preston. At least, that's where she bicycled from this afternoon." He now directed his words to Meredith and went on. "But you originally hail from Australia, don't you?"

She nodded. "Sydney. But how did you know? Oh, my awful voice, that's how, isn't it?"

"It's not awful," Amelia said. "But you do have a

slight twang, one that's distinctly Australian. And tell me, when did you come to live in Connecticut?"

"Last year. I'll have been living here just a year this July. I came with the Paulsons. They're an American family I met when they were living in Sydney. Mr. Paulson's with an advertising agency. I worked for them in Sydney as an au pair."

"And now you wish to leave them. May we inquire why?" Jack probed.

"I want to change jobs, Mr. Silver. But it's a bit more complicated than that. Mr. Paulson has been transferred again, this time to South Africa. The family are about to leave for Johannesburg. They asked me to go too, but I don't want to. I want to live in America. I never want to leave Connecticut. It's the most beautiful place I've ever seen."

"But what about your family? Your parents back in Australia? How do they feel about this?" Amelia seemed slightly puzzled. "Surely they want you to go home?"

"Oh no, they don't . . . what I mean is . . . well, you see . . . they're . . . dead. They died, yes, they did. In a . . . car crash. When I was ten." Meredith nodded to herself. "When I was ten," she repeated.

"Oh you poor girl," Amelia exclaimed, her face changing yet again, filling with sympathy. "How terribly sad, heartbreaking for you. And do you not have other family out there? Relatives?"

"No, I don't. There's no one."

"But how awful for you to be so alone in this world." Amelia turned her chair to face Jack. "Isn't it sad, darling?"

"Yes, it is."

"How old are you?" Amelia asked, giving her a warm, encouraging smile.

"Eighteen. I was just eighteen at the beginning of May."

Jack said, "Have you ever worked as a receptionist? Had any experience in a hotel?"

"No, but I'm good with people. At least, Mrs. Paulson says so, and I've been helping her with her paperwork for two years. You know, her checkbook, household accounts, things like that. She's even taught me a bit about bookkeeping. She says I have the right skills for this job, Mr. Silver. And you can phone her anytime. She's also going to give me a written reference. It'll be ready later this afternoon. I can bring it back to you tonight if you want."

"That won't be necessary," Amelia said briskly, then addressed Jack. "I think you should speak to Mrs. Paulson about Meredith right away. Now. You don't mind if we call her while you're still here, do you, Meredith?"

"Oh no. And she's at home packing. I think she's sort of expecting you to give her a call."

"What's the number, Meredith?" Jack asked as he crossed to the desk and picked up the phone.

She gave it to him; he dialed. And a moment later he was engaged in a conversation with Mrs. Paulson, or, rather, he was listening, saying very little, hardly able to get a word in edgewise.

Amelia sat quietly, waiting for the conversation to come to an end.

Meredith clasped her hands tightly in her lap, suddenly anxious and tense. Even though she knew Mrs. Paulson would say all the right things, she couldn't help worrying a little. This job was important to her.

When Jack finally hung up, he said to Meredith, "She's full of praise for you, says you're a clever girl, diligent, honest, and hardworking, and she told me you looked after her children very well."

Meredith beamed, and relaxed, then looked at Amelia expectantly.

Amelia said, "It's good to know that Mrs. Paulson thinks so highly of you."

"Yes. And she did say she'll come to see you," Meredith volunteered. "She'd like to meet you."

Jack walked over to the window seat, sat down, then said to Amelia, "To continue. Mrs. Paulson's sorry to lose Meredith, but she understands her reasons for wanting to stay in Connecticut. In any case, she thinks Meredith's cut out for better things." Then to Meredith he remarked, "She says you were very good with her children. Apparently they love you."

"I love them," Meredith replied. "I'm going to miss them, Mr. Silver, but I don't want to go to South Africa."

"I can't say I blame you for wanting to stay in Connecticut," Amelia murmured. "The Litchfield Hills, in particular, are very lovely. Now, when would you be able to start?"

"Next week." Meredith sat up straighter and glanced from Amelia to Jack. "Do I have the job then?"

"Yes," Amelia said. "Mrs. Paulson's recommendation is wonderful, and it's good enough for us. I don't think we'll find anyone better than you, Meredith. Isn't that so, Jack?"

"Yes, I agree. However, there's a slight problem, you know."

"What's that, Jack darling?"

"Where is Meredith going to live?"

Taken by surprise on hearing this, Meredith gaped at the Silvers. "Here at the inn!" she cried. "The advertisement said *food and lodging provided if required*. I wouldn't have applied otherwise. That was the thing that pleased Mrs. Paulson . . . that I would be living here at the inn with you. That I wouldn't be out on my own."

"We do have a room, but it's up in the attic," Jack explained. "And it's not very nice. The assistant housekeeper occupies the one good staff bedroom. We're a bit short of staff quarters, if the truth be known."

"I don't mind the attic," Meredith said, suddenly afraid the job would slip through her fingers. "Honest, I don't."

"We were hoping we'd find a receptionist who lived nearby and could come in daily," Amelia smiled. "But no one applied, even though the advertisement's been in for a few weeks. Until you came today, of course." Amelia gave Jack a long, searching look. "Perhaps we could make the attic more presentable, get it painted and wallpapered. We could put in a few pieces of really nice furniture, spruce it up. And let's not forget that it is fairly spacious."

"I don't know . . ." Jack began, and stopped when he noticed the crestfallen look on Meredith's face. Making a sudden decision, he jumped up. "Let me show you the room." Turning to his wife, he explained, "I think we should let Meredith be the judge of the room. Let's hear what she thinks of it."

"You're quite right. Run along with Jack, Meredith. He'll take you to the top floor."

A few minutes later Meredith and Jack were standing in the attic under the eaves. Meredith was relieved to see there were two dormer windows and that the room *was* quite large, as Amelia had indicated. She walked around, then said to Jack Silver, "But I love it, and it's quaint, cute. I'll soon make it look nice. Don't worry, I'll be fine up here."

Jack merely nodded and they went back downstairs.

"Well, what do you think, my dear?" Amelia asked, raising a brow quizzically as they walked in.

"It's unusual, Mrs. Silver, and it'll work nicely for me. I'll make it comfortable. Do you want me to start next week?"

"If you can. I'm really looking forward to your arrival, Meredith."

"So am I. And I'll bring the written reference with me."

"If you wish. Good-bye for now," Amelia said, and wheeled herself behind the desk. "I must get back to all this tedious paperwork that has recently landed in my lap."

Jack and Meredith went out to the front porch and he walked with her down the steps. "The inn's not busy at the moment," he confided, "but it will be in another week or so. What day do you think you can come?"

"Monday. That's only four days from now. Will that be all right, Mr. Silver?"

"It certainly will. You're going to take a huge burden off me, and I'll be able to tackle some of the other chores that Pete O'Brien has been doing. He's the estate manager and he's badly overworked. Amelia will feel more at ease too once you're installed. She gets so tired at times. Try though I have, I've not been able to find anyone to assist her."

Meredith nodded her understanding, full of empathy for the Silvers. "It must be difficult, but don't worry, Mr. Silver, I'll help her with that paperwork. I'd really like to do that in my spare time." She glanced across at him, hesitated, and then asked softly, "What exactly happened to Mrs. Silver? Why is she in a wheelchair?"

"Amelia had a riding accident eleven years ago. Her spine was damaged. She's been paralyzed from the waist down ever since."

"How dreadful, I'm so sorry . . . she's so beautiful."

"Yes, she is . . . inside as well as out. She's a truly good person, Meredith, the best I've ever known. So brave, so patient . . ."

There was a small silence, and then Meredith

said, "Thank you for giving me the job. I won't let you down. And I'll work very hard."

"I'm sure you will."

Meredith walked over to her bike, then suddenly, swinging around, she stood looking across at the lake. She could see it through the trees, glistening in the late afternoon sunlight. "Do you get much wildlife on the lake?" she asked at last in a strangely wistful voice.

"All year round, I'm happy to say. There're probably flocks of birds down there now. Ducks, Canada geese especially. Shall we walk over and have a look?"

Meredith nodded, reached for her bicycle and wheeled it along between them.

At one moment Jack said, "Do you like biking?"

"Sometimes. Why?"

"I have a bike, and I often ride it around the property. I can't claim to have covered the whole hundred and fifty acres, but I've done my best to see as much as I can. And there's a lot to see, most of it interesting."

"It's a big place, isn't it?"

"Yes, but not as big as some of the spreads in the outback, I bet."

She laughed. "The only part of Australia I know is Sydney."

He shrugged. "But it *is* a big country."

"Yes, it is. And is this all your land, Mr. Silver?"

"It is. My great-great-great-grandfather, Adam Silver, and his wife Angharad, bought it in 1832, as I told you. They built the inn, the house next to it, which is the one where Amelia and I now live, and various other small buildings on the property. And, of course, the family's been running the inn since those days."

"An unbroken chain," she said, the awe creeping into her voice again.

Jack simply nodded.

The two of them walked on, taking the wide path. This cut down through the green lawns and flower gardens, which were just starting to bloom; it stopped at the edge of the lake.

"I know it's called Silver Lake because of your name, but the lake *is* silver in color. And it's so calm."

She leaned against the handlebars of the bike and shaded her eyes with one hand. "I've always liked being near water, and for as long as I can remember. I don't know why, but it makes me feel—" She paused, unable to finish her sentence, at a loss for the right word to describe her emotions.

"*What* does it make you feel, Meredith?"

"I'm not sure . . . I can never really put my finger on the feeling."

"Happy? Content? Secure? It's surely a *good* feeling you experience, or you wouldn't like being near the water at all."

"That's true. I suppose it makes me feel . . . well, all of those things you've just mentioned. But sometimes I feel sad, as if I've lost something . . . something precious. The water reminds me of it."

He made no response, merely looked at her closely before focusing on the lake. Suddenly he pointed and cried excitedly, "Oh look! Over there!

That's the blue heron that comes every spring. It flies away after a few days and rarely comes back to the lake until the next year. But it's marvelous and I'm certain it's the same bird."

"How strange. I can't imagine why it does that. If I were a bird, I would never want to leave Silver Lake. I would want to live here forever and ever, it's so beautiful."

Jack Silver stared at her, taken by her words so softly spoken.

Meredith met his eyes. She was quite startled by their intensity. They did not leave her face and there was an expression in them she could not fathom. And she discovered that she could not look away . . .

It was Jack who broke the spell between them. He said suddenly, gruffly, "I'm glad you're coming to work at Silver Lake Inn, Meredith. I have a feeling things will go well. Amelia likes you. I like you. I sincerely hope you like us."

"I do, Mr. Silver, and *I'm* glad I'm coming here too."

They walked back to the inn in silence, both lost for a few moments in their own thoughts.

"See you on Monday, Mr. Silver," Meredith said, climbing onto her bike and riding away.

"Call me Jack," he shouted after her.

"All right, I will," she answered, half turning, waving before disappearing down the long drive.

He stood watching her until she was out of sight, and he was amazed at himself when he suddenly realized he had not wanted her to leave. There was something most appealing about this girl; she was fresh and sweet and very beautiful, although he knew *she* did not realize just how beautiful she truly was. Nor did she understand the impact she made with her long legs, sun-streaked brown hair, and smoky-green eyes. He discovered he missed her already and he had known her for only a couple of hours, and he was further amazed at himself.

The insistent ringing of the telephone awakened Meredith with a sudden start. As she jumped up and went to answer it, she realized she had fallen asleep on the sofa earlier.

"Hello?"

"Good morning, Mrs. Stratton. This is your wake-up call. It's five o'clock," the hotel operator informed her.

"Thank you," she answered, putting the phone back in the cradle and turning on a lamp. Glancing at her watch, she saw that it *was* five; it surprised her that she had spent the entire night on the sofa without waking up once. She must have been extremely tired. On the other hand, the big, over-stuffed sofa was as comfortable as the bed.

Patsy will soon be here, she thought, hurrying into the bedroom, slipping out of her dressing gown, then heading for the shower. She was filled with relief that she had packed the night before.

An hour later she was standing in the lobby of Claridge's waiting for her partner, who was going to drive them to the north of England.

# Chapter Eight

It was a dull morning, gray and overcast, when Patsy and Meredith drove away from Claridge's hotel. Leaden skies threatened rain, and by the time Patsy was pulling onto the motorway, pointing the Aston-Martin in the direction of the north, it was already pouring.

Meredith leaned back against the car seat, only half listening to the radio, her mind preoccupied with business. At one moment she closed her eyes, and then, almost against her own volition, she began to doze, lulled by the warmth in the car and the music on the radio.

"Go to sleep if you feel like it," Patsy said, glancing at her quickly before focusing on the road ahead again. "I don't mind, and we don't have to talk if you're tired."

"I'm fine," Meredith replied, opening her eyes

and sitting up straighter. "Even though I spent the night on the sofa I did in fact have a good rest."

"Why did you sleep on the sofa?"

"I was still wide awake at one in the morning, too much on my mind, I guess. So I decided to get up, then I must have dozed off a bit later on."

"I hope you weren't up in the middle of the night fretting about Reed Jamison." Patsy frowned, throwing her a concerned look.

"No, of course not."

"Good, because he's certainly not worth worrying about."

"I agree, and I'm relieved I told him how I felt, Patsy." Meredith laughed dryly. "It's probably the only time I've had his full attention."

"What do you mean?"

"I always thought Reed wasn't really listening to anything I had to say. It seemed to me that he was very busy formulating his reply, preoccupied with what he was going to say rather than with the meaning of my words."

"A lot of people suffer from that particular ailment," Patsy muttered. "It's a kind of self-involvement, I suppose. Then again, nobody seems to *really* listen anymore. Except you. You're the best listener I've ever known."

"I learned that from Amelia. She taught me how important it is to listen, and she was always saying that you didn't learn anything if you were the one doing all the talking. How right she was, but she was generally right about most things, and she taught me such a lot." There was a small pause, and then Meredith added, "She was quite the most remarkable person I've ever known."

"I'm sorry I never knew her," Patsy said. "And it's funny you should mention her this morning, because I was thinking about her only last night, thinking what an influence she's been on both our lives, although indirectly on mine, of course. Just think, if John Raphaelson hadn't been her lawyer and then yours, you would never have met his brother, who was one of my father's best friends, and therefore we would never have met, would we?"

Meredith smiled. "That's true, and I wish you'd known Amelia. She was so special." Meredith let out a little sigh. "You know, if she'd lived, she'd be only sixty-two this year. Not that old at all."

"And Jack? How old would he have been?"

"He was four years younger than Amelia, so he would have been fifty-eight . . . at the end of this month, actually."

"How sad for you that they died so young."

"Yes . . . Amelia struggled to keep going after Jack's death, but the light had gone out for her. She just gave up in the end, and I've always thought she died of a broken heart, if that's possible."

"Oh I think it is, Meredith. I believe my mother did . . . she went so quickly after my father passed away. I've always thought she just lost all interest in living once he was gone. In fact, I found out from my aunt, after Mummy had died, that she was always saying, 'I want to go to Winston,' and she stopped eating, well, she ate very little. It was as if she lost her appetite . . . for everything, including life. I do think she'd made up her mind to die."

"Amelia was a bit like that too, although she did live for a year after Jack's death. Not surprising really, when you think about it. People who have been together for a long time are so dependent on each other, and when one of them is suddenly alone, it's traumatic."

"They're lonely, and loneliness is a pretty unbearable state to be in."

"Amelia once said the same thing. Actually, she said loneliness was another kind of death. She loved me and she loved Cat, but Jack was the light of her life. Without him she seemed to lose her purpose, her raison d'être. Did I ever tell you that they'd known each other since their childhood?"

"No, you never did. And did they grow up together?"

"Part of the time, yes. Her parents had a summer home in Cornwall Bridge, not far from Silver Lake, and they were friends of the Silvers. Jack and Amelia met when they were children. Amelia was fourteen and Jack ten. They became best friends. They were both only children, you see, only children of only children, so there were no brothers and sisters or cousins. 'I'm going to marry you when I grow up,' Jack was forever telling her, and she'd laugh and say she couldn't possibly marry a younger man. But they did marry when they were in their early twenties. And then Amelia had the riding accident . . . how different their lives would have been if she hadn't been thrown by her horse. But that was her destiny . . . at least, that's what she used to say to me."

"What did she mean?"

"Exactly that, Patsy. She said that none of us could tamper with fate. Or avert it. *Ché serà serà* she would constantly murmur, *what will be will be*. That was her motto in a way, and her philosophy too. She said it was fate that brought me to Silver Lake that day in May of 1969. She said I was simply living out my destiny, just as she was doing, and Jack too. 'I'm meant to be in this chair, Meri, I don't know why, but I am,' she would tell me over and over again." Meredith paused, looked at Patsy through the corner of her eye. "According to Amelia, fate brought me to them. And as I've told you many times before, they changed my life, just as I changed theirs, and in so many different ways. For the better . . . for all of us. They gave me love and warmth and understanding, and the only real home I'd ever known until then. And I gave them something they'd always wanted, always missed . . ."

"You were like a sister to them, the sister neither of them ever had."

"Yes, I *was* a sibling, in a sense. But what I meant was that I gave them Cat. My baby was like their child as well as mine. And how much they loved her."

"I know, and just think how happy they'd be if

they could see her today. She's really grown up to be such a fine young woman. Do you think she *will* get engaged to Keith?"

"I do, and it'll be soon. Catherine has very good instincts, and she wouldn't have said anything to me the other night if she hadn't felt Keith was on the verge of proposing."

"I hope I get an invitation to the wedding."

"Don't be so silly, of course you will. Cat loves you, and she's never forgotten how marvelous you were to her the year she lived with you in London. And neither have I, for that matter. Because of you, I was able to sleep every night. I didn't have to worry about my daughter being alone in a foreign country."

"I was happy to look out for her, be a big sister. Will you have the reception at Silver Lake?"

"Oh, yes, I'm sure of that. Cat wouldn't want it anywhere else, she loves that place the way I do. And it's the perfect setting for a wedding. Blanche is all excited, planning it already in her mind. The other evening she was talking about marquees and the menu and no doubt she's got everything planned by now, from the flowers to the parking arrangements. Anyway, you're going to come, and you'll stay with me at the house."

"How lovely, thank you. Oh gosh, Meredith, being in love is wonderful, and I'm thrilled for Cat, thrilled that she's found the right man. I wish I could."

"When you're looking, there's never one around."

Meredith leaned her head against the back of the seat, closed her eyes. "And a man isn't always the answer, you know."

"Only too true!" Patsy peered ahead, cursing under her breath. The heavy rain was slashing against the windshield, so that everything looked blurred despite the wipers. "I hope this awful weather is going to let up soon. It's just miserable."

"Do you want me to drive?"

"No, no, I'm okay. And I know this road like the back of my hand. Don't forget, it leads to the north of England."

"Your favorite place."

"One of them anyway," Patsy said, smiling to herself.

Meredith fell silent, her thoughts taking over.

Patsy concentrated on her driving. There was a strong wind blowing, and she suspected it was bitterly cold outside; the road had recently grown slick, icy, suddenly slippery because of the freezing rain and sleet.

As she drove on, her eyes fixed ahead, she thought of Meredith and how she had gone to Silver Lake all those years ago, how her life had been transformed overnight. What an extraordinary story it was. She knew that Meredith had become indispensable to Amelia and very quickly; the two women had developed a symbiotic relationship. Meredith had once told her how Jack had come to rely on her as well, teaching her so much about the management of the hotel, teaching her everything he knew about business. Yes, Meredith had confided a great deal about her years with the Silvers, but not much else about herself. She never talked about her earlier life in Australia. In fact, everything before the Silver Lake years seemed to be clouded in mystery. It was as if there were another part of her life, a secret part that Meredith did not want anyone to know about. Patsy had no inclination to pry, ask questions; that was not her way. She respected Meredith's desire for privacy.

Meredith turned to her and said, "This may sound funny to you, but I have a feeling you prefer the inn in Ripon. Skell Garth is your favorite of the two, isn't it?"

Taken aback, Patsy exclaimed, "Why do you say *that?*"

"I just know. I've put two and two together from the few things you've said. Anyway, you love Yorkshire so much, it's where you grew up."

"As I've been telling you all along, I want you to be the judge, Meredith, I really do. I don't want to influence you, set you up in advance."

"What's wrong with the one in the Lake District?"

"Nothing. You've seen the pictures."

"Yes, and it does look gorgeous, and so do the gardens and the view. You've said it's luxurious, beautifully done, and yet there's a *but* in your mind; I know you."

"Too many cushions," Patsy muttered.

Meredith began to laugh. "I'll never live that

down, will I?" she said, remembering a comment she had made about another inn they had considered six months earlier. "So what you're saying really is that it's *overstuffed, overdecorated.*"

"Sort of . . . lots of luxury and comfort, and I think the place does make you feel terribly pampered. But despite all the lovely fabrics and rugs and nice antiques, there's nothing unique or different about Heronside. There's nothing there that's gone awry. You've always told me that it's important for a room to be slightly askew, a bit 'off.' You said it makes a place interesting."

"Oddities add character, and that's something we have always taken into consideration." Meredith looked at her partner and friend, and nodded to herself. "I *feel* you don't like Heronside."

"I don't *dislike* it," Patsy answered, speaking the truth.

"Look, why are we going there? Why not go directly to Ripon?"

"Because it is a wonderful inn, and I want you to see it for yourself. It doesn't need much money spent on it, since it was redone two years ago, and the views are magnificent. Also, I'm not sure I'm right about it. Truly, Meredith, I want *you* to make the decision."

"All right, I will. But you're not often wrong, Patsy. We have very similar tastes."

# Chapter Nine

The morning was clear and cold, the kind of crisp, bright day that Meredith liked. The sky was a dazzling blue, without a cloud, and the sun was shining; while this offered little warmth, it added radiance to the day.

Just as the clock turned nine on Tuesday morning, Meredith was bundled up in boots and a sheepskin coat, walking through Studley Park. The stately avenue of lime trees down which she hurried led to Studley Church, just visible on top of the hill at the end of the avenue. She knew, from Mrs. Miller's directions, that within a few minutes she would be at the abbey.

Yesterday afternoon, when she and Patsy had arrived in Ripon, they had gone directly to Skell Garth House. Situated between the tiny villages of Studley Royal and Aldfield, the house stood on the banks of the little River Skell, as did Fountains Abbey on the opposite bank.

After the Millers had been introduced to her, Patsy had explained to the couple that they would like to stay the night at Skell Garth. Since it was midweek in winter, this had not presented a problem. There were plenty of available rooms and Claudia Miller had given them a choice.

"I think we'd like those two that adjoin each other on the top floor," Patsy had said as they had followed the owners up the wide main staircase. "You know, the two that face Fountains."

The minute they walked into the first of the rooms, Patsy dragged Meredith to the window. "Now, isn't that the most spectacular sight!" she cried. "Behold Fountains Abbey! One of the two most beautiful ruined abbeys in the whole of England."

Meredith stared out across the sloping lawns and gardens of Skell Garth House, now obliterated by a covering of snow, her eyes fastening on the abbey. It rose up out of glistening white fields, huge, dark, monolithic, silhouetted against the fading greenish sky, an ancient tribute to God. And she caught her breath, struck by its beauty. She agreed that it *was* magnificent. That was the only word to describe it, she thought.

"And it's one of the best preserved abbeys in the country," Bill Miller had pointed out. "There are stonemasons working on it all the time, trying to keep it from crumbling away. It's a national treasure, you know."

At that moment, and for a reason she could not fathom, Meredith had made up her mind to take a closer look, feeling oddly drawn to those ruins.

After they had taken tea with the Millers, the rest of the afternoon had been devoted to a complete guided tour of Skell Garth House, which dated back to the nineteenth century. By the time they finished talking with the owners, going over all aspects of the inn and the pros and cons, it had grown dark outside. I'll go tomorrow, before we leave, Meredith resolved, filled with determination to visit the ruins, a determination she did not quite understand.

This morning, when she was finishing her breakfast, Claudia Miller had come into the dining room to see if Meredith needed anything else. She seized the moment and asked her how to get to the abbey from the inn.

"You'll have to approach it on foot, that's the best way. Wear a pair of wellies, if you've got them with you, or boots. There's still a bit of snow out there by Studley way." Claudia then gave her explicit directions.

And I'm almost there, Meredith told herself as she finally reached the top of the hill at the end of the avenue of limes. She glanced over at Studley Church, so picturesque in the snow, and at the obelisk nearby; she then directed her gaze to the lake below, glittering in the sunlight. The river Skell flowed beyond it, and there, just a short distance upstream, was the abbey.

Meredith stood for a moment longer on top of the hill, shading her eyes against the sun with one hand, thinking that Fountains looked more imposing than it had the previous afternoon. But of course it would, she told herself. She was, after all, much closer to it now, viewing it with the naked eye, not through a glass window from a distant house.

Unexpectedly, Meredith shivered. She felt as though a cold wind had blown around her, through her. But there was no wind that morning. Someone walked over my grave, she muttered under her breath, and then wondered why she had thought this, wondered how she knew such an odd phrase. She had never used it in her life before.

A strange sensation came over her. She stood very still, all of her senses alert. Instantly, she knew what it was . . . a curious feeling that she had been there before, that she had stood in this very spot, on this very hill, gazing down at those medieval ruins. It seemed to her that the landscape below her was familiar, known to her. She shivered again. Déjà vu, the French call it, *already seen,* she reminded herself. But she had not been there before; she had never even been to Yorkshire.

Yet this ancient place stirred something in her. The ruins beckoned, seemed to pull her forward urgently; she set off, began to hurry down the hill, her boots crunching on the frozen snow. She was almost running, slipping and sliding in her haste to get there. Several times she almost fell but managed to recover her balance and go on running.

At last, somewhat out of breath, she was hurrying into the center of the ruined Cistercian monastery.

It was roofless, open to the vast arc of sky floating above it like a great canopy of blue, and the glassless windows were giant arches flung against that empty sky. Meredith stood there, turning slowly, her head thrown back as she gazed up at the soaring stone walls, jagged and broken off at the top . . . the immense columns only partially intact . . . the cracked flagstones covered now in pure white snow. A sense of timelessness enveloped her.

As she looked around, absorbing everything, her heart clenched, and she felt a strange sense of loss. So acute, so strong, so overwhelming was this feeling, tears came into her eyes. Her throat closed with such a rush of emotion she was further startled at herself.

Something was taken from me here . . . something of immense value to me. *I have been here before.* I know this ancient place . . . somehow it's part of me. What was it I lost here? Oh God, what was it? Something dearer than life. Part of my soul . . . part of my heart. Why do I feel this way? What do these ruins mean to me? She had no ready answers for herself.

Meredith stood perfectly still in the middle of the ruined abbey. Unexpected tears ran down her face, warm against her cold cheeks. She closed her eyes, not understanding what was happening to her; it was as though her heart were breaking. Something had been taken from her. *Or someone.* Someone she loved. Was that it? She was not sure. The only thing she really knew at that moment was that she was experiencing an immense sense of deprivation.

Opening her eyes, moving slowly, she went and stood near one of the walls of the monastery, resting her head against its timeworn stones. There was a stillness here, a quietness that was infinite; it calmed her.

Far away, in the distance, she heard the call of a lone bird high on the wing. There was a sudden rush of wind through the ruins, a moaning, sighing wind, and then everything was still, silent again.

She began to walk toward the cloisters, moving like a somnambulist. She knew the way. Once inside, she was protected from the wind. And there was no sound at all. Just perfect silence in these great vaulted halls of the cloisters.

Pain, she thought. Why do I feel pain and hurt and despair? What is it about this place that makes me feel like this? What does Fountains mean to me? She did not know. It was a mystery.

When Meredith returned to Skell Garth House an hour later, Patsy was waiting for her in the sitting room.

"My God, you look frozen to death!" her partner cried as she walked in. "Come and sit by the fire and have a hot drink before we leave for the airport."

"I'm all right." Meredith took off her coat and

walked across to the fireplace, warming her hands in front of the flames for a moment.

"I couldn't believe it when Claudia told me you'd gone to Fountains Abbey. And in this weather. If you'd waited for me to come down for breakfast, I would have driven you there. At least, I would have driven you as close to the abbey as I could get."

"I enjoyed the walk." Meredith sat down on a chair, turned her head, gazed into the flames burning so fiercely.

"I'll go and order a pot of tea," Patsy said, jumping up. "Would you like something to eat? Pikelets, maybe? I know you enjoy them as much as I do."

"No thanks, not now. The tea would be nice though."

When Patsy came back, she threw Meredith a curious glance. "This may be a strange thing to say, but you look quite white, as if you've seen a ghost." Then she grinned and added, "A couple of Cistercian monks perhaps, walking around the abbey's ruins with you?"

When Meredith did not respond with a gale of laughter, as she usually did, but looked at her oddly and remained silent, Patsy stared at her harder.

"*Is* there something the matter, Meredith?" she probed.

At first Meredith was silent, then said, "No, there's nothing wrong. But I did have a funny experience at Fountains."

"What happened?"

"I was drawn to the ruins. It was as though a *magnet* were pulling me forward. I practically ran there from Studley Church. I almost fell a couple of times. The thing was, Patsy, I couldn't wait to get there, to be in the middle of those ruins. And once I was standing in the center of them, I felt as if I knew that place so well. It was curiously familiar. And then something happened to me . . . I had this immense sense of loss. It was so overwhelming, I was shaken. I can't explain it, I really can't." Meredith stared at Patsy. "You probably think I'm crazy . . . Anyway, Fountains Abbey *does* mean something to me, of that I'm sure. Something special. And yet I can't tell you why that is so. I'd never heard of it until the other day. And I've never been there in my life."

For a moment there was no response from Patsy, then she said, "No, you never have. Not in this life, at any rate. However, maybe you were there in another. In the past . . . in a past life. Do you believe in reincarnation?"

"I don't know." Meredith shook her head. "To say I don't believe sounds so arrogant . . ." She shrugged, looking suddenly baffled. "Who knows anything really about this strange world we live in."

"Perhaps you saw a movie—a documentary about Yorkshire that featured the abbey. Perhaps that's why it's so familiar to you," Patsy suggested.

"I don't think so. And how do you explain that peculiar sense of loss I experienced?"

Patsy said, "I can't."

A young waitress came in with the tray of tea; the two women fell silent.

Once they were alone again, Patsy remarked quietly, staring closely at Meredith, "You were pretty excited last night . . . I mean about buying Skell Garth House. I hope your odd experience this morning hasn't made you change your mind."

"No, it hasn't, Patsy. Quite the contrary. It's obvious that Fountains Abbey is meaningful, although I don't quite understand why. Still, I see that as a good omen for the future. Anyway, I like the inn. You were right about it." She gave her partner a warm smile. "It's a little gem in its own way, and certainly it's got a lot more going for it than Heronside. Too many cushions *indeed*. Skell Garth is quaint and charming, and it has a great atmosphere, is loaded with comfort. Of course, it's a bit shabby, but it doesn't need any big money spent on it."

"All Skell Garth House needs, in my opinion, is a good decorating job. And you're the best person to do it, Meredith."

Meredith nodded, but made no comment.

Patsy lifted her cup of tea. "Here's to our new inn, then. May it be ever prosperous."

"To Skell Garth House."

# CHAPTER TEN

L uc de Montboucher looked from Agnes D'Auberville to Meredith and said, "You must allow six months at least for the remodeling. To cut the time down to four months will only mean disaster."

Agnes said, "We'd hoped to have the inn open by the summer—"

"That is not possible!" he exclaimed, cutting in swiftly. "There's too much to do, and some of the work is major, such as the architectural changes you want. And which are necessary, I might add. Then there's new wiring, plumbing, windows, and floors. Most of the walls have to be replastered and sanded." He lifted his hands in a typically Gallic gesture, and finished, "To be honest, Agnes ... Meredith ... six months is going to be a tough schedule for the contractor, please let me alert you to that fact right now. I sincerely hope he can keep to it."

"But the Manoir de la Closière is not such a large house," Agnes remarked, and turned to Meredith. "You've now been there twice this week, what's your opinion?"

It was Friday. The three of them were having lunch in the Relais Plaza of the Plaza Athénée hotel in Paris, having spent the morning going over ideas for the transformation of the old house.

Now Meredith put down her fork and returned her French partner's penetrating look. "You're right, Agnes, inasmuch as it's not a huge house, but it is in terrible disrepair, in much worse shape than the château was. I happen to think Luc is correct. And I doubt very much that we can get the remodeling finished in less time than he suggests. In fact, I believe it's a bit foolhardy to allow only six months." Glancing at Luc, she asked, "Don't you think it would be wiser to settle for eight?"

Before he had a chance to answer, Agnes exclaimed somewhat heatedly, "But we remodeled and redecorated Château de Cormeron in a year! And that's a much bigger place."

"I know. However, the manor house at Montfort-L'Amaury hasn't been so well cared for," Meredith pointed out. "I think it's unfair of us to expect Luc to work with unrealistic time schedules. He's right, we're only going to end up with a disaster."

Agnes was silent.

Luc nodded, gave Meredith the benefit of a

warm smile. "Thank you for understanding my problems."

Meredith liked him. He was an attractive man, with a great deal of continental charm, yet sincere.

"When *would* we open the inn then?" Agnes asked.

"I think it will have to be next spring . . . the spring of 1996. I don't believe we have any other alternative. Luc's pretty clear in his mind about what we want, and he will soon know what's feasible. I suppose he could start the work in a month from now. Am I correct, Luc?"

"You are. I will complete my plans for your approval as quickly as possible. If you like them and give me the go-ahead, I can have the contractor in there by the end of January. He can start demolition of some of the interiors. And if there are no unforeseen problems, we should be able to finish by June. I will endeavor to complete the job in six months, not eight, as you suggested. Thank you for offering those extra two months; however, I don't think we'll be needing them."

Meredith said, "That's good to know." Addressing Agnes, she continued. "As soon as the contractor is finished, we can bring in the other trades . . . the painters, paperhangers, et cetera, and they will be finished in four months quite easily. Starting next week, you and I can begin to create the decorative schemes."

"Well, all right," Agnes murmured, "If you think it's going to take a whole year, then it will." She laughed, suddenly relaxing, and shrugged. "I must admit, you're rarely wrong when it comes to a remodeling job." Digging her fork into a piece of fish, she concluded, "The problem with me is that I'm overanxious. I can't wait to get the new inn running properly and open to the public."

"There's nothing wrong with that," Meredith responded. "But if we try to do it at breakneck speed, it's asking for trouble."

"I'm glad we're all agreed," Luc said. "And let me just add that the manor is charming, and has endless possibilities, especially since the grounds are also so pleasant. I think you've made a good choice."

"Thanks to you, Agnes," Meredith said. "You spotted the house."

Looking pleased, her nervousness about the schedule now abating completely, Agnes took a long swallow of white wine. "Then it's settled. Luc will get the plans done quickly and once they're ready he can send them on an overnight to New York. Now—" She paused, reached out, and squeezed Meredith's arm. "What are *your* plans for the weekend?"

"Nothing special, really. I thought I'd take it easy, do a little shopping, and maybe go to the Marché aux Puces on Sunday. But please don't worry about me, Agnes, I know you've got your hands full."

Agnes grimaced. "I'm afraid I do, with Alain and Chloe both down with the flu. Thank God I haven't caught it from them."

"I'm sorry they're not well, and you mustn't fuss about me, I'll be all right on my own this weekend."

Luc lifted his glass, drank a little of his wine, and

sat back in his chair, scrutinizing Meredith across the luncheon table. Eventually he said, "If you really don't have anything special to do this weekend, I would like to invite you to my house in the country. I'm leaving tomorrow morning; we could drive there together, and I would bring you back to Paris early on Monday."

"That's so nice of you, Luc," Meredith murmured and hesitated. "I don't know . . . I don't want to impose . . ."

"But you're not imposing, I invited you. And I would *like* you to come. It's not going to be a very fancy weekend with lots of guests, if that's what is worrying you. In fact, I must warn you, we will be there alone and you might find that boring. Although the countryside is beautiful, and perhaps you would enjoy it."

"Well, thank you . . ." Meredith began and stopped, still uncertain.

Agnes looked from one to the other and jumped in, saying swiftly, "Luc has the most charming old house. In the Loire. It's really unique, Meredith, you'll love it. You *must* go for the weekend."

"Yes, do please come, Meredith," Luc insisted.

"All right, then, I will," Meredith said, suddenly making up her mind. "And again, thank you very much for inviting me."


After lunch Agnes and Meredith walked back to the Havens offices which were located in a narrow street off the Rue de Rivoli.

"I've been collecting fabrics and wallpapers for the past few weeks," Agnes explained once they were ensconced in her cluttered private domain.

Flopping down onto a sofa, she dragged two large shopping bags toward her and said, "Come on, Meredith, sit here next to me and we'll go through some of these. I thought it would be a good idea to have something on hand, so we can start formulating our decorative schemes well in advance."

"You must have scoured the whole of Paris," Meredith laughed, joining her, plunging her hands into one of the shopping bags. "I've never seen so many samples." She took out a blue-and-red fabric and stared at it. "I like this . . . it looks like a Manuel Canovas . . . oh yes, so it is."

"He's very eligible, you know," Agnes said, also delving into one of the bags.

"Who? Manuel Canovas? I thought he was married."

"No, not Manuel Canovas. *Luc de Montboucher.* That's who I'm talking about."

"Oh."

"Why do you say *oh* like that? In that surprised tone?"

"Are you trying to be a matchmaker, Agnes?"

"Not really." Agnes laughed. "It hadn't really crossed my mind until he invited you for the weekend. Then it suddenly hit me . . . he's attractive, successful, and, most important, single."

"Divorced?"

"No, I don't think he's been married." Agnes

frowned and bit her lip. "No, wait a moment . . .
perhaps he *was* married and she died. I can't remember. He's a friend of Alain's, I'll have to double-
check that."

"How old do you think he is? About forty?"

"I think he's a bit older than that, if I remember
correctly. About forty-three perhaps. I'll ask Alain
when I get home tonight and I'll call you at the
hotel."

Meredith laughed, shook her head. "He's only
asked me to go to his house for the weekend, he
hasn't proposed marriage."

"I know, on the other hand, my dear Meredith, I
believe he's rather taken with you. I've noticed him
looking at you over the past few days, and looking
at you with great interest, I would like to add. In
that certain way."

"What do you mean by *certain way*?"

"With curiosity. It's perfectly obvious he wants
to get to know you better. Do you like him?"

"Of course, otherwise I wouldn't have accepted
his invitation to go to the Loire with him."

"He is a very talented architect. But you know
that from the examples of his work he showed you
at his office yesterday. We've been lucky to get him
for this job. And as I said, he's very eligible, which
is most important."

"The way you spoke, you must know his
house," Meredith murmured, changing the subject.

"Yes, Alain and I have been there a couple of
times. In the summer . . . never at this time of year.

But it's a lovely old place. Between Talcy and Menars."

"Where's that in relation to our inn?"

"It's higher up, just up beyond Blois, closer to Orléans than Cormeron. Do you remember that time Alain and I took you to Chambord?"

Meredith nodded.

"Well, Chambord is in a direct line to Talcy across the river Loire."

"I think I know where you mean. What kind of house is it?"

"Big . . . Clos-Talcy has been in his family for hundreds of years. It's been well looked after, kept in good repair. I think Luc goes there most weekends; it's only a few hours drive, closer to Paris than Cormeron."

"I'm glad I brought some country clothes," Meredith said, now suddenly wondering what she had let herself in for this weekend.

"Oh you don't have to worry, I think he lives quite casually," Agnes remarked, and handed her a swatch of fabric. "Do you like this?"

Meredith examined it and nodded. "You know I love red toile de Jouy. It would work well with black furniture or black accessories."

"Luc really was looking at you in that certain way, *chérie*," Agnes remarked, eyeing Meredith. "I'm not inventing that."

"I believe you," Meredith answered, and began to laugh, amused by Agnes and her romantic notions.

# CHAPTER ELEVEN

Her first sight of Clos-Talcy was of a double image—the house itself and its reflection in the large ornamental lake in front of it.

"Oh how beautiful!" Meredith cried when Luc de Montboucher walked her around the bend in the driveway and directed her attention across the lake, pointing out the house in the distance.

"I wanted you to see it from here, not from the car," he said. "This view surprises everyone, and I must explain to you that it's one of my own special favorites . . . it's the reflection, of course, that intrigues me."

"What a perfect house in a perfect setting," Meredith murmured, almost to herself. She stood next to Luc, surveying the great château with interest. It was built of pink brick and pale stone, topped with a roof of dark gray slate. There were a number of tall, slender chimneys rising up from the roof, and she counted thirty-eight windows and five dormers.

The many tall trees surrounding the château were reflected in the lake, along with the facade of the house itself. To Meredith, there was a marvelous symmetry to the two in combination. Certainly it was the loveliest initial view of any house she had ever seen.

Turning to Luc, she asked, "How old is the château?"

"It was built in the early seventeenth century, and the gardens were designed about fifty years later by Le Nôtre, the famous landscape artist of the time."

Taking hold of her arm, he continued. "But come, let us go back to the car. Later, after lunch, I'll drive you around the park, and we can go for a walk in the gardens if you would like. I must warn you, though, they are rather bereft looking at this time of year."

"Oh I don't mind that; in fact, I like gardens in winter. Very often they're interesting, different naturally, but still eye-catching." She gave a wry little laugh. "Well, some of them, anyway."

"I happen to like winter gardens myself," Luc remarked, opening the car door, helping her in, then going around to the other side.

Starting the car, he drove up the majestic avenue lined with plane trees, continuing. "Fortunately, we haven't had much snow here this year, so we'll be able to have a pleasant stroll later in the day."

Meredith nodded and turned her head, glancing out of the car window. She saw another lake, this one smaller than the first, and it prompted her suddenly to confide, "I've always been drawn to houses that are on water, or very near it, although I've no idea why."

"Oh I understand that feeling very well," Luc replied, giving her a swift look, then immediately swinging his eyes back to the road. "I have the same attraction myself. There's something wonderful about water in the middle of a land mass, and it enhances natural surroundings as well as any buildings that might be nearby. We have a lot of water here in Talcy. Aside from the ornamental lake, there's the smaller one you just noticed, plus a fish pond near the orchard, a stream that runs through the woods, a waterfall, and innumerable fountains." He began to chuckle. "I had an ancestor who was obviously extremely fond of those . . . we've got over a dozen of them in the park, and some are quite magnificent, even if I do say so myself. You'll find you're never very far from running water at Talcy."

Meredith smiled. "That's nice . . . you know, Luc, all of my inns are near water too, except for Montfort-L'Amaury. That's the only thing I wasn't happy about when I first saw the manor earlier this week."

"If you wish, I could create a lake or a pond at the new inn," Luc volunteered. "It's not so difficult to do, and there is a fair amount of land attached to the manor house. What do you think?"

"That might be rather nice. I'll talk to Agnes, and perhaps you could give me some idea of the cost."

"*Mais certainment* . . . of course. Ah, here we are, Meredith, we've arrived at the house at last."

Luc had driven into a large cobbled courtyard and parked; it was apparently the front entrance to the château. Wide steps led to a huge double door made of dark wood embellished with iron ornamentation. Before they had even alighted, a middle-aged man in his shirtsleeves, wearing a black waistcoat and a green-striped apron, had come out of the house. He ran down the steps, a broad smile ringing his cheerful face.

"*Bonjour,* Vincent!" Luc called as he climbed out of the car and hurried to assist Meredith.

"*Bonjour, Monsieur,*" the man responded.

Luc and Meredith walked toward him. He shook Luc's hand.

Luc said, "Meredith, this is Vincent Marchand, who, with his good lady, Mathilde, runs this place. Vincent, this is Mrs. Stratton."

"*Madame,*" the man said, inclining his head reverentially.

Meredith smiled at him. "I'm pleased to meet you, Vincent," she said, stretching out her hand.

Shaking it vigorously, he responded, "*Grand plaisir, Madame.*" With a nod he hurried to the trunk of the car and took out the luggage. Grasping several bags, he followed them up the front steps.

Luc led her into a vast entrance hall that was almost cavernous, with soaring stone walls and a stoneflagged floor. The pale-colored limestone walls were hung with two Gobelin tapestries, and a bronze and crystal chandelier floated down on chains from the high ceiling. The only piece of furniture was a long, ornately carved and gilded console upon which stood two large stone urns filled with dried flowers; a huge gilded mirror hung above the console, and there was a stone statue of a knight in armor in one corner.

Luc said, "Let me take your coat," and after she had shrugged out of it he carried the sheepskin over to a cupboard built into one of the walls.

A split second later, a door at the end of the hall flew open and a tall, plumpish woman came hurrying toward them on fast-moving, nimble feet.

"*Monsieur!*" she exclaimed, beaming at Luc before flashing Meredith a glance filled with undisguised curiosity.

Luc kissed her on both cheeks. "*Bonjour, Mathilde.* I would like to introduce Mrs. Stratton. As I told you on the phone, she's my guest for the weekend."

Nodding, smiling, Mathilde stepped forward. The two women shook hands, and Mathilde said, "I will show you to your room, *Madame.*" Glancing at Luc, she continued quickly. "As you suggested, *Monsieur,* I have given Mrs. Stratton the room of your grandmother."

Luc guided Meredith toward the staircase, saying, "I do hope you like your room, it was my grandmother's favorite. I'm sure you will . . . it overlooks water . . . the ornamental lake, actually, which was your first glimpse of Talcy. It was a lucky choice on my part, I think."

"Yes, it was, and I'm sure I'll love it."

Mathilde led the way upstairs, followed by Meredith and Luc, with Vincent bringing up the rear, carrying Meredith's two suitcases.

Mathilde marched them down a long corridor, thickly carpeted and lined with windows; the walls were hung with many paintings. Meredith sneaked a look at them as they hurried by, realized they were family portraits, probably of minor members of the family, since they were relegated to this corridor.

"*Voila!*" Mathilde suddenly cried, flinging open a door. "Here is the room of *Grand-mère* Rose de Montboucher. Whom everybody loved."

"And feared," Luc added, winking at Meredith. "She was quite a terror at times. But also very, very beautiful."

Noticing her glancing around, Luc explained: "This is the sitting room, the bedroom and bathroom are through that door over there. But to continue, my grandmother fell in love with this suite of rooms when my grandfather brought her to Talcy for the first time. And she made them hers. And that's a portrait of her, by the way. The one hanging over the mantelpiece."

Meredith followed his gaze.

Her eyes settled on the painting of an extraordinarily lovely young woman. Red-gold curls framed a piquant face set on a long white neck. Her eyes were bright blue under arched auburn eyebrows, and her wide mouth had a generosity about it.

Walking over to the fire, Meredith gazed up at the portrait with great interest. The artist had captured something of the woman's personality ... there was an inherent warmth in the smile, and happiness dwelt in that face as well. Rose de Montboucher wore a dress of palest pink chiffon with a softly draped collar and a string of pearls, and Meredith decided the portrait had been painted in the 1920s.

"Your grandmother was absolutely gorgeous, no two ways about it," she said, looking over her shoulder at him. "I think she was probably a bit mischievous, there's a certain glint in those rather remarkable eyes and in her infectious smile."

Luc nodded. "Quite an accurate assessment of her. *I* believe she had a lot of mischief in her, as well as a special kind of joie de vivre. It was a true gaiety that people found irresistible. I knew her as a much older woman than she is in that portrait, but even then I felt she was up to something, and all the time. Up to no good, my father always said. He was her firstborn and her favorite of her four children. I recall that she had a good sense of humor and was a marvelous raconteur. I think she must have kissed the Blarney Stone."

"Was she Irish?"

"She was. My grandfather met her in Dublin. At a ball. He had gone there to shoot."

Mathilde bustled in from the bedroom with

Vincent in her wake. "Would you like to have help with your unpacking, *Madame* Stratton? I will send Jasmine to assist you."

Meredith shook her head. "Thank you, Mathilde, but I can manage."

The housekeeper nodded, gave her a quick smile, glanced at Luc, and inclined her head, then flew out of the room. Vincent hurried after her, endeavoring to keep pace.

"He's her shadow," Luc murmured in a low voice, once they were alone. "They're both the salt of the earth, and have worked at Talcy all of their lives, and their parents before them. They have two daughters, Jasmine and Philippine, and a son Jean-Pierre, who all work here at the château. I'll leave you now, Meredith, so that you can freshen up. Are you quite sure you wouldn't like Jasmine to come upstairs and help you with your clothes?"

"No, really, I'm fine, thanks."

Luc pushed his jacket sleeve away from his watch, peered at it. "Ah, it's only just a little after twelve. Let us meet, then, in the library, in an hour, shall we say? Does that give you enough time?"

"Of course."

He half smiled, turned on his heel, and headed toward the door.

Meredith said, "Luc, where *is* the library?"

He swung around, grinning, and answered apologetically, "So sorry, I forgot you don't know the house. The library is the middle room of the *enfilade* . . . that's the series of rooms which adjoin each other, off the entrance hall on the right-hand side. We'll have a drink in there before lunch."

"Yes, that'll be nice."

The door closed softly behind him. Meredith turned back to the portrait of his grandmother; she studied it again for a moment or two.

"Irish eyes are smiling," Meredith murmured aloud, thinking of the famous old ballad. And indeed Rose de Montboucher's eyes *were* full of laughter, and it was very much an Irish face, of course. It couldn't be anything else. Stepping back, Meredith stared at the portrait for a second longer, her head held on one side. Her eyes narrowed slightly; she squinted at the picture. Rose de Montboucher reminds me of someone, she thought, but she had no idea who that was. Rose's grandson perhaps. No, not Luc. He was dark haired with dark brown eyes. A woman with red-gold hair and clear blue eyes . . . this image and a tiny fragment of a memory leapt into her mind, but it was fleeting, disappearing before she could grasp it properly. Shaking her head, she gave the portrait a last glance and went into the adjoining bedroom.

The minute she entered it, a smile settled on Meredith's face. It was charming, welcoming, with a fire burning brightly in the grate and the silk-shaded lamps turned on. The room was decorated in a mélange of grays and soft grayish-blues. The walls were covered with silver-gray moire silk, the flowing, bouffant draperies at the three tall windows were of silver-gray taffeta, and the large four-poster was hung with the same taffeta that looked as if it had been hand-embroidered. On closer inspection, Meredith realized that the pink, red, and yellow roses and trailing green vines had been hand-painted on the gray silk. There were several chairs and a love seat covered in pearl-gray cut velvet arranged around the fire, and in a corner stood an unusual antique dressing table made entirely of Venetian mirror.

Fascinated, Meredith walked slowly around the bedroom, looking at everything closely, admiring its style and elegance, nodding to herself as her glance lighted on a particular painting or an object of art. Certain things in the room were worn, even a little shabby, but the overall ambiance was one of old world elegance, luxury, and a bygone age. It also had a restful feeling, as did the adjoining sitting room, which was decorated in a mixture of grayish pinks, smokey blues and greens, all taken from the colors of the Aubusson rug on the floor.

Moving across the bedroom, Meredith finally came to a standstill in front of the Venetian dressing table. Silver brushes with Rose de Montboucher's initials were lined up on the mirrored surface, and there was a collection of crystal perfume bottles, silver-topped powder bowls, and rouge pots grouped together.

To one side of them stood a silver-framed photograph of a darkly handsome man in evening dress. Meredith bent down, stared at it, and for a split second she thought it was a picture of Luc.

Then she realized it was not he; the evening suit be-
spoke the 1920s. It was obviously his grandfather,
Rose's husband. That's who Luc must resemble, she
decided. His grandfather . . . he's the spitting image
of him.

After unpacking her two suitcases, Meredith
picked up her toilet bag and went into the bathroom. Immediately she came to a standstill, taken
aback by its size and by the fire burning merrily in
the white marble hearth.

The bathroom was enormous, with a soaring
window draped with white lace curtains, an old-
fashioned tub on feet, and bell pulls dangling over
it to ring for the maids. She wondered whether they
still worked but refrained from pulling one, just in
case they did.

# Chapter Twelve

Downstairs in his office at the rear of the château, Luc de Montboucher sat at his drawing table, a series of blueprints spread out in front of him.

The plans had been done by a colleague in his architectural firm, and Luc had fully intended to go over them before lunch, hoping to give his approval. But so far he had paid scant attention to the blueprints.

His mind was not on work. It was focused on Meredith Stratton.

From the moment he had met her on Wednesday morning, at the manor house in Montfort-L'Amaury, he had been intrigued by her; he was very taken with her, in point of fact. Being an architect and a designer, he was an extremely visual man, and so it was her looks that had initially attracted him to her.

He liked her height, her blondness and fair skin, those smoky-green eyes that told him so much about her.

She was a good looking woman with a great deal of personal style. He experienced a jolt of genuine pleasure whenever his eyes rested on her. He also appreciated her self-confidence and composure, found them reassuring. Skittishness in women invariably made him nervous.

Luc had realized within the first couple of hours of being in her company that she was businesslike, practical, professional, organized, and decisive, and, not unnaturally, these traits appealed to his love of order.

He couldn't abide chaotic women who dragged trouble in their wakes, who lived in perpetual mess and created mess in other lives. Also, he found Meredith's energy and effervescent personality most appealing; they buoyed him up, gave him a sense of *élan*, the like of which he had not experienced in a long time.

What a pity she lives so far away in New York, he thought, tapping his pencil on the drawing table. But it was not so far away that it made a relationship impossible. There was, after all, a supersonic flight. He could be in Manhattan in three and a half hours, four at the most, on the Concorde. He had made the trip from Paris to New York only three weeks earlier, to visit a client. It had been easy.

Luc wanted, had the *need* to know Meredith Stratton better. Much better. *Intimately*. He found her sexually attractive, and more so than any woman he had met in some years. He realized on Wednesday night, after their first business meeting, that he desired her. If a man didn't know that after the first encounter, then when would he ever know? Luc suddenly wondered. And he felt certain it was the same way for a woman.

Almost against his own volition, he had confided in Agnes, but only to a degree. He had merely told her of his interest in Meredith, his wish to know her better. These confidences had been passed on Thursday evening, when he had called her at home. He had not been able to help himself. Then he had invited the D'Aubervilles and Meredith to Talcy for the weekend, but Agnes had been obliged to decline because Alain and Chloe were ill with the flu.

Agnes had said he should issue the invitation to Meredith anyway. "Don't worry," Agnes had promised, "I'll suggest we all have lunch after our Friday morning meeting, and you'll find a way to invite her to the château. I'll lead you into it quite naturally."

When he had demurred, Agnes had exclaimed, with a laugh, "Don't be so fainthearted, such a coward, Luc. Meredith has absolutely nothing to do this weekend, and she has no friends in Paris other than us. I happen to know she likes you, so she'll accept the invitation. And you're going to enjoy being with her. She's wonderful. Everyone loves her."

*Love,* he thought to himself. Will I ever find love again? He wanted to, and very seriously so. He

liked women, admired and respected them, and he
wanted a wife. Certainly he did not relish the idea
of living alone for the rest of his life.

So far love had proved elusive. After Annick his
life had stopped. He had been numb. But eventually
he had tried to start over, God knows he had, to start
life anew, to have a worthwhile relationship. But
there had been no success. Only abundant failure.

It was true he had known a couple of women in
the last few years, and they had been perfectly nice
human beings, but neither of them had ignited a
spark in him. He had begun to wonder if the spark
had left him forever, had quite recently decided that
it had, convinced himself of it, really. Until
Meredith. But she had so enthralled him, without
even trying, he had actually been startled at himself.
So rare was this feeling, so strong this desire, this
need to become part of another person, part of her
life, he felt bound to pursue her.

How often did a man feel like that? Once in a
lifetime perhaps. Instantly he corrected himself. It
was twice in his case; he had felt the same way
about Annick.

Meredith Stratton, he said under his breath, and
wrote her name on the notepad in front of him,
stared down at it.

Who are you, Meredith Stratton? And why are
you so troubled? Where does that deep well of sadness inside you spring from? Who was it that hurt
you so badly they've scarred your soul? Who broke
your heart? Instinctively, Luc knew Meredith had

experienced great unhappiness. He saw pain mirrored in those smoky eyes, saw infinite sadness dwelling there. He wanted to ease the pain, chase away the sadness if he could; he was sure he could, given the chance.

Luc had not wished to ask Agnes questions about Meredith, although he longed to do so. He had felt awkward about prying, which went against the grain. In certain ways, he felt that he did *know* Meredith, knew what she was truly like, the kind of person she was inside. A good woman.

What was that phrase his lovely Irish grandmother had always used? "True blue," Rosie de Montboucher would say to him, "Your grandfather is true blue, Luc."

And so was Meredith.

The small black clock on the drawing table told him it was almost twelve-thirty. Throwing down the pencil, suddenly impatient, he stood up, stretching his long legs. He was tired of sitting, and he felt cramped after the drive from Paris that morning.

Leaving the office, he ran up the back staircase and down the corridor to his bedroom. Shrugging out of his blazer, he went into the bathroom, where he splashed his face with cold water, dried it, and combed his hair.

Luc peered at himself in the mirror. There were a few silver strands in his black hair these days; he stared harder, thinking he seemed drawn, fatigued. There were lines around his eyes. He decided he looked older than forty-three.

Meredith was also in her early forties, he was certain of that. It was something Agnes had said about her age, before Meredith had arrived from London. He wondered if that was too old to have a child, then supposed it depended on the woman. He had always wanted a child. To carry on the line. But if he didn't have one, it wouldn't matter in the long run. Life was such a struggle, and Luc suddenly understood that he wanted to reach out, grab life, grab happiness. Loving someone was not about progeny.

*Meredith.* She could make me happy. I know it in my bones. Bones don't lie, Luc, Grandma Rosie used to tell him when he was a boy growing up. You can tell a lot by the bones, child, she would add. Breeding's in the bone, Luc. Look at horses. Even when the stamina's there, it's not enough. Got to have breeding in a racehorse. I know my horseflesh, Luc, I'm a good judge. *Oui, Grand-mère*, he'd answer dutifully. Luc, please speak English today. Yes, Grandmother. Always trust your bones, she would repeat. They never lie, Luc, never. Oh Grandma Rosie, he thought, smiling inwardly at this lovely memory of her, you were a genuine original.

Turning away from the mirror, Luc hurried into his bedroom, took a gray tweed jacket out of the armoire, put it on over his black sweater and dark gray slacks, and left the room.

He ran down the front stairs at a rapid pace, crossed the front entrance hall and strode into the library, glancing around as he did.

The fire crackled in the hearth, the drinks tray was well stocked, and there was a bottle of Dom in the silver ice bucket, just as he had instructed Vincent. There was nothing to do but wait for Meredith to appear.

Walking over to one of the French windows, he stood looking out at the garden, thinking how arresting the parterres looked; the clipped, dark-green hedges were covered with a light frosting of snow that highlighted their intricate geometric shapes. He thought how lucky it was that his sisters had decided not to come to Talcy this weekend. He loved them dearly and liked their husbands, but he was relieved, and glad to have the house to himself. He had no great seduction plans, that was not his style; he liked everything to happen naturally. But he did want Meredith to feel relaxed, at ease, not on display for his family.

There was a slight noise, the sound of a step.

Swinging away from the window, he looked toward the adjoining living room expectantly. Meredith was walking toward him, and he felt that same jolt of pleasure at the sight of her, the rush of excitement inside.

Moving forward, he exclaimed, "There you are! Come in, Meredith, come to the fire, where it's warmer. Now, would you care for a glass of champagne?"

"That would be lovely, Luc," she answered, gliding across the floor.

He went to open the bottle of Dom Pérignon, but

could not resist looking at her surreptitiously out of the corner of his eye. She was wearing a beige checked jacket over a cream cashmere sweater and pants, and he thought she looked stunning. He bit back a smile. Of course she did. There was no question in his mind that he was quite prejudiced when it came to Meredith Stratton.

After bringing their flutes of champagne to the fireside, Luc sat down on the sofa opposite Meredith and said, "I hope you have everything you need, that you're comfortable in Grandma Rosie's rooms?"

"Oh yes, I am, thank you very much. I love them, and that bathroom. My goodness, a fireplace, no less." She laughed and added, "What a luxury. I feel thoroughly spoiled."

He laughed with her. "All of the bedroom suites on that floor have fireplaces in the bathrooms, but we don't often use them, only for guests really, and only when it's cold weather. It's such a lot of work, keeping all the fires going. In my great-grandfather's day, even Grandfather's, they had armies of servants to do that, to look after everything. Nowadays it's hard to get staff, and expensive, so I keep such things as fires down to a minimum."

"I can't say I blame you." She looked across at him, smiling warmly. She liked him a lot, wanted to know more about him. "Did you grow up here?" she asked, filled with curiosity.

"Yes, I did. With my sisters Isabelle and Natalie. They're younger than I, but we had great times together, and an estate such as this is a wonderful place for young children."

"It must have been an idyllic childhood."

"I suppose it was, although it didn't always seem so at the time. My father was rather strict. And rightly so."

He observed her over the rim of the flute for a brief moment. "You're looking rather wistful. Is something wrong?"

"Oh no, not at all," she replied swiftly. "I was just thinking how different my childhood was—" Meredith stopped abruptly, wondering what had induced her to say this. She rarely confided details about her childhood to anyone.

Although he had no way of knowing her thoughts, Luc suspected that Meredith had said more than she had intended. He could tell from the startled expression on her face. Quickly he said, "But you grew up in the country, too, didn't you? In Connecticut?"

She shook her head. "No, I didn't. I suppose Agnes told you I come from Connecticut, that I have a family home there and an inn, and that's true, I do. But I grew up in Australia. My childhood was spent in Sydney."

"You're an Australian?"

"Yes. At least, I was born there, and that's my original nationality, but I became an American citizen when I was twenty-two." Leaning back against the tapestry cushions, she gave him a very direct look and finished, "That was exactly twenty-three years ago."

"You're forty-five? But that doesn't seem possible. You certainly don't look it." Luc was genuinely surprised.

"Thank you, I'm still forty-four, actually, Luc. I'll be forty-five at the beginning of May."

"And I'm forty-three . . . I'll be forty-four on June third." There was a small pause, and then he said carefully, not wanting to stir up bad memories, "From the tone of your voice, I rather got the impression you didn't have a very good childhood."

"I didn't. It was terrible. Horrible, really. No child should have to go through that," she blurted out, and then bit her lip, averted her face, stared into the fire.

So that's the source of the pain, he thought, at least some of it. There's much more that she is concealing. He remained silent for a few moments, allowing her the space and time to compose herself.

Eventually, Luc said, "I'm sorry to hear that you were unhappy, Meredith. What happened to you?"

"I was orphaned when I was young. Ten years old. My parents were killed in a car crash. I got pushed around a lot after that . . . it was rough, hard—" She cut herself off again, shrugged, forced a smile, met his direct gaze. Hers was equally as candid as she finished. "But that's such a long time ago. I've forgotten about it really."

Not true, he commented to himself, and asked, "When did you go to America?"

"When I was seventeen. I went to Connecticut as an au pair with an American family who'd been living in Sydney. Later I worked for Jack and Amelia

Silver. They sort of . . . turned my life around." A lovely smile spread across her face. "What I mean is, I was like a younger sister to them. You see, Luc, they weren't much older than me, in their early thirties. Anyway, they treated me like a member of the family. Amelia and Jack made up for . . . well, for all those bad years."

Luc nodded, refrained from commenting. He sat staring into her smoky-green eyes. The sadness of the moment before had lifted, but he knew it still lurked at the core of her. He wondered if he could make it go away entirely; he was not sure. All he knew was that he wanted to try.

Meredith said, "You're staring at me, Luc. Do I have a smudge on my nose or something?"

"No, you don't." His dark brown eyes suddenly twinkled. "I was just admiring you, if you want the truth. You're a beautiful woman, Meredith."

She felt the color rising up from her neck to flood her face and was mortified at herself. Men had paid her compliments before; why was she blushing because Luc had? "Th-thank you," she managed to stammer, and was relieved when the telephone began to shrill.

Luc rose, went to answer it. "Clos-Talcy. *Bonjour*." After listening for a second, he said: "Hold on for a moment, please," and looked across at her. "It's your daughter, Catherine."

Meredith's face lit up and she jumped to her feet, stepped over to the desk, took the receiver from him, thanking him as she did.

Luc merely nodded, walked over to the window, stood gazing out, his head full of this woman. He felt he knew her intuitively, and yet she baffled him. There was an air of mystery about her. He found her irresistible.

"Hello, Catherine, how are you, darling?" Meredith asked, then listened attentively as her daughter's voice floated to her across the transatlantic wire from New York. Her smile widened. "Yes, I'm happy for you, darling, I'm thrilled, actually." She clutched the phone tightly, continued to listen, then said into the mouthpiece, "Yes, I'll be back in Paris on Monday, and no, I won't be home for at least another week." There was a pause at Meredith's end before she answered, "Yes, all right, I'll call you on Wednesday. Give Keith my love. Don't forget to tell Jon. Have a great weekend. I love you, Cat. Bye now."

She replaced the receiver and smiled at Luc when he turned around to face her, an expectant look in his eyes.

"My daughter just got engaged. Last night. She's floating on cloud nine." Meredith blinked and looked away, pushing back sudden tears. She was so happy for Catherine, her emotions got the better of her for a moment.

"What wonderful news! It calls for a toast and another glass of bubbly, as Grandma Rosie used to call it."

After filling their crystal flutes, Luc raised his and clinked it against hers. "Here's to love . . . and happy endings," he murmured, staring at her closely, his dark eyes riveted on hers.

Meredith stared back, felt the warmth rising to fill her face again. "Love and happy endings, Luc," she repeated, and took a sip of champagne. Then she went over to the sofa, where she sat down. She was very conscious of Luc de Montboucher all of a sudden.

Luc followed her but remained standing, his back against the fire. "How old is your daughter?" he asked.

"Twenty-five. And I have a son, Jonathan, who's twenty-one. He's studying law at Yale."

A smile flashed across his face, and he exclaimed, "I studied architecture there. Graduate school after the Sorbonne. What a coincidence! Does he like it?"

"Yes, he does."

"I'm glad. I did, too. Best years of my life." He chuckled.

"Were they really?"

"Up to a point. I had some other good years. Before. After." He took a swallow of his drink, a reflective look washing over his face.

"Luc?"

"Yes?"

"Have you ever been married?"

"Oh yes. Didn't Agnes tell you about me?" He raised a brow questioningly.

"No." She frowned. "What makes you think she would?"

"Oh no special reason," he answered and

shrugged. "I thought she might have, that's all. And yes, I was married. My wife died six years ago. Annick was in good health one day, dying of cancer the next. It was virulent, she went very quickly. Just six months after being diagnosed. She was only thirty-seven." He paused, cleared his throat. "We were married eight years."

"Luc, I'm so sorry. How tragic. What a terrible loss for you." Meredith looked up at him worriedly, hoping she had not upset him. How stupid she had been, thoughtless, to bring up his wife.

"We didn't have children," Luc volunteered.

Meredith said nothing, gazed across the room, lost in thought.

Luc put down his drink on the coffee table between the two sofas; he threw a couple of logs onto the fire, straightened up. Lifting his drink, he took a sip.

The room had gone very quiet. The only sounds were the crackling logs, the ticking clock.

At last Meredith said, "Nobody's life is ever easy, whatever we might think. There's always pain and heartache, trouble, problems, ill health. Loss . . . of one kind or another."

"That is so . . . yes, it's very true what you say. My Irish grandmother was not only beautiful but also very wise. She was forever telling us, when we were growing up, that life had always been hard, was meant to be hard, and that it would never be anything else but hard. That is the earthly lot of us poor mortals, she would say, and therefore we should grab what bit of happiness we could when-

ever we could. And if we found the right person we
must hang on to them for dear life. Forever. That's
what she said, and I strongly suspect that Grandma
Rosie spoke the truth."

"I've never met the right person," Meredith said,
surprising herself, instantly regretting these words.

"I did. But she died." Luc stared off into the distance for a moment, as if he could see something
visible only to himself. Then he said, "I've never
met anyone else. But I haven't given up hope. . . ."
He looked at her pointedly, but Meredith did not
appear to notice his meaningful glance.

"Catherine's father died," she suddenly answered,
"but he was a married man anyway . . . I would
never have been able to marry him. I divorced Jon's
father . . . that was all wrong . . . we weren't right
for each other at all. . . ." She let her sentence float
in midair, unfinished.

"Was that a long time ago? Your divorce?"

"Sixteen years." Confessions, she thought. And
more confessions. What's suddenly got into me?
Why am I telling him all these private things about
myself? This man is a stranger.

Luc said, "You will meet the right person,
Meredith. I know you will." He wanted to add that
perhaps she already had, but he refrained.

Mathilde appeared in the doorway at the far end
of the library. She cleared her throat.

Luc glanced at her. "Ah, Mathilde. Is lunch
ready?"

*"Oui, Monsieur."*

"*Merci.*" Turning to Meredith, he said, "I don't know about you, but I'm ravenous."

"Yes, I am too."

As he led her across the library in the direction of the dining room, Luc explained, "I asked Mathilde to make a fairly simple lunch. Vegetable soup, plain omelette, green salad, cheese, and fruit. I hope that's to your taste."

"It sounds perfect," Meredith answered, looking at him.

Luc smiled at her warmly, took hold of her arm, and led her into the dining room, where Mathilde was waiting to serve lunch.

Suddenly Meredith did not care what she had told him about herself. She knew he would not judge her; she trusted him.

And she felt safe with Luc de Montboucher.

# Chapter Thirteen

fter lunch Luc took Meredith on a tour of the park in which Clos-Talcy stood. As they walked they talked about a variety of things, but eventually the conversation came back to his grandmother. Luc told her several amusing stories about Rose de Montboucher, keeping her thoroughly entertained.

At one moment she said, "The way in which you speak about *Grand-mère* Rose really brings her to life for me. I wish I'd known her."

"You would have enjoyed her," Luc answered, glancing at Meredith. "She was a true original. Strong of character, spirited and courageous, and she truly ran our family. Ruled it with an iron hand. In a velvet glove, of course." He chuckled, continued. "My father loved to tease her, and when her birthday came around he always used to lift his glass and say, 'Here's to that great man whose name is Rosie,' borrowing the line from Voltaire."

"Who said those very words to Catherine the Great, when he met her in Russia for the first time," Meredith remarked. "She's one of my favorite characters in history, and I've read a number of biographies about her. *She* was strong and courageous too. And she made her own rules."

"That's true, she did, but then most strong women do do that, don't you think?"

"Yes, they do . . . sometimes they have to, because they have no other choice."

Luc took hold of her arm and led her down a side path, heading for the orchard ahead of them. "In 1871, when my great-great-grandfather acquired Talcy from the Delorme family, he built the fishpond over there. It's actually fed by the stream that flows through the wood, and it was a marvelous bit of engineering on his part."

They came to a stop by the edge of the pond, and Meredith peered down into its murky depths. "There really are fish in it," she said, sounding surprised.

"*Of course*. When I was a little boy, I used to fish here. My sisters and I all had rods and lines, and sometimes Grandma Rosie joined us. She was rather good at fishing."

"I can just imagine." There was a silence between them as they walked around the pond, turned, and headed toward the woods. After a moment, Meredith murmured, "Your grandmother was a great influence on you, wasn't she?"

"Oh yes. She brought us up, you see. My mother died in childbirth, giving birth to our little brother Albert, who was premature. He also died that same week. It will be thirty-three years ago this summer, to be exact."

"How sad for you and your sisters . . . for your whole family."

"Everyone took it very hard, especially my father. He never remarried, and I believe he mourned my mother until the day he died."

"When was that, Luc?"

"Almost two years ago. He wasn't very old, only seventy-one, which is no age at all these days. He dropped dead suddenly of a stroke. He was in the stables, didn't know what hit him, thankfully. It would have been terrible if he had been an invalid, he was a very active man, a great sportsman."

"And your grandmother? When did she die?"

"In 1990 at the age of ninety. She was wonderful right to the end, not a bit senile or decrepit, and she was very active, had all of her faculties. Oh yes, *she* was still the boss around here. One night she went to bed and never awakened, just died in her sleep, very peacefully. I was glad of that, glad she didn't suffer. Neither did my father, for that matter."

"I think that's the best way to go, with your boots on, so to speak," Meredith said, thinking out loud. "Or when you're asleep, as your grandmother was. Dying of old age is the most natural thing." Meredith turned to Luc, smiled at him. "That paint-ing of her in my sitting room is very lovely, isn't it? I was trying to figure out how old she was when it was painted."

Luc's brow furrowed as he said, "I'm not exactly sure. However, she'd just married Arnaud de Montboucher, my grandfather, and come to live at Talcy when she sat for the portrait. So she must have been in her early twenties."

"That's what I thought. She reminds me of somebody, I'm not sure who."

"My sister Natalie favors her, but you've never met Natalie. Or have you?"

Meredith laughed, shook her head, "No, I haven't."

"Natalie resembles Grandmother physically, she's really rather beautiful, but she's not like her in character. Neither is Isabelle. I'm the one who inherited Rose's basic character," Luc confided.

"She really put her imprint on you, didn't she?"

"*Absolutely*. I have come to realize that I think like her, and I have a tendency to do things the way she did. When someone really influences you in childhood, you carry her imprint. Always, I think. It's like an indelible stamp. And who was it who put their imprint on you, Meredith?"

"No one did," she answered almost fiercely, and bit her lip, suddenly aware that she had sounded angry. Speaking in a softer tone, she went on. "I just muddled through on my own, doing the best I could, teaching myself. Nobody influenced me. There was no one in my life to do that, no one at all, I was completely alone."

They had stopped walking a few seconds before, had paused near one of the fountains, now stood face-to-face as they spoke. The sadness invading her touched Luc; he wanted to reach out, pull her into his arms. But he did not dare. He was about to say something comforting to her, when she suddenly smiled. The bereftness vanished instantly.

Meredith said, "But there was someone later, when I was a bit older . . . eighteen. Amelia Silver. She showed me how to do certain things, taught me about antiques and art. She had wonderful taste and was very artistic, actually, and her husband, Jack, influenced me in certain ways, too."

"Are the Silvers still living in Connecticut?"

"Oh no, they're both dead. They died years ago, over twenty years ago. Sadly, neither of them was very old."

"I'm sorry. They were like family, weren't they?"

She nodded, half turned away from him. "I was twenty-two when Jack died, twenty-three when Amelia followed him to the grave. I had them in my life for only a few years."

Aware that the sadness had surfaced again, Luc took hold of her hand. "Come on, let's walk down to the ornamental lake, it's so picturesque, one of the prettiest parts of the park."

By the time they reached the lake situated at the far side of the house, Meredith was beginning to feel unwell. A wave of nausea passed through her and a peculiar kind of exhaustion seemed to settle in her bones. Unexpectedly, she thought she was going to collapse, and she grabbed hold of Luc's arm, said in a faint voice, "I don't know what's wrong with me, but I feel awful. Nauseated, and suddenly very tired."

Luc looked at her in concern. "I do hope you're not getting the flu, that Agnes hasn't passed on any germs."

"I doubt it, and Agnes wasn't ill."

"No, but her family was. Do you think it was the wine at lunch? Could that have upset you?"

She shook her head. "I didn't drink very much. Anyway, I remember now that I felt a bit queasy when I arrived in Paris on Tuesday night. I'd spent the morning wandering around an old ruined abbey in Yorkshire, and it was bitterly cold. That night I thought that I'd probably caught a chill. But I was all right the next morning, so perhaps I'm just tired in general, run down."

"Perhaps. Let us return to the house. You must rest for the remainder of the afternoon." So saying, he put his arm around her and together they walked back to the château.

Luc accompanied Meredith upstairs to her rooms and fussed around her. He made her take off her boots and forced her to lie down on the sofa. After adding more logs to the fire, he brought her a thick cashmere throw and laid it over her.

"Don't go away," he said, smiling down at her. "I'll be back in a few minutes with a pot of hot lemon tea laced with honey. It'll do you the world of good . . . one of Grandma Rosie's cures." He left the room, closing the door quietly behind him.

Meredith leaned her head back against the pile of soft velvet cushions and closed her eyes; she was so sleepy, she could barely keep her eyes open.

She must have dozed off, for she awakened with a start when Luc bent over her and moved a strand of hair away from her face. This intimate gesture on his part startled her for a moment, and then she realized that she did not mind that he did this. It suddenly seemed perfectly natural to her.

"I put the tea here on the ottoman," he said, his voice low, concerned still. "Drink some of it while it's hot. Now I shall go and let you rest." He squeezed her shoulder.

"Thank you, Luc, you're so kind. I'm sorry I cut short our walk, but I—"

"Think nothing of it," he said swiftly. "It's not important."

"Would you turn off the lamp, please?"

"Of course. Now rest." He left the room.

Meredith turned on her side, lay curled in a ball under the cashmere throw, staring into the fire's bright flames. The logs hissed and crackled and sparks flew up the chimney. She raised her eyes at one moment and gazed for a long time at the portrait of Rose de Montboucher.

The afternoon light was fading rapidly, the room filling with shadows, but the roaring fire and its dancing flames introduced a rosy glow. In the soft incandescent light it seemed to Meredith that the painting of Rose came alive. Her face was full of life, her delphinium-blue eyes brilliant, sparkling with joy, and the red-gold curls framed the sublime face like a halo of burnished copper. How beautiful she was . . . so radiant.

Meredith's eyelids drooped. She drifted on a wave of warmth. Her mind was filled with that face . . . memories jostled for prominence . . . fragmented into infinitesimal pieces. She fell into a deep sleep. And she dreamed.

The landscape was vast and it stretched away endlessly, as far as the eye could see, miles and miles of desolation. There was something oddly sinister about this place where there were no trees and nothing bloomed on the parched, cracked earth.

She had been walking and walking for as long as she could remember. It seemed like forever. She felt tired. But some inner determination pushed her forward. She knew they were here somewhere. The children. She had followed them here. But where could they be? Her eyes darted around. The land was empty; there was nowhere for them to hide.

Help me to find them, please. Oh God, help me to find them, she pleaded. And immediately she understood that her prayers fell on arid ground. There was no God here. Not in this empty void. It was godless, this netherworld.

And then unexpectedly she saw something moving near the pale rim of the far horizon. She began to run. The cracked dry earth suddenly gave way to mud flats and her shoes squelched and sank into the mud and sometimes stuck and her progress was slowed. She persisted. Soon the land was dry again. She ran and ran.

The specks on the horizon grew closer and closer, loomed up in front of her as if they had jumped backward. She saw a young boy holding a girl's hand. Just as they had drawn closer to her, now they withdrew, moved forward again, and rapidly so. She ran, almost caught up to them once more. They walked on slowly, the two of them, still hand in hand, perfectly in step. She called out to them, called for them to wait for her. But they did not. They went on walking as if they had not heard her. The sky changed, turned a strange grayish-green, and a high wind began to blow, buffeting her forward. Suddenly the boy flew into the air, as if blown upward by a gust of wind. He disappeared into the sky.

The little girl was alone now. She suddenly turned around and began to walk toward her. Meredith hurried forward to greet the girl, so wan, so pathetic, with her pale, pinched face and big sad eyes. She wore black stockings and shoes, and a heavy winter coat. There was a small black beret on her head and a long striped scarf was wrapped around her neck. The label pinned to the lapel of her coat was huge. The girl pointed to it. Meredith peered at it, trying to decipher the girl's name written there, but she could not.

Suddenly, taking her by surprise, the girl began to run away. Meredith tried to run after her but her feet were stuck, encased in the mud. She cried to the girl to come back, but she did not stop, just went on running and running and running until she was gone out of the landscape.

There was a cracking sound and then a terrible noise like shell fire and everything exploded around her . . .

Meredith sat up with a jolt. Her face and neck were bathed in sweat. She was disoriented, and it took her a moment to get her bearings. Then she realized she was in Grandma Rosie's sitting room at Talcy.

Outside, a storm was raging, lightning streaking through the darkening sky, thunderbolts rattling the windows. She shivered and huddled under the cashmere throw Luc had wrapped around her earlier, stared at the fire, grown low in the grate. And the fear was there inside, ravaging her.

Closing her eyes, she tried to push the fear away, not understanding why she was so frightened. She was here at the château, perfectly safe from the violent storm raging outside.

And then it came to her. She knew why she was so fearful. It was the dream. The dream that had recurred so many times in her life. She had not dreamed it for years now. Suddenly, the old, familiar dream had come back to haunt her, to frighten her again, as it always had in the past.

# Chapter Fourteen

O nce she had returned to Paris, Meredith's thoughts frequently focused on her weekend at Clos-Talcy. And most particularly, Luc de Montboucher was at the center of her reflections.

She liked him, more than liked him, in fact, and his kindness to her had left a lasting impression.

Kindness had always been important to Meredith, perhaps because she had experienced so little of it in her life. None at all when she had been a child, and growing up without kindness had made her acquire a carapace of iron. Only Mrs. Paulson had been able to break through this tough protective shell; and then, of course, the Silvers, when she had gone to work for them at Silver Lake.

And just as kindness was important to a child, so it was to a grown woman, and especially a woman over forty. But this characteristic aside, she found him extremely attractive as a man.

Luc was very good-looking, darkly handsome and fine of feature, but that was not his most important asset as far as she was concerned. Just a pretty face had long ago ceased to hold her interest.

She admired his intelligence and talent, and his integrity, which instinctively she knew was unassailable. He also had a good sense of humor, and she discovered they liked so many of the same things— good books, classical music, a glass of icy champagne in front of a blazing fire on a wintery night, not to mention houses built on water, stained-glass windows, and the delicate paintings of Marie Laurencin. All in all, Luc was an impressive man and she was glad she had met him, glad she had accepted his invitation to go to the château in the Loire.

They had driven back to Paris early on Monday morning, and she had spent most of the afternoon with him and Agnes out at the Manoir de la Closière in Montfort-L'Amaury, going over the changes they wanted to make. That evening Luc had taken her to dinner at the Relais Plaza, and the night before they had eaten at Grand Vefour.

They had laughed a lot over the past few days, and she had begun to realize what an enormous impression he was making on her, and just how much she really did care about him.

Meredith had known Luc only a week, but he was already under her skin, and she knew she was going to miss him when she returned to New York. In her mind

she was already planning her next trip to Paris. There
was business to attend to in Manhattan; also, she had to
sign the initial documents for the sale of Hilltops to the
Morrisons. And she couldn't wait to see Cat, to hug her,
fuss over her, and celebrate her engagement to Keith.

But all of this would take only ten days at the
most, she had calculated, and then she would fly
back on the Concorde. In any case, she was needed
in Paris because of the remodeling and renovation of
the old manor house. The three of them had agreed
on Monday that it must be modern and up-to-date
in every way, while still retaining its basic character
and charm. And of course it required her decorative
imprint, the look and the stylishness that pro-
claimed it to be a creation of Havens Incorporated.

In the quietness of her hotel suite the previous
night she had wondered what would happen after the
inn was finished; she had an immediate answer for
herself. The inn would take a whole year to complete,
therefore she would be spending a great deal of time
in this city. Paris. The City of Light. And of lovers.

Things will work themselves out, she reassured
herself in the early hours of the morning. A long
time ago Meredith had come to understand that life
had a way of taking care of itself.

Day by day, step by step, she decided, as she prepared for bed. It's the only thing I can do, and we'll see
what happens. Everything must take its normal course.

Meredith knew only too well that a relationship
that looked promising could quite easily come to
naught, fizzle out in a flurry of recriminations and

bad feeling. After all, that had happened with Reed Jamison. Her face had changed at the thought of him. What an unpleasant encounter that had turned out to be in the end. But then, Reed and Luc were as different as any two men could be, poles apart, and anyway, to make comparisons was foolhardy, even odious.

Luc was so straightforward, so honest, she believed she would always know exactly where she stood with him. No game-playing there. And he was a thoughtful, responsible, mature man whom she knew respected her; certainly she respected him.

Meredith had spent most of Tuesday with Agnes, and she had been surprised that her French partner had not probed too deeply about the weekend; Agnes had asked only a few cursory questions. But then, they had been very preoccupied with their plans for the inn and busy rushing around Paris. They had visited innumerable antiques shops and fabric houses, taking Polaroids of furniture and collecting samples of fabric and wallpaper. Since they had similar tastes and the same ideas about the decoration and furnishing of the inn, there were no problems in this respect.

It was on Wednesday afternoon, when they were sitting in Agnes's office at Havens, that Meredith mentioned Luc. The two of them were selecting fabric swatches and lining them up on a flat board, endeavoring to create viable color schemes.

Quite suddenly Meredith said, "Last night Luc invited me to the château again. This weekend."

Agnes glanced up. "I'm not surprised, he likes you a lot."

"And I like him."

Agnes laughed. "Most women do. He's irresistible. I've always wondered why he's never remarried."

"Perhaps it's taking him a long time to get over his grief for his wife."

"Oh, so he told you about her?"

"Yes, which is more than you did, after you'd promised. I sort of blundered in on that one, and I was afraid I'd upset him."

"I'm sorry I didn't phone you, as I promised, but Chloe was so sick, I had my hands full. Anyway, Alain and I had a chance to talk only on Sunday afternoon, and I certainly didn't want to call you at Talcy to gossip about your host."

"No, I understand that, and I'm glad you didn't, I would have been embarrassed."

"Alain has known Luc off and on for many years, Meredith, but not really well. We became a bit closer to him only in the last year, mainly because he was designing a house for Alain's sister. And even so, he never discussed Annick . . . his past was sort of . . . well . . . *vague* to us, and we're not the kind to pry. . . ." She did not finish her sentence, merely looked across at Meredith and shrugged.

Meredith said, "I understand. You can know people, be very friendly, and yet not know too much about their private life at all." She leaned back in the chair and crossed her long legs. "There's so much I like about Luc, Agnes. I mean as a person, and he's very straight, honest. Also, he really listens, pays attention. That's a rarity these days."

"I believe him to be the kind of man who's worth taking seriously. I know for a fact he's not a playboy. Not at all, not one bit the philanderer." Agnes eyed Meredith and probed. "Could you become involved with him? On a serious level?"

There was a brief hesitation on Meredith's part and then she said, "Yes, I could, Agnes. He's the type of man I like, the kind I thought I'd never meet again. Men like Luc are usually well and truly spoken for."

"You are indeed correct, *ma chérie*, but I think Luc has chosen not to be spoken for. Until now. He did tell me he liked you, wanted to get to know you better."

Meredith stared at Agnes. "*Oh*. And when was that?"

"Last week, just after he met you."

"And you never told me. Thanks a lot, friend!"

Agnes burst out laughing. Shaking her head, her gray eyes full of merriment, she said, "He didn't tell me not to say anything, but I thought discretion was the better part of valor, and all that. In any case, I didn't want to frighten you away from him. I thought you'd probably bite my head off and tell me I was a romantic fool. Consider them, Meredith, the various men I've introduced you to in the past eight years. They were attractive, eligible, but you never seemed interested in them. Not one little bit."

"I wasn't."

"But you *are* interested in Luc?"

Meredith nodded.

"*Mmmm*, I can't say I blame you, he is very sexy looking. Sensual, I think, no?"

# CHAPTER FIFTEEN

T hey worked together in Luc's office from the moment they arrived at Talcy until seven on Thursday night. And then they started again at nine the next morning.

Once more it was a long day, broken only by lunch. Late on Friday afternoon Luc put his pencil down and looked across the room at Meredith. She was seated at a small desk, pasting fabric, carpet, and paint samples onto boards, creating her first schemes for the inn.

"I shouldn't have done this to you," he said, leaning back in this chair, his eyes lingering on her.

"What do you mean?" she asked, looking up.

"I've kept you cooped up in this office since yesterday morning, and all because I wanted to work and wanted you near me while I did so."

She said nothing, merely stared back at him.

He went on. "I've been rushing, trying so hard to finish the plans for the pond and complete this drawing of it. I feel guilty, though, about you. I should have sent you walking or riding, or at least let you rest—"

"Luc, I enjoyed being here with you," she interrupted, "working alongside you. And I would have been doing the same thing in Paris anyway, sorting through the swatches, making my boards. Truly, it's been wonderful sharing this time here with you."

"Has it?"

"Oh yes."

"Meredith?"

"Yes, Luc?"

He opened his mouth to say something, changed his mind, and stood up, walked over to her. He placed the sheet of paper he was carrying in front of her on the desk. "This is the drawing of the pond, as it will look when it's finished."

"Oh Luc, how marvelous! It resembles the fishpond here!"

"I positioned the pond near the small wood behind the manor in Montfort-L'Amaury, in the same way the pond is next to the orchard at Talcy. I think it is picturesque, don't you?" As he spoke he bent over her, his finger tracing the drawing of the pond, the copse, and the manor house in the background.

She could feel his warm breath against her neck and she held herself perfectly still, hardly daring to breathe. Her cheeks flamed and she felt an unexpected warmth spreading through her, desire flooding her.

He said, "I wanted to please you, Meredith."

Meredith half turned her shoulder to look at him, tilted her face up to his. "I love it, Luc, it's perfect."

She smiled.

He was dazzled.

He said nothing. He was unable to speak. *I want you.* Those were the words on the tip of his tongue. It was the only thing he could think of at the moment. He had been thinking of it for days. He was about to tell her so, but instead he leaned closer to her and before he could stop himself he kissed her on the lips, lightly at first, and then, as she responded ardently, his kisses became more intense.

He paused after a moment, but only briefly, in order to pull her to her feet. She was in his arms instantly. He held her close; her arms went around his neck. They were clinging to each other, their passions rising.

Meredith thought: Oh Luc, my darling, I've longed for this, longed to hold you in my arms. But her thoughts were unspoken; his hungry kisses stopped her words.

And then he stopped abruptly and said in a voice thickened by emotion, "I want you, Meredith, I've desired you since the day we met."

"Oh Luc—"

He was kissing her again, greedily, as if he were about to leave her forever. He pulled her closer to him, fitting himself to her body, and he thought how perfectly they blended together; she was almost as tall as he was.

She knew this was how it should always be between a man and a woman. He was kissing her cheeks, her eyes, her brow, her neck, her ears. His mouth went back to her mouth, and then he whispered against her neck, "I've thought about you so much, I feel as if we've already made love. Do you understand what I mean, how I feel?"

"Yes."

"I'm serious about you, Meredith. Say no to me now if you don't feel the same way. Because once we start this, there's no going back. Not for me."

"I want *you,* Luc, I feel as you do."

He held her away from him, his hands firm on her shoulders, and looked deeply into her eyes. Smoky-green eyes, always mirroring her thoughts, her feelings, mirroring her soul. He had seen intelligence shining there, and reflectiveness and merriment, but also a deep-rooted sadness. Now he saw only desire and longing, and it was for him.

He took hold of her hand and led her across the room, and still gripping her tightly he hurried her up the back stairs and down the corridor.

Once inside his bedroom, he locked the door with one hand, drew her into his arms, kissing her over and over as he walked her in the direction of the bed. Releasing her at last, he pulled down the quilt, threw his jacket on a chair, struggled out of his sweater and jeans. She did the same.

Luc reached for her, pulled her to him, repeating her name as they fell onto the bed. They lay together, still half dressed, their bodies entwined. He ran his hands up into her thick golden hair, caught hold of it, wrapped his fingers around it, brought his face down to hers, his mouth, his tongue grazing her lips, touching her tongue lightly, tantalizingly.

Meredith responded to him eagerly; she knew this was right, that it was meant to be. She harbored no qualms about this man. The desire in his voice, the yearning in his dark eyes, had told her everything she needed to know.

Her heart lifted. She wanted him, wanted to feel his hands all over her like this, taste his kisses, savor his passion. She wanted to be with him, joined to him.

Luc was fully aware of her desire for him, her growing ardor, and this further inflamed him. The most sensual sensations rolled over him; he wanted to give himself up to them entirely.

Somehow they hastily shed the rest of their clothes, came back into each other's arms. He looked down into her face for a moment, took pleasure from seeing her pleasure reflected there, now just visible in the fading afternoon light. He brought his hand to her face, traced a line down her cheek and across her mouth, and he did so with tenderness.

Arms entwined, legs entwined, mouth on mouth, hands smoothing and stroking, caressing and exploring, each of them hungry for the other. It had been too long for them both.

Luc gave himself up to the pure joy of her touch,

of her kisses falling on him. On his mouth, his face, his eyelids. He rolled on top of her, aligning his body to hers.

Silken arms, silken legs wove themselves around him, bound him to her, the most welcome and softest of ropes. He moved into her deeper, harder, heard the soft moans escaping her throat. Deeper and deeper he sank, reveling in the sheer pleasure of her, knowing he had found the right woman. At last. The woman he had known would one day come to him . . . to fill the darkness, fill the void in him, and as he buried himself yet deeper in her, there was, miraculously, the total cessation of pain. She had liberated him, set him free. He soared. Higher and higher.

Meredith was moving against him, matching his rhythm; they were joined, became one entity. A perfect mating, he thought, and it was exactly as he had imagined, had known it would be.

And as she had known too. Luc was touching the core of her, reaching to her heart, filling her as she had never been filled, not since she was a young girl . . . so long ago . . . time past. He slipped his hands under her buttocks, brought her closer to him. I want you closer still, she cried out silently, all of you, Luc, I want all of you. And she willingly abandoned herself to him.

Luc could feel his heart pounding as he moved against her, almost violently now, caught up in the rhythm of their moving bodies; their joy was mounting.

Oh God, he thought, there is only this. Only this

woman. Only me and her and this joining. She is all I will ever want. For the rest of my life, until the day I die. With her I am made whole again. And then he stopped thinking as they moved together in a sudden frenzy, flying higher and higher until they reached that peak of pure sensation. He wanted it to last forever, this ecstasy.

And Meredith understood that she had found her true mate at last, after all these years. He carried her upward with him.

He was shuddering, racked by spasms, shouting her name as he lost himself in her. And she answered him, calling out, "Luc, oh Luc."

Later, when their frenzy had ceased, he held her in his arms, stroking her hair. She moved closer to him, draping her leg over his, and he tightened his hold on her.

Her face was against his chest. She kissed it, then he felt her smile.

"What is it?" he asked.

"What do you mean?"

"Why are you smiling?"

"Because I'm happy, Luc."

"This is only the beginning," he answered, and bent over her, kissed the top of her head. "I thought I would never find you."

"Were you looking for me?" Her voice was light, filled with happiness.

"Oh yes, *ma chérie*, ever since— For a long time."

"And I've been looking for you, although perhaps I didn't realize it. I was beginning to think I'd never find the right man."

"Am I?"

"Are you what?" she teased, knowing what he meant.

"The right man, Meredith?"

"Oh yes, Luc, very much so, and in every way."

"We're good together, Meredith, very good. I enjoy every minute we are together, and just now, well, you gave me such pleasure, I'm still reeling. And you? Did I please you?"

"Of course. You must know that."

"Yes, I suppose I do, but it's nice to hear it from your lips, Meri."

He felt her stiffen against him. "What's wrong? Don't you like me to call you Meri?"

"I don't mind," she replied quickly, catching the note of concern in his voice. "It's just that few people do."

Pulling her around and up into his arms, he touched her face lightly, gazed into her bright eyes, and said in the softest of voices, "I don't want to see that terrible sadness in your eyes ever again. There's been too much hurt and pain in your life, too much sorrow."

She did not respond.

"I'm here for you, Meri, if ever you want to talk about it. Sometimes it is helpful to unburden oneself."

"One day, perhaps."

He nodded, leaned forward, and kissed her on the lips. "You have become very dear to me and in such a short time. I've fallen in love with you, Meri."

Meredith stared at him. Unexpectedly, tears welled in her eyes. She swallowed hard, trying to push them back, but she could not. Slowly they rolled down her cheeks.

"Oh, *ma chérie*, don't weep, there's nothing to weep about." Luc lifted his hand, wiped away her tears with his fingertips. "Do you think you could fall in love with me?"

"I already have," she whispered, and began to cry again.

"Thank God!" Luc exclaimed, and kissed her on the lips. And as he kissed her cheeks and her eyes he tasted the salt of her tears. "No more sorrow. I'm going to make sure of that," he said against her damp face. "Only happiness from now on, Meri."

But he was wrong.

# PART TWO

# TIME PRESENT, TIME PAST

# Chapter Sixteen

Meredith stood at the far end of the drawing room, leaning against a Sheraton breakfront. The interior of the antique piece was illuminated, its shelves filled with priceless Meissen figurines.

A few minutes before, she had wandered over to look at this unique collection and had suddenly felt weak. Reluctant to maneuver through the crowded room looking for somewhere to sit down, she had stayed where she was, nursing a glass of champagne.

She took a deep breath, hoping she was not going to have one of her attacks, which was what she had begun to call them. There had been two in January when she was in France, then three last month, and she wondered how many she would have in April.

They passed as quickly as they occurred, and she

was never the worse afterward; nonetheless, they made her nervous. She never knew when one would strike her.

The other day, in the office, she had told Amy about them, had explained how they had started in Paris and had continued off and on.

Amy had said at once, "They're becoming too frequent. I think you should get medical advice. Let me make an appointment for you with Jennifer Pollard."

Meredith had shaken her head, told Amy not to call the doctor. Now she asked herself if she had been foolish. Perhaps she should have listened to her assistant. At that moment her legs were weak, she could feel the fatigue slowly creeping through her entire body, and she could not help wondering whether she would be able to last through the evening.

She must do that, no matter how she felt. Tonight was a very special occasion in her daughter's life, and in hers. It was Cat's engagement party, and she had been looking forward to it.

Meredith believed that by rights *she* should have been giving the party, but Keith's sister, Margery, and her husband, Eric, had insisted on hosting it at their Park Avenue penthouse; she had had no alternative but to acquiesce.

She fully intended to plan a celebration dinner for Cat and Keith, which she would give in the next few weeks. She hoped Luc would be able to attend. He had spent the past week in New York with her, and had planned to stay on for the engagement party. Then at the last minute he had been called back to France. A problem had developed with one of his larger architectural jobs, a shopping complex in Lyons, and his presence on the site had been imperative.

They were both disappointed he had been forced to leave, but he was coming back to New York in ten days to spend a long weekend with her at Silver Lake. She could hardly wait for his return. They were very much in love, and in the past two months had grown extremely close. They were rarely apart when they were in the same city, and when separated by the Atlantic they spoke every day by phone. He's everything I want in a man, she thought now, missing him. How she wished he were there with her tonight.

Meredith constantly marveled at her luck in meeting Luc; and at their extraordinary compatibility. Her children knew him now and liked him, and he was very taken by them. He and Jon got on extremely well; aside from having Yale in common, they were both sports aficionados and especially addicted to football. And Cat was equally at ease with Luc since they both had artistic natures. He was impressed by Cat's talent as an illustrator, thought her an accomplished artist. Meredith had been very proud when he had congratulated her on her fine children, noting the admiration in his voice.

She now peered into the milling crowd filling the drawing room, wishing Cat or Jon would reappear.

There were about sixty people present and she hardly knew any of them, only the immediate members of the Pearson family: Anne and Paul, Keith's parents, his sisters Margery, Susan, Rosemarie, Jill, and Wendy, and his two brothers, Will and Dominick. And Eric Clarke, Margery's husband, one of her hosts this evening.

The Pearson family was a large and boisterous American-Irish clan. As big as the Kennedy tribe, Cat had informed her recently. However, the Pearsons did not hail from Boston; they were dyed-in-the-wool Yankees from the heart of Connecticut. It suddenly struck Meredith that the Pearsons were out in full force this evening, since there were innumerable aunts, uncles, cousins, and their offspring present.

And we are only three, such a small family, she thought. Not much of a match for a crew like the Pearsons. Meredith felt unexpectedly overwhelmed, and then she experienced such a sudden sense of loss, she was startled. It was a feeling she could not rightly explain to herself.

Blanche and Pete O'Brien had come in from Silver Lake to attend the party, and they were extended family. Even so . . . Meredith snapped her eyes shut, endeavoring to shake off that awful feeling.

Opening her eyes a moment later, she scanned the room, wondering where Blanche and Pete were. Somehow she had lost track of them in the last hour. Perhaps they were in the crowded dining room, where a buffet table groaned with all manner of fancy hors d'oeuvres.

Meredith felt strangely isolated, standing there alone, propped up against the breakfront. I must sit down, she thought, and decided to head for a chair near the fireplace. It was then that she spotted her daughter.

Catherine was glancing around, obviously looking for her.

Meredith raised her hand, waved.

Instantly Cat saw her, smiled, waved back, and hurried across the drawing room.

"Mom, there you are, I've been looking all over for you," Catherine said, rushing up to Meredith. "Isn't this a wonderful party? I'm so excited tonight. I can't stand it." She looked down at her left hand, gazed at her sapphire ring admiringly, then flashed it at Meredith. "It's gorgeous, isn't it, Mom?"

"Beautiful, darling," Meredith answered, and caught hold of Cat's arm to steady herself.

Catherine gave her a quick look and exclaimed, "Mom, are you all right?"

"Yes."

"But you seemed to stagger just now, and you're very pale. Not only that, you look taut, tense. Are you sure nothing's wrong? Look, if you're not ill, is there something else the matter? You're not angry, are you? I mean because Margery and Eric insisted on throwing the party?"

"Don't be silly, you know I'm not like that. I feel a bit tired, that's all. I've probably been overdoing it at the office."

"Let's go and sit on the sofa over there, Mother.

My feet are killing me anyway. These shoes are fab, but gosh, they're agony."

Meredith allowed her daughter to guide her to a sofa near the fireplace, and she sat down gratefully. A moment earlier she felt as though all of her strength were ebbing away. The last thing she wanted was to pass out here. She would be humiliated in front of all these people.

Turning to Catherine, she said, "Perhaps a glass of water would help. Could you get me one, please?"

"Of course, Mom. I won't be a minute." Catherine threw her mother a reassuring smile and glided across the floor toward the large entrance foyer, where a bar had been set up.

No one would know her feet are killing her, Meredith thought, watching her daughter float through the room as if she were walking on air.

How beautiful Catherine looked tonight, so elegant in her short midnight-blue taffeta cocktail suit and Amelia's pearls. Her brown hair was cut in a sleek shape, and her lovely, open face looked so young and fresh, her wide-set eyes very blue. Cat was tall, as she was, with long, shapely legs. I can't imagine why she wants to wear five-inch heels, Meredith thought in bafflement, then leaned back against the sofa, trying to relax.

Suddenly, there was her son, pushing forward through the throng. She watched him walking rapidly toward her, tall, slender, as blonde as she, with her green eyes. Cat resembled her father, while Jon took after her.

As he drew closer, she saw that he wore a worried expression on his lean face. "Mom, what's the matter?" he asked, drawing to a standstill by her side. "I just saw Cat getting you a glass of water, and she thinks you're not well. Are you ill?"

"No, Jon, I'm not," she answered evenly in a firm voice. "Truly, darling. I felt a bit queasy earlier. Perhaps I'm tired."

"You work too hard," he said, bending his lanky frame over her, resting his hand on the sofa's arm. Bringing his face closer to hers, he dropped his voice. "If you want to leave, I'll go with you. I wouldn't mind splitting this scene myself."

"I'm fine," she replied swiftly. "And I don't think we can leave. It wouldn't be polite, and anyway, we can't abandon Cat to all these Pearsons."

"She's got Keith to protect her, and anyway, she'll be a Pearson herself soon."

Meredith frowned, searched his face. "Aren't you having a good time, Jon?"

"Sure, it's okay, but . . ." He shrugged. "I'm just here for Cat and you, Mom. I don't have a lot in common with this group."

"*Oh*." She drew back, looked at him closely. "Are you trying to tell me something?"

Jonathan shook his head and grinned. "No, not at all. And don't get me wrong, I like Keith. I think he's a pretty nifty guy, and he's great for Cat. But I'm not particularly close to their friends, my group's different, that's all." He looked directly at his mother, grimaced, and finished, "The Pearsons are a nice family, just a bit too social for me."

"I know," Meredith murmured. "And I'm glad you came . . . for my sake and Cat's."

"You can always depend on me, Mom. I wish Luc were here, he'd liven things up a bit."

Meredith laughed. "Here's Cat now."

"With Keith hot on her heels," Jon said, straightening up, glancing over his shoulder at his sister, who was heading their way.

"Here's your water, Mom." Cat handed her the glass and sat down on the sofa next to her.

"Thanks, darling."

"I'm sorry you're under the weather, Meredith," Keith said, bending over her as Jon had done a moment before. "Is there anything else I can get you?"

Meredith looked up into his freckled face, as always thinking how honest his light gray eyes were, and shook her head. "Thank you, Keith dear, but I'm feeling much better." She smiled at him warmly, liking him, knowing he would make her daughter a good husband, just as Jon knew. Cat would be safe with Keith Pearson; he was devoted, loyal, and loving.

Clearing her throat, Meredith said, "The three of you are beginning to make me feel like an invalid."

Keith grinned at her. "We don't mean to, we just care about you, that's all."

"You're very sweet, Keith," she answered.

"You will come to dinner later, as planned, won't you?" Keith went on, fixing her with his serious gray eyes. "I don't want to pressure you, but we'll all be disappointed if you don't. It won't be the same without you."

Meredith answered, "I wouldn't miss it," and patted his hand reassuringly. "Jon is my escort, he'll look after me."

"Keith's right, Mother, and the evening would certainly fizzle for me without *you* at the engagement dinner," Catherine said.

"I'll be there." Meredith smiled at her daughter, loving her.

Catherine smiled back, lifted her left hand, tightened a loose pearl earring. The sapphire engagement ring flashed in the bright lamplight.

It's the color of her eyes, Meredith thought. Jack's eyes.


"You're a good sport, Mother," Jonathan said several hours later as he helped Meredith out of her coat and hung it in the hall closet.

"It was a lovely dinner in many respects, and generous of the Pearsons to have it in the private room at La Grenouille. But they're a bit—"

"Overwhelming," Jonathan interrupted, and shook his head. "My God, all those Pearsons, Mom! My sister's pretty brave, taking on that clan. I wouldn't want to, I can tell you that."

"I know what you mean, but individually they're very nice really, and Keith's parents are lovely, Jon."

"True, but Keith's sisters are a pretty rowdy bunch."

"The problem is, darling, we're used to a whole

different kind of family life, so much quieter. After all, there's only been the three of us all these years."

"And thank God for that," he answered, hanging up his overcoat. "In my opinion you deserve a medal, sitting through the dinner the way you did, all those toasts. *Mind boggling.*"

Meredith laughed. "Yes, it was a bit much. But I began to feel better once we left the apartment, and I got some fresh air. And I do like the food at La Grenouille."

"You didn't eat very much."

She smiled at her son. "I'd like a cup of tea, Jon, how about you?"

"Great idea."

He followed his mother into the kitchen, took the kettle off the stove, filled it with water, put it back, then turned on the gas. He glanced out of the kitchen window. The lights of the Fifty-ninth Street Bridge twinkled brightly against the dark night sky; beyond he could see another bridge glowing in the distance. Beautiful glittering city. He had always loved Manhattan. Jonathan stared down at the East River flowing far below and then across at Roosevelt Island. Funny how his mother always wanted to live near water, needed to, really. This was the second apartment she had owned on Sutton Place. He liked this one the best; they lived in the penthouse and the views of Manhattan were spectacular.

Meredith said, "When are you going back to New Haven?" and put two cups and saucers on a tray as she spoke.

"Tomorrow morning. Early. I'll do it in under two hours. It's not that bad a drive. By the way, has Cat indicated when she wants to get married?"

Meredith nodded. "This year, certainly. They don't want to wait too long, she told me. I've suggested September. It's very lovely at Silver Lake at that time of year."

"Early October's better, Mom, when the leaves are turning. I think a fall wedding would be picturesque."

"You're right, and I did suggest that only the other day. Cat's going to let me know sometime next week, so we can get the invitations engraved and sent out, make proper plans."

"Aunt Blanche is all worked up about the reception," Jon said, laughing. "She's been planning it for weeks. In her head, that is . . . she told me tonight that she wants to top your wedding reception, which she was apparently involved in."

"Very much so. In fact, she really designed and planned the entire thing by herself. She has such a talent for that kind of occasion. Make the tea, Jon, the kettle's screeching its head off."

"Okay. Why don't you go and sit in the library. I'll bring the tea."

"Thanks, darling," she said, and did as he suggested, walking out of the kitchen, across the entrance foyer and into the library, which overlooked the water. She went to one of the windows, stood staring out. A great barge was floating down, loaded with cargo, heading for the docks, no doubt.

Meredith never got tired of looking at the East River. There was a great deal of traffic on this waterway and something was always moving on it, going up or down.

Her thoughts turned to Catherine as she swung away from the window and went and sat down near the fireplace. She was going to give her the best wedding any girl had ever had, make sure that she—

Jon interrupted her thoughts when he said, "Where do you want the tray, Mom? Over there by you, I guess."

"Yes, that's fine, put it here on this coffee table." Meredith moved a pile of large art books to make a space.

Meredith poured, and they sipped their tea in silence for a few minutes, and then Jon suddenly said, "Are you going to make it permanent with Luc?"

Startled, Meredith gaped at him.

Jon said, "What I mean is, are you going to marry him, Mom?"

"He hasn't asked me," Meredith replied.

"But would you if he did?" Jon pressed.

"I honestly don't know."

"*Why?*"

"Why don't I know? Is that what you mean?"

"Yes."

Meredith lifted her shoulders in a small shrug. "I just don't, that's all. It would be a big step for me to take, it would mean rearranging my life completely."

"So what. I think you *should* marry him."

"You do, do you?" A blonde brow lifted expressively.

"Sure. You're in love with him, he's in love with you. I bet if you gave him half a chance, he'd ask you."

Meredith said nothing.

"You've been used to having *us* with you always, Mother. The Three Musketeers, remember? That's what you used to call us. Cat's getting married, starting a whole new life soon, her own family. And I expect I'll get married when I meet the right woman. I just don't want you to be all alone one day."

Meredith stared at her son, touched by his words, then her brows drew together in a furrow. "You're worrying about my old age, is that it, Jon?"

Laughing, he shook his head. "You'll never be old, Mother. You'll be beautiful forever. You're the greatest looking forty-four year old I've ever seen."

"And you've lived such a long time," she shot back, laughing with him. "Known so many women."

Jonathan's face sobered as he continued. "I just don't want you to be by yourself, lonely later in your life." He cleared his throat and gave her a piercing look. "When I was little I used to hear you . . . *crying,* Mother. Sobbing as if your heart were breaking, at night in your bedroom. I used to stand outside the door and listen, hurting for you inside. But I didn't dare come in, even though I wanted to comfort you."

"You could have," she said softly, further touched by his words.

"I was afraid. You could be very fierce, you know,

in those days. Do you remember, I once asked you why you cried at night, when I was a bit older?"

"Yes, vaguely."

"Do you recall what you said?"

Meredith shook her head.

"You told me you cried because you'd lost someone when you were a child. When I asked you who, you wouldn't answer me, you just turned away."

Meredith stared at her son, speechless.

"Mom, who was it that you lost? I've always wondered."

"I don't know," she replied after a long and thoughtful pause. "If I did, I would tell you, Jon. Truly I would."

Her son rose and came and sat next to her. He took hold of her hand, looked into her face. His own had a loving expression on it. Slowly, he said, "It broke my heart to hear you crying. I wanted to help you and I didn't know how. It's always worried me that you cried in that way."

"Oh Jon."

"That's why Luc is so important to me . . . I want him for you, Mom, he's such a great guy, and he loves you. Maybe he can make up for . . . everyone that hurt you."

During the night Meredith awakened.

Immediately she slipped out of bed, put on a dressing gown, and went into the library. There was a tray of drinks on a console table and she poured herself a small brandy in a tall glass, added soda water, then carried it over to a chair. She sat down, made herself comfortable, took a sip of the drink.

Lately she had discovered that it was far better to get up when she awakened in this way. It was easier to think through what was troubling her when she was sitting in a chair, rather than lying down in bed.

Now, placing the glass on the coffee table, she sat back, relaxing, thinking of her son's words.

Jon had taken her by surprise, but she had also been moved by his words, his loving concern. Although she did not want him to worry about her, it was gratifying, in some ways, that he did. Her son cared about her well-being, and that was important to her.

She had tried to bring up her children properly, had always striven to do the right thing for them, and she believed she had succeeded. Catherine and Jonathan had turned out to be good human beings, with all of the right values. They functioned, were well adjusted, very normal young people, and thank God they had never been tempted by their peers to experiment with drugs, nor did they drink much. She had been lucky with her children.

It was startling to her that Jonathan remembered how she used to weep at night, when she thought her children were fast asleep. The odd thing was, she had no recollection of ever telling him she cried for someone she had lost when she was a child. Yet she knew he was not lying. Why would he? She must have forgotten what she had said to him all those years ago. And whom had she meant? She had no idea; she was truly baffled.

Sighing to herself, finishing the drink, Meredith got up, walked back to her bedroom. Perhaps now she would be able to fall asleep. Certainly she must try. She had a busy day ahead of her. She took off her dressing gown and got into bed. Almost immediately she began to doze, drifting off into a deep sleep.

There were many children. Boys and girls. Some of them were very young. Three and four years old. Others were older, perhaps seven and eight. They were all walking across the vast landscape. Some were hand in hand, boys and girls, and girls together. Many walked alone. Too many children, she thought, filling with fear. I'll never find that little girl again. Or the boy. They are lost to me. Where are they? They must be among these children. I must find them.

She was frantic, running in among the children as they walked, perfectly in step, toward the distant horizon. She peered into their faces. She did not know them. They marched across the parched, cracked mud flats like automatons, staring straight ahead, paying no attention to her. Their faces were glazed, empty of expression, their eyes dull, lifeless. Where are you going? she cried. Where are you heading? None of them answered her.

Have you seen them? she cried. The girl with the long striped scarf? The boy with the cap? Please tell me if you've seen them.

The children turned en masse, veered to the right, began to walk toward the sea. She had never seen the sea before. The water was black, the color of oil. She shuddered and called to the children to come back. They did not heed her. She was afraid, shivering with fright. The children marched on. No! she cried. Stop! Still they paid no attention. They marched on and on, marched right into the sea. Slowly they sank, disappeared from sight. Oh God, no! she cried. Nobody heard her.

The landscape was empty. She was the only one left. And then she saw them. They were skipping toward her holding hands. The little girl with the scarf and the boy in his school cap. She waved. They waved back. She began to run. She was getting closer and closer. The labels pinned to their coats were huge, bigger than before. They fluttered in the wind, blew against their necks, obscuring their faces. Suddenly they turned around, veered to the right and began to walk toward the sea. No! she shouted. No! Stop! Don't go there! They did not listen. She ran and ran. Parts of the arid landscape opened up, cracking in half. She jumped over the cracks. Went on running. Her breathing was labored. Finally she caught up with the children. She reached out, grabbed the boy's shoulder. He resisted. Then slowly he swung around. She screamed. He had no face. She grabbed the girl's arm. The girl turned. Meredith screamed again.

"Mother, what's wrong, what is it?" Jon exclaimed, bursting into her room, snapping on the light as he did. He hurried over to the bed.

Meredith was sitting up, her eyes wide with fright, her face and neck damp with perspiration. She shook her head.

Her son sat down on the bed. He stared at her closely, took hold of her hand, wanting to comfort her. Again he asked, "What is it, Mom?"

Meredith took a deep breath. "I had a strange dream, a nightmare, actually."

"It must've frightened you. I heard you screaming."

"Yes, it must have. I'm sorry I woke you, Jon."

"That's okay." He frowned. "What was the nightmare about?"

"It doesn't make sense, it was very muddled." She forced a smile onto her face, hoped it reassured him. "Let's forget it. I'm all right, really. Go back to bed, honey."

Jonathan leaned forward, kissed her lightly on the cheek. "I'm just across the hall if you need me."

"I'm fine," she replied.

Long after Jonathan had returned to his own room, Meredith lay awake, remembering every detail of the dream, pondering on it.

It was a dream she had first dreamed many years before, when she was young and still lived in Sydney. It had recurred off and on over the years, and then it had stopped all of a sudden when she was in her thirties. Unexpectedly, she was having the dream again—twice in the space of two months.

The details were always the same. The barren landscape, sinister, and godforsaken. The children marching to their doom in the sea. Her desperation as she tried to find the little girl and boy.

She always woke up in a cold sweat. And she was always fearful when she awakened. Why? What did the dream mean?

# Chapter Seventeen

"How many of these attacks have you had?" Dr. Jennifer Pollard asked, scrutinizing Meredith across her desk.

"I had two in January, two in February, three in March, and two this month . . . last Thursday at Catherine's engagement party and again on Sunday. The last was the worst one yet. It lasted most of the day, and I felt more debilitated than usual. So much so, I didn't go to the office yesterday. When I went to work this morning I was still feeling very tired. I thought I'd better come to see you."

"I'm glad you did," the doctor answered. "Earlier, on the phone, you told me the symptoms are always the same—nausea and a feeling of total exhaustion. Are there no other symptoms, Meredith?"

"None at all."

"No vomiting, fever, pains in your stomach, diarrhea, high temperatures, headaches, migraines?"

Meredith shook her head. "No, nothing like that. I just feel sort of queasy, but mostly very tired, exhausted really."

"I see." Jennifer brought her hand up to her chin, looking thoughtful.

Meredith leaned forward intently. "Jennifer, what do you think is wrong with me?"

"Frankly, I'm not sure. First we must give you a very thorough examination, then I'll be able to make a proper diagnosis." As she was speaking, the doctor opened the folder in front of her and scanned the top page. "I looked at your records just before you arrived, and you had a checkup three months ago, at the end of December. You were in perfect health then, Meredith."

"Yes, I know, that's why I'm so baffled."

"We'll get to the bottom of it, don't worry." Closing the folder, the doctor went on briskly. "All right, then, let's start by getting the tests done."

She stood up, walked around the desk.

Meredith also rose.

Jennifer Pollard put her arm around Meredith's shoulder. "Don't look so apprehensive. We'll get to the bottom of the problem."

"What do you think it *could* be?"

Jennifer hesitated, then said, "Any number of things, but I don't want to make guesses. Also, I'm not going to pretend it's nothing, Meredith, I've too much respect for your intelligence, and in any case, you know that's not my way. I believe in being very honest with my patients. The kind of exhaustion you've described can mean any number of things. It could be caused by anemia, a hormonal disorder, or a chronic infection of some kind. Then again, it might be tiredness due to burnout."

"Not burnout, no!" Meredith exclaimed. "Most of the time I'm full of energy and vitality."

"Let's go in to Angela," Jennifer said, leading the way out of her office and down the corridor. "You know the routine after all these years. Angela will take blood samples, do the EKG and a chest X ray. We'll also need a urine sample from you. Once these tests are completed, I'll give you a thorough physical examination."

Opening the door of the small examination room, Jennifer said, "I'll send Angela in with a gown, so you can get undressed."

"Thank you," Meredith murmured.

Exactly one hour later Meredith was dressed again and sitting in her doctor's office, once more staring at Jennifer Pollard. Her expression was worried and there was a questioning look in her eyes. "What did you find?"

"Nothing." Jennifer smiled at her confidently. "As far as I can tell, there's nothing physically wrong with you. No lumps, no swelling anywhere, and you didn't flinch when I put pressure on your abdomen. And your reflexes and blood pressure are normal. Of course, I don't know what the blood and urine tests are going to reveal, and I won't have the results for a couple of days. But frankly, I'm pretty sure they're going to be normal too. It seems to me that you're as physically fit as you were three months ago."

"Then how do you explain the attacks?"

"Not sure." Jennifer leaned back in her chair, focused her eyes on Meredith. "Nerves, maybe? Stress? You push yourself very hard. For as long as I've known you, which is a good ten years now, you've been a workaholic, to use a nasty word. And stress can play havoc with a person's nervous system."

"I realize that, but I don't feel stressed out, not at all. Very honestly, Jennifer, I've been taking it a lot easier lately, especially when I'm in France. I'm remodeling an inn there, but I have a very good French partner who takes a load off my shoulders. And I spend long weekends with my boyfriend in the Loire. He has a country house there." Meredith leaned forward and finished, "I've never been happier on a personal level. Business is good, the kids are great."

"I'm glad to hear it," Jennifer answered. A reflective expression flickered in her eyes, and after a moment she asked, "Is there anything at all worrying you?"

"No. And as I just said, my life has never been better."

Jennifer nodded. "Let's see what the blood tests tell us. I'll call you as soon as they come in. Probably by Thursday, Friday at the latest."

\*　　　\*　　　\*

Meredith was signing a batch of letters late on Thursday afternoon when the private line in her office rang. Picking up the phone, she said, "Hello?"

*"C'est moi, chérie."*

"Luc!" she exclaimed. "How are you, darling?"

"Not so good, I am afraid."

"What's wrong?" she asked, her voice rising slightly, her concern apparent.

Luc sighed over the transatlantic line and explained. "I am so terribly sorry about this, Meredith, but I cannot now come to New York this weekend. I am afraid I am stuck here in Lyons. Because of the job, I am needed here."

"Oh Luc, what a shame, I was so looking forward to it," Meredith said. "I'm very disappointed, darling, but I understand. Work has to come first." She, too, sighed resignedly.

"I have to be on the spot," he continued. "There is an unanticipated condition in the foundation that is going to require major redesign. I can't just delegate this particular part of the job. We have run into subsurface ledgerock that requires redesigning the foundation in the first of the buildings. It is vital that I am here. I'm meeting with the contractor and structural engineer tomorrow. We'll complete the design on Saturday and bring in the crew next week." There was a fractional pause before he laughed quietly and said, "I don't suppose you could come to Lyons, could you?"

"I'd love to, but I can't. I told you, I have the closing on the inn tomorrow. And I have to be in New York on Tuesday for a meeting with the bank. Henry Raphaelson is going to the Far East the following day, so I can't change that appointment. Next week is a bit tough for me, Luc. I'm due in Paris soon, in case you've forgotten."

"I hadn't, *ma chérie,* I was just hoping to see you before."

Meredith glanced at the calendar on her desk. "I was planning on being there at the end of April, and I will be staying the whole month of May, you know."

"Well, that is wonderful! I am happy. But I shall miss you, Meri."

"And I will miss you too," she said. They went on talking for another ten minutes. For a moment Meredith almost confided in him, almost told him about her visit to the doctor, then changed her mind. She did not want to worry him. He had enough problems with the shopping center in Lyons.


"There's absolutely nothing physically wrong with you, Meredith," Jennifer Pollard said, leaning back in her chair, smiling at her. "I'm happy to tell you the blood and urine tests are normal."

Meredith smiled back, filling with relief and then she frowned and asked, "But this morning when you called the office you told Amy you wanted to see me, talk to me."

The doctor nodded. "I do." Jennifer cleared her throat and went on. "There's still something wrong. Those attacks. Now, in my experience, people who suffer from the kind of exhaustion you described to me earlier this week usually do so all the time. In other words, it's chronic. And permanent. It doesn't come and go the way you have described *your* attacks."

"Meaning what?"

"Meaning that your attacks could easily become increasingly frequent, until, in the end, you, too, have the exhaustion on a permanent basis rather than only occasionally."

Meredith was silent; she sat staring at the doctor.

"Let me explain something to you, Meredith," Jennifer said. "Very often this kind of exhaustion is due to psychological causes."

"Do you think that's the case with me?"

"Possibly. You could be suffering from *psychogenic fatigue.*"

"What does that mean?"

"That the cause of your tiredness is an emotional problem. Or, alternatively, you could be depressed without knowing it."

"I'm definitely not depressed!" Meredith answered with a dry laugh. "When I was here on Tuesday, I told you my life was on an even keel and rather wonderful these days. I'm in love with a fabulous man, he with me."

"I believe you, and I'm happy for you. However, let's not dismiss the idea of psychogenic fatigue due to an emotional problem, or an upset mental state. What's causing it, the thing that's bothering you, doesn't necessarily have to be of this moment. It could go back in time."

"How do you treat something like that?" Meredith asked nervously, eyeing her doctor warily.

"We have to determine the nature of the actual problem, get to the root of it, then treat it."

"*Psychiatry*. Is that what you're getting at, Jennifer?"

"Yes, it is. If you are suffering from psychogenic fatigue, I recommend that you see someone immediately. The illness, and it *is* an illness, is not going to go away on its own. Furthermore, it could become chronic."

"Who . . . who would you recommend?" Meredith asked quietly.

"Dr. Hilary Benson. She's very sympathetic, you'll like her. And she's a brilliant psychiatrist. Her office is just around the corner from me on Park and Sixty-ninth."

Meredith leaned back in the chair, looking worried.

"There's nobody saner than you, Meredith," Jennifer said swiftly, responding to the look in Meredith's eyes. "I can testify to that. Listen to me, you might not have psychogenic fatigue at all. It could be stress . . . I said that to you earlier in the week."

"I don't think so."

"Then you will go and see Hilary Benson?"

Meredith nodded.

# Chapter Eighteen

Meredith was nothing if not decisive. Once she had agreed to see the psychiatrist, she told Amy to make an appointment for the following week.

After that she endeavored to put the matter out of her mind; she had always had the ability to pigeonhole problems until it was the appropriate time to deal with them. And so she managed to get through the next few days without dwelling too much on her health or mental state. Fortunately, there were no more attacks.

On Tuesday afternoon, when she walked into Dr. Hilary Benson's private office, her first impression was of a good-looking but stern woman. The doctor had a rather lovely face with high cheekbones, and the palest of blue eyes that appeared almost transparent. But her mouth had a severe set to it and her dark brown hair was pulled back in a plain chignon that was singularly schoolmarmish.

There was a no-nonsense, businesslike air about her, and for a split second Meredith was put off, thinking that she might be a cold fish. Then she recalled her physician's words. Jennifer had told her that Hilary Benson was a sympathetic person as well as a brilliant psychiatrist.

I must give her a chance, give this a chance, Meredith decided. She needed to understand what was wrong, why she was having these attacks on a regular basis. According to Jennifer, only a psychiatrist could help her get to the root of the problem.

After greeting Meredith pleasantly and shaking hands, Dr. Benson said, "Come and sit down, Mrs. Stratton."

"Thank you," Meredith answered, and followed the doctor over to the desk, where they sat facing each other.

Meredith, studying the doctor, decided that she was probably the same age as Jennifer and herself; in her early forties.

The psychiatrist said, "Dr. Pollard and I have spoken at length. She has filled me in, given me your medical history in general. Apparently you're a very healthy woman."

"Yes, I am, thank goodness," Meredith replied, smiling faintly.

Dr. Benson nodded and sat back in her chair, taking stock of Meredith for a moment. Beautiful woman. Puts up a good front, she thought. But there's pain in her, hurt. I can see it in her eyes. Getting straight to the point, she said, "Jennifer believes you could be suffering from psychogenic fatigue."

"So she told me."

"Let's talk about that fatigue, the attacks you've been having. When did the first one occur, Mrs. Stratton?"

"Early in January. I was in Paris on business. I'd been traveling part of the day, and that night, after I'd checked into my hotel, I felt quite ill. Exhausted, a bit queasy . . . nauseated."

"Where had you traveled from?"

"England. Not a long trip by any means, and traveling doesn't affect me usually. I have a lot of stamina and tremendous energy, Dr. Benson."

"So feeling ill was unusual for you. I understand." There was a moment's pause, then Hilary went on. "Had anything happened to upset you that day?" She put her elbows on the desk, steepled her fingers, and looked over them at Meredith.

"No, it hadn't. To tell you the truth, I thought I was probably coming down with the flu. That morning I'd been outside for a long time in the cold, in the snow. I'd been wandering around a ruined abbey. I thought that—" Meredith stopped short, abruptly cutting herself off.

"You thought what, Mrs. Stratton?" Dr. Benson asked, giving Meredith a quiet, encouraging smile.

"I was going to say that I thought I'd caught a chill when I was lingering at the abbey. But come to think of it, something odd *did* occur that morning, something quite strange really."

"And what was that?"

"I had a peculiar sense that I'd been there before. It was a feeling of déjà vu."

"But you had *not* been there before. Is that what you're saying?"

"Yes, it is."

"Can you recall how you actually felt?"

Meredith nodded.

"Will you tell me about it, Mrs. Stratton?"

"Yes. But let me explain something, Dr. Benson. I saw the abbey for the first time the day before . . . I was looking at it from the window of an inn, viewing it across snow-covered fields. It was beautiful. And I realized I was curiously drawn to it. The next morning I had a little time to spare, I was waiting for my English partner to get up, come down to breakfast. Well, anyway, not to digress . . . I had a little free time, so I went to look at the abbey close-up. As I approached the ruins I felt that I was literally being pulled toward them, and that even if I'd wanted to, I couldn't have turned back. A short while later, when I finally walked into the actual ruins, I had the queerest feeling that I'd been there before. It was strong, rather overwhelming."

"And you *are* positive you didn't know this place?"

"Oh yes. I had never been to Fountains Abbey before; I was visiting Yorkshire for the first time in my life."

"I see. Did you experience anything else? Did you have any other emotions that morning?"

"Yes, I did, as a matter of fact. I felt a great sense of loss. And sadness . . ." Meredith paused. There was a reflective look on her face when she added quietly, "I experienced a feeling of true sorrow."

"Have you any idea why?"

"Not really, although I do recall that I had a sudden flash of clarity at that moment. I was sure that I had lost someone there, someone very dear to me. Or, rather, that someone had been *taken* from me. It seemed to me that I *knew* those ruins, and I sensed a tragic thing had happened there. Yet it didn't feel like a bad place. Quite the opposite. I had a sense of belonging, and I was at ease."

"Do you know England well, Mrs. Stratton?"

"Not really, although I've been going there for more than twenty years. However, as I just said, I had never been to Yorkshire." Meredith leaned forward, gave the psychiatrist a piercing look. "How do you explain what happened to me that morning?"

"I don't think I can. At least, not at this moment."

"Do you think my experience at Fountains Abbey triggered the first attack?"

"I don't know." Hilary Benson shook her head. "The human mind is a strange and complex piece of machinery. It takes a lot of understanding. Let's leave your experience at the abbey alone for the moment and go in another direction. I understand from Dr. Pollard that you're an Australian. Please tell me a little about yourself, about your background."

"I'm from Sydney. I grew up there. My parents were killed. In a car crash. When I was ten years old. Relatives brought me up." Meredith sat back in the chair, crossed her legs, and gave the psychiatrist a cool, very direct look.

Hilary Benson returned this glance and thought: Her expression is candid but she's lying. I know it. What she's just said has been well learned. She's repeating it by rote to me, just as she's done so before, to countless others.

After a short pause Hilary said, "How sad for you to be orphaned so very young. Who was it that brought you up?"

"Relatives. I just told you."

"But *who* exactly?"

"An aunt."

"I see. Did you have any siblings?"

"No, I didn't. There was just me. I was always on my own."

"Is that actually how you felt, that you were on your own, even though you had an aunt?"

"Oh yes, I always felt that way."

"Tell me how you came to this country, Mrs. Stratton."

"I'll be happy to," Meredith replied, and then added, "I'd like you to call me Meredith, Dr. Benson."

The doctor nodded. "Of course. Please give me a little background about your arrival in America."

"I came with an American family who'd been living in Sydney. The Paulsons. I'd been working as an au pair for them since I was fifteen. Mr. Paulson was transferred back to the States two years later, when I was seventeen, and they asked me to go with them. So I did."

"And your aunt didn't object?"

"Oh no. She didn't care. She had four daughters of her own. She wasn't interested in me."

"And so she gave her permission for you to travel to America with the Paulson family? Am I understanding this correctly?"

Meredith nodded. "She helped me get my passport." Meredith made a small grimace. "She was glad to be rid of me."

Hilary Benson frowned. "You were not very close, then?"

"Not at all."

"And what about your parents? Were you close to them?"

"Not really."

"But you were an only child. Only children are usually very close to their parents."

"I wasn't, Dr. Benson."

The psychiatrist was silent. She looked down at the pad in front of her, made a few notations on it. She was more convinced than ever that Meredith was lying about her background. It seemed to her that everything was too well rehearsed, and Meredith spoke in monosyllables, as if she were afraid to elaborate in case she made a mistake. Or revealed something she was trying to hide.

Hilary put down her pen and looked up, smiling

at Meredith. "You came to New York with the Paulson family. Did you ever go back to Australia?"

"No, I didn't. I stayed here. In Connecticut. That's where we lived, near New Preston. Up above Lake Waramaug. I was with the Paulsons for another year and then Mr. Paulson was transferred to South Africa. He was a troubleshooter for an international advertising agency, and he was always moving around."

"And did you go there with them?"

"No, I didn't want to go to Johannesburg. I stayed in Connecticut."

"*Alone?* You were only eighteen."

"Well, Mrs. Paulson agreed I could stay on, because I had found myself a job. At the Silver Lake Inn. She came to meet the Silvers and liked them. They were providing room and board as well as a wage, and she approved. The Silvers were from an old family and well known, very respected in the area."

"So at the age of eighteen you were on your own, working at an inn. How did you feel about this? About being so . . . so independent."

"I was pleased, but I wasn't really on my own, Dr. Benson. The Silvers treated me like family right from the beginning, and they made me extremely welcome. I felt at home, as I'd never felt before in my life, actually."

"If I am understanding you correctly, they treated you like a daughter. Am I right, Meredith?"

"Not a daughter, no, they weren't that much older than I was. More like a sibling, a younger sister."

"How old were the Silvers?"

"Amelia was thirty-six when I went to work there, and Jack was thirty-two."

Hilary Benson nodded. "And what was your job at the inn?"

"I started as a receptionist, but it was always understood, right from the beginning, that I would help Amelia with the office work. She was very overloaded, and since she was paralyzed, things weren't easy for her. I became her assistant as well as the receptionist. And I helped Jack a lot with the management of the inn."

"What had happened to Amelia Silver? Why was she paralyzed?"

"She'd had a riding accident when she was twenty-five, just after they were married. She injured her spine and she lost the baby she was carrying. It was a great tragedy. But she coped very well."

"Tell me more about her. She was obviously someone you cared about."

"Oh yes, I did. She was remarkable, and she taught me so much. Not only that, Amelia was the most beautiful woman I've ever known, ever seen. She was like Vivien Leigh in *Gone With the Wind*. That was the first thing I said to Amelia . . . that she resembled Vivien Leigh."

"Then she must have indeed been beautiful. You say she taught you many things. Would you explain this to me, please?"

"She loved art, antiques, and decorating, and I learned about those things from her. But I also learned about courage ... she was so courageous herself. And I learned about dignity and decency from Amelia Silver. Those were some of her other qualities."

"What you're saying is that she gave you certain values."

"Yes. And so did Jack. I learned about true kindness from him, and he encouraged me, helped me to understand business. He taught me a great deal about running an inn, almost everything I know, in fact. He was a very smart man."

"Was it a busy hotel?"

"Only on weekends. It was quiet during the week. Silver Lake Inn was and is very much a weekend retreat, and all the year round. But more people came in the good weather, in the spring and summer, than they did in winter. And we were always full in the fall, of course, when the leaves changed color. People loved to come and see the foliage. They still do."

"You describe the inn in a very loving voice, Meredith."

"I do love Silver Lake. I always have, from the very first moment I saw it. And it was the first real home I ever knew. My first safe haven—" Meredith stopped. She had said too much. She shifted slightly in the chair and focused her eyes on the painting above Hilary Benson's head.

Hilary said, "*Safe* haven ... had you not felt safe before then, Meredith?"

"It's just an expression," Meredith hedged.

"You speak so beautifully about the Silvers, I know you must have loved them, obviously still do. How are they—"

"They're both dead!" Meredith exclaimed, interrupting the psychiatrist.

"I'm sorry to hear that. Their passing must have been a great loss to you."

"It was. I was heartbroken."

"When did they die?"

"Jack died in 1973. He was only thirty-six. And Amelia about a year later, just a bit longer than a year, actually, late in 1974. She was young too, only forty-one."

"How truly sad for you to lose two people you cared about so close together. They must have loved you very much."

"Oh, yes, they did," Meredith said softly, remembering them, cherishing them inside. "That's why it was so hard for me when they died. Jack was the first person to ever show me any affection in my life, put his arms around me, comfort me."

There was a brief silence before Hilary Benson asked softly, "Are you saying that there was a sexual relationship between you and Jack Silver?"

"I'm not suggesting anything of the sort!" Meredith shot back, her voice rising. "Amelia also loved me and as much as Jack did. She showed me a great deal of affection too, but it was verbal. The poor woman was in a wheelchair. *She* couldn't very well put *her* arms around me."

"I understand," the psychiatrist replied quietly,

noting Meredith's anger, her overreaction, realizing
that there had indeed been a sexual relationship between Meredith and Jack. But it was far too early to
probe this. Meredith Stratton was not ready.

Meredith looked at her watch; it was four
o'clock. She had been there almost an hour. "I have
an appointment at my office at four-thirty, Dr.
Benson, and in any case I think our first session is
finished, is it not?"

"Yes, you are correct," Hilary answered, glancing
at the clock on her desk. "I believe we have another
appointment on Thursday of this week."

"Yes, we do," Meredith replied, standing up. As
she shook the doctor's hand and then left the private office, she wondered if she would keep it.

# Chapter Nineteen

Despite her misgiving, Meredith did keep her Thursday appointment with Dr. Hilary Benson. And she agreed to three more sessions the following week.

So far, the psychiatrist had not pinpointed the cause of her attacks of fatigue.

It was at her fifth appointment, at the end of the second week, that Meredith finally decided to make it their last meeting.

"I don't think we're getting anywhere at all, Dr. Benson," she said slowly. "I've talked endlessly and you've listened, and we've not really progressed or come up with anything of real value. We don't even know if I'm suffering from psychogenic fatigue."

"I think you are," the psychiatrist said firmly.

"But I haven't had any more attacks."

"I know. But that doesn't mean very much."

"Let's make this our last session."

"I think that would be foolish of you," Hilary answered quietly, observing her closely. "Something is troubling you. I am certain of that. We just haven't uncovered it yet."

"I can't come again for several weeks. I'm going to London and Paris for a month."

"When are you leaving?"

"On Wednesday or Thursday of next week."

"Shall we see how we do today, Meredith?"

"All right," she agreed. She did so because she had grown to like Hilary Benson, felt at ease with her and she trusted her. Even though they had not discovered the root of her problem, she knew she was partly at fault. For years she had lived with half-truths, had hidden so much, it was difficult to unearth all of this now.

Hilary said, "I'm not going to mince my words today, Meredith, I'm going to be brutally honest with you. I know you are lying to me. I know you had a sexual relationship with Jack Silver. I want you to tell me about it."

Meredith was so taken aback, she blurted out, "It wasn't just sexual. We loved each other—" Breaking off, she swiftly averted her face, regretting these words.

"You mustn't be embarrassed," Hilary murmured in an understanding tone. "I'm not here to judge you, I'm only trying to help you. . . . Talk to me, tell me about Jack, tell me what happened all those years ago at Silver Lake Inn. I *know* you'll feel better if you do, and having more information about your past will help me to trace the cause of your illness."

There was a very long silence. Meredith did not answer. Instead, she rose, walked over to the window, stood looking down onto Park Avenue, thinking about Jack and Amelia and herself, and all that had happened between them so long ago. It had shaped her life, changed her life. She had had so much from them. She did not want Hilary to think badly of Jack. Or of her.

Turning around, she walked back to the chair and sat down opposite Hilary, who was behind the desk. "Yes, it's true. We did have a sexual relationship, but we also loved each other very much. I haven't wanted to talk about it to you because I don't want you to misunderstand. Words can sound so cold when they're said. Perhaps you could never understand the love, the emotions, the feelings, there were between us, because you were not a witness to them. No one could understand." Meredith gave her a long, hard stare.

Hilary nodded. "I appreciate everything you're saying. I know exactly what you mean. But as I just told you a moment ago, I'm not a judge or juror, just your doctor. And if I am to help you, I must understand your past."

"Do you think that's troubling me? Our love affair? Jack's and mine?"

"I'm not sure, Meredith. I have to hear everything first before I can make an assessment."

"Because I'm sure it isn't. However, I will tell you about Jack, and what happened between us when I went to work at the inn in 1969."

"Are you comfortable? Would you prefer to sit over there on the sofa?"

Meredith shook her head. "No, I'm fine here. I just want to preface what I have to say about Jack with something else. A couple of weeks ago, my son, Jon, told me he used to listen to me crying at night when he was very young. And I did, I wept endless tears until I thought I had none left in me, but I always did. I cried for a lot of things in those days, but especially for Amelia and Jack. I missed them so much."

Meredith paused, cleared her throat, then she went on softly. "Jack Silver was my true love. I loved him from the first day I met him. He had fallen in love with me too that day. He called it a *coup de foudre*. I'd never heard that phrase before. He told me what it meant . . . struck by lightning. But we kept our love at bay for weeks, never disclosed our feelings for each other. Then Amelia had to go away. She had to visit her mother in Manhattan. The old lady was very ill, probably dying, and Jack drove Amelia into the city. When he returned on that July night, he came looking for me. He found me down by Silver Lake, lying in the grass, endeavoring to cool off. It was extremely hot that month, blistering. He said he needed to talk to me about Amelia; he was worried because he had left her alone with her sick mother, and with only two young maids in attendance. He wondered out loud if he ought to drive me into the city the next day so that I could stay with Amelia, look after her. I told him I would be happy to go, that I'd do anything for him.

"And then suddenly, without either of us understanding exactly how it happened, we were in each other's arms, kissing each other. I'd never experienced anything like it before, the surging passion, the desire, and the love I felt for him. I hadn't had any previous sexual encounters, Dr. Benson, and Jack was upset when he discovered I was a virgin, scolded me for not telling him. But by then it was too late. We had already made love."

Meredith fell silent for a split second.

Hilary Benson said nothing; she knew it was wiser to wait until Meredith was ready to continue her story.

After a few moments, Meredith said softly, "And we went on making love to each other even after Amelia returned to Silver Lake. We just couldn't help ourselves, we were so crazily in love. Jack had been terribly deprived for years, before my coming on the scene. He told me that he had once gone to a call girl in New York, but that it had been a failure, a waste of time because he had no feelings for her. But Jack loved me, and he loved Amelia, and we were scrupulous. We never displayed our intense feelings for each other in front of her. Jack always said that Amelia must never know about us, that we must not hurt her in any way whatsoever, and we never did."

"She never knew?" Hilary asked.

Meredith did not answer. Instead, she went on, "Then one day I missed my period. I knew I must be pregnant. I was terrified, convinced Amelia would guess the baby was Jack's child. But he reassured me, told me Amelia would never suspect. I believed him, why wouldn't I? I loved him beyond all reason. When I asked him what I would say to Amelia, how I would explain my pregnancy, he said I must invent a boyfriend, say that my new young man was the father. Later I could explain to her that my boyfriend had let me down, gone away and left me in the lurch, left me to fend for myself. And this is what I did tell Amelia, and she believed me.

"Actually, Dr. Benson, Amelia was so thrilled I was pregnant, she was in seventh heaven. When I became really heavy, six months into my pregnancy, she insisted I move into the apartment over the garage adjoining their house. I had been living in the attic of the inn, and Amelia just decided one day that the stairs were too much for me, and this was true. And so we all settled down in the house together. Naturally, Jack and I were as careful as we'd always been in front of Amelia.

"One afternoon, when I was eight months into my pregnancy, Amelia asked me if I intended to go away once the baby was born. I told her I didn't want to leave, that I hoped I could stay at Silver Lake, continue working for them. She was very happy to hear this, and I remember how she placed her small hand on my stomach and smiled and said, 'Our baby, Meri. It'll be our baby, we'll all bring it up, and we're going to be so happy here together.' And we were, that's the truth. Sometimes I wondered out loud to Jack whether Amelia suspected the baby was his, and he assured me she did not.

"Finally, our daughter, Catherine, was born. The most perfect baby any of us had ever seen. Beautiful, with Jack's bright blue eyes. And then three years later tragedy came to Silver Lake. Jack died, just like that, in the flick of an eyelash. He had a heart attack when he was talking to Pete O'Brien on the front lawn. And he never knew he had a heart problem, none of us did." Meredith sat back in her chair, stared off into space, lost again in that faraway time.

"And then what happened?" Hilary asked after a few seconds had elapsed. "Please continue."

"What happened? We *grieved*, Amelia and I. We were so sorrowful. But I had the baby to look after and the inn to run for Amelia . . . so much work in those days, but I was young, strong . . . I had my hands full but I coped. And poor Amelia was in such a bad way, I had to take care of her as well. You see, she did not really want to live after Jack's death, and by the following spring she was fading. I knew she was not long for this world. At least, I felt that, felt that she was literally willing herself to die. My heart grew heavier and heavier as the months passed. I couldn't bear the thought of losing her so soon after Jack . . . the very idea of it filled me with dread.

"One day, a Friday it was, Amelia and I were sitting together in the mud room of the hotel, arranging daffodils for the restaurant tables. Cat was playing on the steps in the spring sunshine. Suddenly Amelia looked at me in the most peculiar way, and she told me she had made a will. 'It's all for you and Cat, Meri. I've no one else to leave all this to, and besides, Catherine is a Silver. The last of the Silvers, at this moment in time, until she grows up and has a Silver of her own. So all this belongs to the child, Jack's child. *You* must keep it safe for her. I trust you to do the right thing; you're smart, Meri. If you ever have to sell the inn for any reason, then do so. Or rent it out, if running it gets to be too much for you. But keep the land, keep the Silver Lake property, no matter what. It is already worth millions, and can only increase in value. That's what Jack would want you to do, Meri, he'd want you to keep the land. It's belonged to the Silvers for almost two hundred years.' As you can probably imagine, I was stunned, Dr. Benson. Aghast that she knew Catherine was Jack's child.

"Once I'd recovered from my surprise, I asked Amelia how she had guessed about the baby, and she gave me that weird look again and said, 'But I've always known, Meri, since the day you became pregnant.' I suppose I must have looked extremely baffled, and so she went on to explain. 'Jack told me, Meri dear,' she said, and then took hold of my hand, held it tightly in hers. 'He loved me from childhood, but he loved you, too, and he needed you desperately, Meri. He was a virile young man, full of passion. I was of no use to him as a woman anymore, not after my accident. He never looked at another woman and for years he was celibate, until you came here. He fell for you, Meri. And once you were pregnant he wanted the child, oh how he wanted it, my darling. And I've never begrudged the relationship he had with you. I knew he would never hurt me or leave me. And I also knew you would always be loyal to me. I loved Jack so much, Meri, and I love you and the baby, too. She's like my child.' And she meant every word, Dr. Benson, Amelia always spoke the truth."

Meredith fell silent again. Remembering that particular day with Amelia, so long ago now, still affected her deeply. Her eyes were bright with tears when she eventually focused her gaze on the psychiatrist. "Amelia died later that year—1974—and she made me a wealthy woman and Cat an heiress. She did leave us everything, and there was so much more than the Silver Lake Inn and the land. There was her own estate, which she had inherited from her mother. She made a few bequests, to Pete O'Brien, who had run the property for years, and his wife, Blanche, and other people who worked at the inn. But the bulk of the Silver estate and her own inheritance came to us. And yet I would have given it all up just to have Amelia back. I longed for her, grieved for her for years. And I also grieved for Jack."

"It's a most unusual story, very moving," Hilary said, her voice low, compassionate. She had noted Meredith's emotions a moment before, and she fully understood how much Meredith had cared for the couple. It was on the tip of her tongue to ask Meredith if she thought the Silvers had used her as a surrogate, and then she instantly changed her mind. In her heart of hearts, Hilary knew this was not the case. She believed that Meredith had told her the story of her life with the Silvers exactly the way it had happened. Her words had the ring of truth to them. She might well be lying about other parts of her life, but not about these particular years.

There was a carafe of water on a console table nearby, and Meredith rose, went to pour herself a glass. Turning to look at Hilary, she murmured, "I am convinced my attacks of fatigue have nothing to do with my early years in Connecticut. I was very happy with the Silvers, they were very good to me."

"I know," Hilary replied. "And I think you are right. The attacks are not related to that time at all. So we must dig deeper, go further back. But I don't know when we can do this. Unless you come in for another session before you leave for London and Paris. That would give us a start, at least."

Meredith hesitated momentarily, and then she made a decision. "All right," she said, "I'll come tomorrow afternoon if you can fit me in."

"Let me check my other appointments with my secretary," Hilary responded, pressing the button of the intercom.


That night Meredith dreamed the dream of her childhood again.

After a light supper she had gone to bed early.

She had a number of important appointments the next morning, and she also wanted to clear her desk before her afternoon session with Hilary Benson.

Almost immediately she fell into a sound sleep,

and it was a dreamless sleep for most of the night. Then just as dawn was breaking she awakened with a start and sat bolt upright in bed. Her face, neck, and chest were covered with beads of sweat, and she was filled with apprehension.

Snapping on the light, she glanced around the room, and then she lay back against the pillows. After a moment, she reached for a tissue on the bedside table, wiped her neck and face, and then crumpled the damp tissue in a ball in her hand.

She had just had that awful dream again, and as always, it alarmed her. She focused on it, remembering.

> She was alone in the vast, parched landscape. She was looking for the little girl and boy. But she could not find them. They had disappeared, had fallen through a giant crack in the earth's surface. She had seen them dropping away, and she was afraid for them. Now she must find them again. They knew. They knew the answer to the secret.
>
> She walked and walked, her eyes scanning the landscape. Just as she gave up hope of ever finding them again, they appeared at the edge of the dried mudflats. She was so happy she had found them. The boy took off his school cap and waved it in the air. Suddenly they were all together, the three of them holding hands, walking across the vast and arid

landscape toward the far horizon. Now she was dressed like the little girl. She wore a dark coat, a long, striped scarf around her neck and a beret on her head. They all had giant labels on their coats. Luggage labels. She peered at the little girl's label. The writing was smudged from the rain. She could not read the name. Or the name of the boy. She looked down at her own luggage label. This, too, was indistinct. What was her name? She did not know.

Ahead of them was the great ship. It was so huge it loomed up high on the docks. The little girl was afraid. She did not want to go on the ship. She began to cry. The boy cried and so did she. None of them wanted to go on board. Tears rolled down their cheeks. It was so cold the tears froze on their skin. It began to snow.

The sea was like black oil. They were afraid, terrified. They clung to each other, weeping. They were led off the ship. They had reached their destination. It was the gray cracked landscape where nothing grew. The sky was very blue; the sun blistering. They walked and walked. There were many, many children, all walking until they came to the black sea once more. And they all walked into the sea. She pulled back; she would not move. She tried to stop the little girl from walking into the sea, walking to her doom. But she could not. The girl moved away from her, and so did the boy. Together the two of them walked into the sea. She tried to shout at them to stop. But no words came out of her mouth. She was alone again on the mudflats. And she was afraid. They knew the answer to the secret. She did not. Now they had gone. Forever. And so she would never know.

This time the dream had been different, Meredith realized that as she examined every detail of it. She wondered what it meant; she had no idea. But she now resolved to tell Hilary Benson about it. Perhaps the psychiatrist would have an explanation for her.

"There's something I haven't told you," Meredith said to Dr. Benson later that afternoon.

Hilary looked at her alertly. "Oh, and what is that, Meredith?"

"It's something to do with my attacks. At least, I think that's so. Certainly it started again after my second attack."

"What started again?"

"The dream. It's a nightmare, in fact, and I've had it on and off for years."

"How many years?" Hilary asked, leaning forward over the desk, scrutinizing her patient intently.

"For as long as I can remember. Since I was

about twelve, thirteen, perhaps even a few years younger. The dream stopped when I first came to Connecticut. In fact, I had it only once in the early years there, when I first started working for Jack and Amelia at the inn. Then it occurred a couple of times in my twenties, again in my thirties. But I hadn't had it since then until January of this year."

"And the dream occurred after you had an attack of fatigue?"

"Yes. I was in the Loire Valley, staying with a friend. I suddenly felt ill that afternoon and I went upstairs to rest in my room. I fell asleep, I was so tired. And I had the dream. When I awakened I was startled that it had come back after so many years, and also that I felt the same way."

"How did you feel?"

"Frightened, alarmed."

"Try to recount the dream for me, please, Meredith."

Meredith nodded and did as the psychiatrist asked. Then she explained that the dream had differed slightly each time she had had it in the past few months.

"So last night in the dream you were finally reunited with the boy and the girl in the arid landscape," Hilary said. "Was there anything else? Anything different?"

"Yes. There was the ship in the dream . . ." Meredith left her sentence unfinished, snapped her eyes shut.

"Are you all right?" Hilary asked.

"Yes, I'm fine," she answered, instantly opening her eyes. "Dr. Benson?"

"Yes?"

"What do dreams mean?"

"I think they are usually manifestations of impressions we store in our subconscious. Then again, sometimes what truly frightens a person can come to the fore in sleep, when the unconscious rises. I personally think that we dream our memories, and also dream our terrors, Meredith."

"So what do you think my recurring nightmare means?"

"I'm not certain. Only by talking, exploring a little more, can we eventually come to some interpretation of it."

Meredith took a deep breath. Unexpectedly and inexplicably she felt as if she were choking. Agitation took hold of her. She had to get out of there; she needed air. She stood up, then sat down again with sudden abruptness. She thought she was going to open her mouth and start screaming. She compressed her lips, striving for control.

Hilary Benson frowned, stared at her. Then she realized that Meredith, who had always appeared the calmest of women, was suffering from acute agitation. She was twisting her hands together anxiously, and her eyes had opened wide.

"You're suddenly extremely upset. What is it, Meredith?"

Meredith said nothing; she began to shake visibly, and she wrapped her arms around her body, hugged herself.

Hilary Benson jumped up, went to her, put a hand on her shoulder comfortingly.

Meredith gaped at Hilary. Her eyes filled with tears. "I've not told you the truth . . . not told anyone . . . not ever . . ."

Hilary hurried to her desk, picked up the phone, and spoke to her secretary. "I can't see any other patients at the moment, Janice. Please reschedule them for another day. I have an emergency with Mrs. Stratton."

Walking back to Meredith, who was bent double in the chair, rocking back and forth, the psychiatrist took hold of her arm, forced her upright.

"Come to the sofa, Meredith, sit with me. You're going to tell me everything. Slowly, in your own time. There's no hurry." She had spoken softly, sympathetically, and Meredith allowed herself to be led to the sofa.

The two women sat down.

There was a long silence.

Finally, Meredith began to speak in a low voice. "I don't know who I am. Or where I come from. I don't know who my parents were. Or my real name. I have no identity. I invented myself. I made my own rules and I lived by them. I had no one to teach me. No one to love me. I was completely alone. Until I met the Silvers. For seventeen years I was a lost soul. I'm still a lost soul in some ways. Help me . . . Oh God. *Who am I?* Where do I come from? Who gave birth to me?"

Meredith was weeping, the tears gushing out of her eyes and falling down onto her hands. She was in an agony of despair, and she started to rock back and forth again.

Hilary Benson let Meredith weep. She said nothing, did nothing, and presently the tears stopped. She handed Meredith a box of tissues in silence. Then she walked over to the console, poured a glass of water, and brought it to her patient.

Meredith took it from her, sipped the water, and said after a moment, "I'm sorry for my outburst."

"I'm not, and you shouldn't be either. You should be glad. It's done you good, I'm sure of that. And it is the first step toward your recovery. Whenever you are ready to start talking again, I am here to listen. Don't rush . . . the rest of the day is for you. The evening too, if that is necessary, Meredith."

"Thank you. Yes . . . yes . . . I must tell you . . ." Meredith now took a deep breath and began:

"I grew up in an orphanage in Sydney. I was eight years old when Gerald and Merle Stratton adopted me. She didn't like my name, so she called me Meredith. They weren't very nice. Cold, hardhearted people. They treated me like a maid. I did all the housework early in the morning and after school at night. I was only eight. They didn't really mistreat me, but he thought nothing of hitting me. She was mean, too, and stingy—with food especially. I grew to hate them. I wanted to go back to the orphanage. Then they were killed in a car crash when I was ten. His sister Mercedes didn't want me. She sent me back to the orphanage. I was there until I was fifteen. I saw Mercedes only once again, when she helped me get my passport. She was glad I was leaving with the Paulsons."

Meredith stopped, leaned against the sofa cushions, and closed her eyes. She took several deep breaths to steady herself. After a short time she opened her eyes and looked directly at Hilary. She began to tremble.

The psychiatrist took hold of her hand, asked softly in a gentle voice, "Was there any sexual abuse when you were living with the Strattons? Did either of them abuse you?"

"No, there was never anything like that. They didn't sexually molest me. There was just this awful coldness and indifference, as if I weren't there. I was there only to be their maid, that's what I thought then. I still think it. I was relieved when they were killed. They never showed me one iota of affection. I had always thought that when I got adopted, somebody was going to love me at last. But no one did."

A bleak look crossed her face, hurt shadowed her eyes, and when she spoke, pain echoed in her voice. "I can never begin to explain to you the horror of being in an orphanage. Nobody cares a thing about you . . . never to be touched, or held, or shown any love. I never knew why I was there. I worried a lot about that. I thought I'd been put there by my parents because I'd been bad. I didn't understand. All I wanted was to find out who my parents were. I never did. Nobody told me anything, they never answered my questions. . . ."

"What is your earliest memory, Meredith? Close your eyes, relax, try to go back in time, try to focus on your youngest years. What do you see? What do you remember?"

After a while Meredith spoke. She said in a quiet voice, "I see a river. But that's all." She opened her eyes. "Perhaps that's why I like living near water."

"How old were you when you went to the orphanage?"

"I don't know, Dr. Benson, I was always there."

"From being a baby?"

"Yes. No. No, I don't think so. In my nightmare last night there was the ship. When I was a very little girl I used to remember being on a ship."

"Do you mean a ship or a boat? There's a difference."

Meredith closed her eyes again, pushing her memory back to her childhood. She saw herself in her mind's eye; she saw boys and girls going up a gangplank. She was one of them. She saw sailors, seamen, docks. She saw a flagpole. The Union Jack flying atop it.

Meredith sat up straighter, opened her eyes, and looked at Hilary intently. "I do mean a ship and not a boat. And an oceangoing ship, too. A British ship, flying a British flag. I *must* have been on a ship, perhaps with other children. Maybe that explains the children who are always in the dream."

"It's possible. Please try and think harder, think back. Could you have been born in England and taken to Australia when very young?"

"Maybe I was. But why don't I remember anything about it? Why don't I remember those years?"

"It's called repressed memory, Meredith. I believe something terrible happened to you when you were a small child, causing deep trauma that resulted in repressed memory. In fact, I'm pretty positive that's what you're suffering from, and I believe it's the reason for your attacks of fatigue. *Psychogenic fatigue.*"

"But why now? Why haven't I had the attacks in the past? Why not years ago?"

"Because the memory stayed deeply buried. That was the way you wanted it. So that you could function. Now something has triggered it. The repressed memory is trying to surface."

"What do you think triggered it?"

"I can't be absolutely certain, but I believe it was your visit to Fountains Abbey."

"You *do* think I was there before?"

"Possibly. Most probably. It would certainly explain a great deal."

"Is there any other way you can trigger my repressed memory, Dr. Benson?"

"Only you can do it really, by endeavoring to go back in time to your earliest childhood years. You're going to England next week. Something else might give your memory a good jolt while you are there. In the meantime, let us talk a little longer about your years in the orphanage."

Meredith shivered violently and threw Hilary a look of horror. "No child should ever have to live like that," she exclaimed, anger surfacing. "But I'll tell you more about it if you want me to."

"I do. I realize how painful it is for you, but it may well give me more clues, something else to go on, Meredith."

Later that night she rang Luc. She could no longer bear to keep the secret of her past from him. Also, she felt the need to confide, share, and in turn receive comfort from him.

# Chapter Twenty

C atherine Stratton sat back and studied the illustration on her drawing board, her head held on one side, her eyes narrowed slightly as she assessed her work.

The watercolor in front of her was of a small boy curled up in a crib, sleeping, with one hand tucked under his cheek. She smiled to herself, liking its innocence, its charm. It was perfect for the last poem in the children's book of verse she had been illustrating for the past few weeks. Now, at last, it was finished and ready to go to the publishers.

Work well done, she thought, taking up a fine-nibbed pen, signing *Cat* with a flourish. She had always used her diminutive on her work, and it was a signature that was becoming well-known these days.

Sliding down off the tall stool, she lifted her arms above her head, did a few stretching exercises, and then walked across her studio and out into the main loft space, heading for the kitchen.

This was a good size, decorated in a crisp blue and white color scheme, and it was equipped with all the latest appliances. It was the perfect kitchen for a dedicated chef, which Catherine was. She had loved cooking since childhood, had been encouraged and taught by her mother and Blanche O'Brien, at Silver Lake, who had always been like a favorite cuddly aunt.

Catherine stood washing her hands at the sink under the window that looked uptown. It offered a unique view of the Chrysler and Empire State buildings. That afternoon those towering skyscrapers sparkled against the blue April sky, and she thought they had never looked better than on this lovely spring day. Except perhaps at night when they were fully illuminated, their glittering spires etched against the dark sky. To Catherine they would always typify Manhattan.

Reaching for the kettle, she filled it and put it on the cooktop to boil. Then she busied herself with cups and saucers, took out various items from the refrigerator, and started to make a selection of small tea sandwiches.

Catherine and her mother had designed her SoHo loft. Her studio was at one end, with big windows and a skylight in the sloping roof; the dining area flowed off the kitchen, and beyond there was a large living room decorated like a library. Two bedrooms were situated to the right of the living room, and each had its own bathroom.

It was a vast loft, cleverly divided to maximize the space and the light and it had a pristine, airy feeling. This was not due only to its grand size and many windows but to the pale color schemes used throughout.

The loft had been Catherine's twenty-first birthday present four years earlier. "But it's not from me, you know," her mother had told her. "It's from Jack and Amelia in a sense, even though they're dead. I bought it for you with money from their estate."

It was then that Meredith had fully explained about Amelia's will, the vast inheritance that was now hers along with Silver Lake Inn, the house she had grown up in, and all of the Silver land: one hundred and fifty acres. All of this had been held in trust for her by her mother ever since Amelia's death; Meredith had effectively increased its value through clever investing of the money Amelia had left. Catherine had suddenly understood that day four years ago that she was an heiress, and a very lucky young woman.

Catherine had always known that Jack Silver was her father. Her mother had told her the truth when she was old enough to understand. She barely remembered him and even Amelia was a shadowy figure in her mind. Her mother had always been the dominant person in her life, and she adored Meredith.

Catherine had never judged Meredith and Jack. She was far too intelligent to do that, and mature enough to realize that no one else ever knew exactly what went on between two people. Three in this case, for obviously Amelia had acquiesced, or had perhaps turned a blind eye to their relationship.

Once, when she had questioned Blanche O'Brien, Blanche had said that she shouldn't waste time dwelling on that old situation. "Nobody got hurt, everybody was happy, they all three loved each other, and you were the crowning point in their lives. They adored you, and Amelia behaved like a second mother to you."

Sometimes she wondered about her mother's past; she understood many things about it, even though Meredith had always been somewhat secretive about her early years in Australia. It seemed to her that her mother started to live her life only when she came to Connecticut.

From odd things her mother had said over the years, Catherine knew that her childhood had been terrible—bleak, without love, or even the merest hint of affection.

Meredith had loved Jon and her with a sort of terrible fury, single-mindedly, with total devotion, and to the exclusion of anyone else.

Perhaps this was because of the deprivation Meredith had endured as a child. Certainly it had always seemed to Catherine that her mother had set out to give them all of the things she herself had never had, and much, much more.

Meredith had always been the most wonderful mother, and probably to the detriment of her relationship with David Layton, Jon's father. She and her brother had always come first with Meredith, and perhaps he had grown tired and resentful of taking second place in her life and her affections.

That marriage had foundered after four years, and within no time at all, David, the country lawyer, had moved to the West Coast. Much to their amazement, he had turned himself into a hot-shot show business lawyer with a string of famous movie star clients. They had never seen him again, heard only infrequently, and not at all after the first year or so. Not that her brother or she cared. Jon had always loved his mother the most, and anyway, David Layton had not been much of a father, or stepfather, for that matter.

Meredith was her best friend. She had not only given her a great deal of love and been supportive, she had encouraged her to chase her dreams and fulfill her ambitions. In fact, she had been instrumental in helping her to do this. And she had been exactly the same with Jon, always there for him, advising him when he asked, rooting for him, cheering him on. Meredith had been mother and father to them both.

She and her brother were delighted that their mother had met Luc de Montboucher. They had taken to him immediately, and had encouraged their mother in this relationship.

They thought he was the perfect mate for her, and Jon was convinced they would get married. She hoped her brother was correct in this conviction. Nothing would please her more than to see Meredith in a happy relationship, especially now that she herself was getting married. She hated to think of her mother alone. It was about time she had some personal happiness in her life.

Luc had been to New York a number of times,

and her mother was virtually commuting to Paris, and this seemed to bode well for the future. Also, she had put the Vermont inn up for sale, and had confided only the other day that she was not looking to make a big profit. "I just want to get out unscathed financially," Meredith had said. "Fortunately, I've several potential buyers."

When Catherine had told Jon about this conversation he had grinned and said, "See, I told you so! Mom's going to marry Luc and move to France, or at least spend most of her time there. Just you wait and see, Cat."

Her mother was leaving for Europe that night, first stop London. She had business with Patsy, but she was planning to spend time in France.

Catherine covered the plate of tea sandwiches with a dampened linen napkin, the way Blanche had taught her as a child, and pushed the plate to a corner of the countertop; then she rinsed the strawberries and hulled them.

Her mind was still on her mother. She had been seeing a psychiatrist for the past few weeks, trying to discover why she had these peculiar attacks of fatigue. During the weekend, they had talked on the phone, and Meredith had said that Dr. Benson was helping her to unearth repressed memories of her childhood. Finally she believed she was getting somewhere, making headway.

Catherine hoped so. All she wanted was for her mother to come to terms with her past, gain peace of mind, as well as a bit of happiness for once. After

all, she was going to be forty-five years old next
month.

"Everything looks beautiful, darling," Meredith said
an hour later as she walked into the loft, glancing
around. "You've added a few things since I was here
last. That painting over there, the lamp, the sculpture in the corner." Meredith nodded approvingly.
"You've given it a wonderful look, your many new
touches have really worked."

"Thanks, Mom. Like mother like daughter, I
guess. I take after you, you know, always fiddling
with rooms, adding accessories and stuff. I'm a real
'nester' just as you are."

"Am I really?" Meredith said, sounding surprised,
giving her daughter a quick glance. "I hadn't realized."

Bursting into laughter, Catherine exclaimed, "Oh
Mom, honestly, how can you say that! You can walk
into the dreariest room, anywhere in the world, and
transform it in a couple of hours, just by adding
flowers, a bowl of fruit, a few cushions and photographs, magazines and books. Other bits and
pieces. You've got a real talent that way. To coin a
phrase, you make wonderful *havens*, Mom."

Meredith had the good grace to laugh.

"Your company is aptly named, I've always
thought."

"I suppose it is." Meredith sat down on the sofa
and continued. "I'm glad I can spend a couple of
hours with you before I catch the night flight to

London; we don't see enough of each other these days. And perhaps we can talk about the wedding a little, come to a few decisions."

"Yes, we can, Mom. Keith and I batted a few dates around this past weekend, and I think we'd like to have the wedding in the fall, as you suggested."

Meredith's face lit up. "That's wonderful, Cat, the perfect time. I suppose you're thinking of early October, just as the foliage begins to turn?"

Catherine nodded. "The second Saturday in October, that would be the fourteenth. Originally, Keith and I toyed with the first Saturday in the month, the seventh. But we weren't sure whether the foliage would have changed by then. What do you think?"

"Better go for the second Saturday, Catherine. The leaves will be in full color, and they don't drop that quickly, remember. I'm assuming you're going to have the ceremony at Silver Lake?"

"Yes. Briefly, and only briefly, Keith and I had talked about the little church in Cornwall, but in the end we came to the conclusion that it's too small." Catherine grinned at her mother. "All those Pearsons, you know."

Meredith smiled. "From the sound of it, I'm going to be giving you a very big wedding."

"Do you mind, Mom?"

"Oh darling, of course not! I'm thrilled. That's what I've always wanted for you, a big white wedding with all the trimmings. Anyway, getting back to the details, I think you'd better call the minister of the church in Cornwall to make sure he will be able to officiate at the marriage, that he's available that day."

"Yes, I'll do it tomorrow." Catherine rose. "Mom, I want to show you the sketches of my wedding gown. Let me get them, they're in the studio."

A moment later she was back, sitting down next to Meredith on the sofa. The two of them pored over the series of drawings Cat had done; all were beautifully rendered and showed the gown from different angles.

"What do you think, Mom?" Catherine asked, eyeing her mother worriedly. "You're not saying anything. Don't you like it?"

"It's absolutely beautiful, Cat. Very . . . *medieval*, wouldn't you say?"

"In a way. But perhaps a bit more Tudor in feeling, Elizabethan. I've spent a lot of time on the design, Mother, and on the details in particular."

"I can see it's quite elaborate." Meredith stared at the sketch she was holding, which was a front view of the dress, and nodded her head. "Yes, I see what you mean about it being Elizabethan . . . the squared-off neck cut very near the edge of the shoulders, the long puffed-up sleeves, tight bodice, and bouffant skirt. Very stylish, Cat, all you need is a white ruff."

"Don't think I hadn't thought of it," Cat laughed. "Because I have, but I decided that might be going a bit too far. The veil will be held by a Tudor-style headdress, and this will fall into a train. I've yet to design the headdress. So, what do you think? Can I get away with it?"

"Of course you can, Cat, you will carry it off very well. I think you'll look stunning. Have you decided who's going to make it?"

"I thought I'd go to Edetta; she's created some lovely evening gowns for us in the past few years."

"Yes, she has, and I'm sure she'll be able to find the right kind of white silk for you. Now, to move on to a few other details, do you know what time of day you want to have the marriage ceremony?"

"Keith and I thought it would be nice to have it at noon. Drinks first, then the ceremony, and a luncheon afterward. With dancing." Cat lifted a dark brow. "Would that be all right?"

"Yes, I think that's a lovely idea, Cat. If I'm going to give you a big wedding, we might as well do it in style. Do you know how many guests you'll be inviting?"

"I think the total will be around a hundred and thirty, or thereabouts. Keith and I counted about eighty, maybe ninety, from the Pearson side, and I figured around fifty from our side."

Meredith laughed. "I'm not sure that we can even rustle up that number, honey."

"Oh we can, Mom, really we can. There are all my girlfriends and their husbands or boyfriends. Blanche and Pete. Some of the new friends I've made in the publishing world, the people from Havens, and Patsy will come from London, I'm certain of that."

"She's already said she's coming. And there will be Agnes and Alain D'Auberville from Paris. Yes, I think you're right, we probably will be about fifty."

"Luc will come, won't he, Mother?"

"I hope so."

"Keith and I like him. So does Jon."

"Oh I know. Your brother's made that only too clear."

"Mom?"

"Yes, darling?"

"Luc loves you."

"I know."

"Do you love him?

"Yes, Cat, I do."

"So what's going to happen?"

"Are you and your brother in collusion?"

"What do you mean?"

"He was asking me the same thing after your engagement party a few weeks ago. And to answer your question, I don't know what's going to happen. Being in love is one thing, getting married another. And there's so much to consider in my case."

"I know, but you will work it out. You're both smart." Catherine jumped up. "I'm glad you came to see me at this time of day. I've made us a lovely tea . . . like you used to do when we were little. A nursery tea, you called it. I've prepared all sorts of tiny sandwiches, cakes, the works, actually. I'll just go and boil the water again. Be back in a jiffy . . ." Cat winked at her mother, laughed, and added, "Before you can even say Jack Robinson," and hurried off in the direction of the kitchen.

Meredith smiled and leaned back against the sofa, thinking about Luc. She would be seeing him soon, once she had completed her business in

England. There were certain matters at the London office of Havens to attend to, and she and Patsy had to make a trip to Ripon. The refurbishing of Skell Garth House was almost finished. They had various things to do before the inn reopened in May. She would then fly to Paris and base herself there, since she had much work to complete on the manor in Montfort-L'Amaury. Good progress was being made there, thanks to Luc and Agnes. Once she was in France she would spend weekends at Talcy with Luc, and they were both looking forward to this.

She wondered what she would do if he did ask her to marry him. Jon and Cat thought it was all so simple, but in reality her life was rather complicated. She lived in America, he lived in France, and they both had businesses, commitments, responsibilities. She couldn't very well walk away from Havens Incorporated, and certainly Luc would never give up his architectural practice in Paris. Nor did she expect him to. So how could they ever work it out . . .

"Mom, let's have tea in here," Catherine called from the archway leading into the dining area. "It's so much easier."

"I'll be right there," Meredith said, pushed herself up off the sofa, and went to join her daughter. "How nice it looks," she said a moment later as she surveyed Catherine's handiwork.

"Thanks, and sit here, Mom." Cat indicated a chair, took the one opposite, picked up the teapot, and poured. "Now, here's this lovely cup of tea, Mother, just the way you like it, and help yourself to some sandwiches. There's cucumber, tomato, egg salad, and ham. Tiny ones but tasty."

"I remember our nursery teas," Meredith said, taking a minuscule cucumber sandwich. "They *were* fun, weren't they?"

Catherine nodded as she munched on a sandwich. After a moment she said, "I tried to get scones today, but no luck. My local bakery sometimes has them. I was hoping to give you warm scones with clotted cream and strawberry jam."

"Thoughtful of you, darling, but this is fine. Not too fattening," Meredith replied with a dry laugh.

Catherine eyed her mother. "*You* don't have to worry, Mom, you look wonderful."

"Thank you."

Catherine stood up. "I won't be a minute, I've got to get something from the kitchen."

When she returned to the table Catherine was carrying a glass bowl and a jug. She stood there, smiling at her mother, her bright blue eyes full of love.

"I have a treat for you, Mom. *Strawberries.* Your favorite."

Meredith stared at Cat.

She felt herself go cold all over.

And then she heard a voice echoing in her head, faintly, as if it came from a very long distance. *"Mari . . . Mari."*

A moment later the same voice was calling, once again echoing in Meredith's head. *"Mari . . . Come on. Come in."*

A scene flashed.

In her mind's eye she saw a young woman with sparkling blue eyes and red-gold hair bending over a small child, her expression loving. *"Strawberries, Mari. A special treat."* The child beamed at the mother. It was such a happy scene; there was such love on the mother's face. Then she heard the child crying. *"Mam, Mam, what's wrong?"*

The scene faded.

Meredith felt icy cold. She stared at Catherine. For a moment she was unable to say anything.

Catherine, who had been looking at her mother intently, now asked in a concerned voice, "What's the matter? Don't you feel well? You've gone awfully white, Mom."

"I'm fine," Meredith managed to say. She shook her head. "I think I've just had what Dr. Benson would call a flashback. My first."

"What exactly is it?"

"It's a memory really, usually a repressed memory coming to the surface. I believe I just had one from my childhood. I saw a young woman of about your age, with bright blue eyes like you, and a small child. Maybe a five-year-old. At first the scene was happy, then suddenly the child was crying. It faded away."

Meredith took several deep breaths. "I think I had a memory of my mother and me. My biological mother, Cat."

"Why do you think you had this flashback all of a sudden?" Catherine asked curiously, sitting down in the chair, her eyes pinned on Meredith's face.

"I believe you triggered it. It was the way you

said *strawberries*, then mentioned *special treat*. And
it was your eyes, Cat, so blue, so full of love."

Meredith paused, shook her head. "Jack had very
blue eyes, and I always thought you had inherited
yours from your father. But perhaps they're my
mother's eyes."

Catherine reached out, took hold of Meredith's
hand resting on the table. "Oh Mom, this is wonderful." She felt her throat tighten, and she said in
an emotional voice, "Maybe you'll keep remembering more and more until you know everything
about your past."

"I hope so, darling." Meredith bit her lip.
"Perhaps I ought to call Hilary Benson, tell her
about this. She would want to know." Glancing at
her watch, she went on, "It's just turned six o'clock.
I'm sure she's still at the office."

"Yes, call her," Catherine exclaimed, getting up.
"The phone in the kitchen is the nearest."

Meredith nodded and followed her daughter, then
quickly dialed the psychiatrist's number from the wall
phone. "May I speak to Dr. Benson please, Janice?"
she said when the secretary came on the line.

"Who's calling?"

"It's Mrs. Stratton."

"Oh, hello, Mrs. Stratton. I'll put you through
right away."

"Good evening, Meredith," Hilary Benson
greeted her a split second later. "How are you?"

"I'm good. As you know, I'm going to London
tonight. I stopped off to have tea with my daughter

this afternoon, and she said something that triggered a memory. I think I've just had my first real flashback."

"This is very good news, Meredith. Very good indeed. What exactly did you remember?"

Meredith recounted the flashback in every detail.

When she had finished, the psychiatrist exclaimed, "This is your first significant memory, a true breakthrough, and I think it's just the beginning. You may find you have more in the next few days. That frequently happens. Try to focus on some of the details you've just mentioned to me, they might lead you into a whole series of significant memories."

"I hope so. I'd really love to unearth the mystery of my early years."

"You will, Meredith, I'm quite certain of that. If you have the need to call me, don't hesitate to do so. And I'll see you in a few weeks."

"Yes, and thank you, Dr. Benson. Good-bye." Meredith hung up the receiver, turned around to face Catherine, who was standing in the doorway, an expectant look on her face.

"What did she say?" Catherine asked.

"That it was a significant memory, and that I'll probably have more now."

"Oh Mom!" Catherine hurried into the kitchen, wrapped her arms around Meredith, and held her close. "I love you so much, Mother, I just want you to have peace of mind. And some happiness in your life finally."

# Chapter Twenty-One

Patsy Canton had been listening attentively to Meredith for the past hour.

Now she said in a low, thoughtful voice, "So what you're saying to me, in essence, is that you believe you were born in England and then taken to Australia as a child."

Meredith nodded. "Exactly. I think I must've been about six years old."

"And you went alone? That can't be so. You must've been with your parents."

"I'm pretty sure I went alone, Patsy. I'm convinced my mother was dead by then."

"No father?"

"I don't remember him."

"But why would you go *alone*? That seems awfully strange to me. And who sent you?"

"I don't know." Meredith gave a light shrug of

her shoulders. "I truly don't have the slightest idea."

"In your recurring dream, there are children . . . could you have been sent with other children, perhaps? You know, the way evacuees were sent in groups to safe places during the Second World War."

"Maybe. But *why*? There wasn't a war on in 1957, when I was six years old, so why was I sent away? Exiled from England?"

Patsy shook her head. "I haven't a clue, my darling, and I want to help you, but I don't know how I possibly can. I'm as baffled as you."

Meredith sighed and took a sip of water. She leaned back in the chair, glancing around the restaurant in Claridge's, and continued quietly. "Last night on the plane, I couldn't sleep. I suppose I dozed off and on, but mostly my mind was racing, trying to remember things."

"And did you?"

"A couple of things came back to me. The first has to do with my name. I was called Mary Anderson in the orphanage in Sydney. It was Merle Stratton who changed my name to Meredith. And of course I took their surname when they adopted me. But I was never Mary—what I mean is, that wasn't *my* name, even though they called me Mary at the orphanage. My real name is Mari, and my last name is Sanderson."

"I see. So how did it get changed?" Instantly Patsy shook her head and exclaimed in a dismayed voice, "Oh God, bureaucracy! Do save me from it.

Your name probably got muddled up by some idiot at the orphanage."

"That's exactly what happened, I think. I had this memory on the plane last night. It was of a woman, a rather stern one, who told me that my name wasn't Mari with an *i*, but Mary with a *y*. I kept telling her that I was called Marigold, but she wouldn't believe me. She scoffed and said that it wasn't a child's name, but the name of a flower."

"There are some bloody awful people running these institutions. It's just terrible what goes on in this world. Despicable." Patsy sighed heavily and gave Meredith a sympathetic look. "So Marigold was your first name, and I suppose they also managed to get Anderson and Sanderson confused."

"Yes," Meredith replied. "And this confusion about my name might well explain the luggage labels in the dream."

"Absolutely," Patsy cried. "*Brilliant*, darling."

There was a small silence between them. Eventually, Meredith looked at Patsy earnestly and said, "My mother's name was Kate—I've remembered that. And I know she's dead, so there's no possibility of my meeting her. But now that I've remembered her at last, after all these years, I need to do something. For myself. I need closure. And so I would like to visit her grave at least. See it, take flowers, be with her there. That would truly help me. And perhaps I'll start feeling better, and maybe—hopefully—the attacks of psychogenic fatigue will go away."

"I'm sure you *would* feel much better, Meredith. And I really understand your need . . . visiting her grave will give you solace in a way."

"At least I'd finally know she really did exist, and that she isn't a figment of my imagination. The only thing is, I don't know where she's buried. I've remembered her name, but I can't remember where we lived."

"Yorkshire," Patsy announced after only a moment's thought. "I'm positive. And certainly it would explain the experience you had at Fountains Abbey. That's always seemed rather significant to me. I haven't forgotten the way you explained it that day, you had a very strong reaction to the abbey. You must have gone there as a child."

"I agree. But I have a feeling I didn't grow up in that area. I remembered something else . . . being taken into a city. On a bus. It was a very big city, bustling, with lots of people milling around. There was a large square in the center, with black statues. My mother used to take me to this city to go to a market. It was huge, covered with a domed glass roof."

"And they sold everything at stalls. Am I correct?"

"Yes, you are."

Patsy nodded. "Vegetables and fruit stalls, fish, meat, cakes, bread, clothes, furniture, crystal and china stalls. Men calling out to passersby to come and look, sample their wares. All of them doing a very loud verbal selling job. Do you remember that?"

"Oh yes, I do, Patsy! We used to stand and listen to them. They all had . . . different pitches for their goods."

Patsy nodded. "Leeds Market. It's very famous, and in Leeds City Square there are black statues of nymphs holding torches. There is also a statue of Edward, the Black Prince, on a horse. Both are life-sized. Does that ring a bell?"

"It does. Let's assume I do come from Leeds . . . how can I find out where my mother is buried? Who would know anything about Kate Sanderson thirty-eight years later?"

"*Somerset House*. Actually, it's no longer called that, they changed its name. Now it's St. Catherine's House, but it is the right place for us to begin. It's the general register office of births, marriages, and deaths, and for the whole of Great Britain. It's a place of records, and it's a mine of information, in fact."

"Where is it located?"

"Here in London, in Kingsway. It's a quick cab ride from here."

"I must go there this afternoon."

"Yes, you must, and I'll come with you, Meredith."

An hour later Meredith and Patsy were at St. Catherine's House in Kingsway. They walked through the glass doors and found themselves immediately in the actual records office itself. On all sides were stacks and stacks of ledgers lined up on shelves.

"It looks like a library," Meredith said as she and Patsy walked up to the security desk.

After the security officer had checked their handbags, Patsy said to him, "How do we go about finding the record of a death?"

The officer directed them to an inquiry desk at the far end of one of the long aisles of ledgers on the left. Five clerks were standing behind the inquiry desk, ready to be of assistance. Patsy and Meredith approached one of them, and Patsy repeated her question.

The young woman clerk handed Patsy a pamphlet. "This tells you how to use the Public Search Room. And it's simple enough. Records of deaths are bound in the black ledgers, stacked on the left. Births are bound in red, and they are on the right. Look for the year of death. You'll find there are four books for the four quarters in each year. And there are three volumes per quarter. These are alphabetical. A to F, G to O, and P to Z."

Patsy thanked her and she and Meredith retraced their steps. Once they were back in the Public Search Room they headed for the black ledgers and found the year they wanted. Meredith took hold of the handle on the spine of the first ledger inscribed March 1957, P to Z, pulled it off the shelf, and placed it on the book stand that ran the length of the aisle in front of the shelves. Opening it, she saw that it covered January to March.

"To save time, why don't you look at the quarter that follows," Meredith suggested. "That would be April, May, June."

"Good idea," Patsy said, and went to look for the appropriate ledger.

Meredith ran her finger slowly down the lists of Sandersons deceased through the first quarter of the year 1957. The name of Katharine Sanderson was not among them. Glancing at Patsy, she said, "She's not listed in this book. How about yours?"

"Give me a minute or two, I haven't quite finished."

Meredith returned the ledger to its shelf, pulled out the one covering July, August, and September of 1957. Once again her mother's death was not shown; nor was her death recorded in the two volumes Patsy perused in quick succession.

"We've covered the whole year," Patsy murmured to Meredith. "Are you absolutely certain your mother died in 1957?"

"Yes. Well, I think so."

"But how do you know this, Meredith? You said you had so little information about yourself. Do you actually remember her dying?"

"Not really. But I do know I went to the orphanage in Sydney when I was six years old."

"You remember that, do you? Are you really sure? How do you know this?"

"Because Merle Stratton told me. She once said to me that I'd been at the orphanage since I was six but they hadn't taught me much in two years."

"All right, so you went there when you were six

years old in 1957. But that doesn't mean your mother died that year. Maybe it was 1956, when you were five."

"I don't think so . . . I know I was six. But let's look at the ledgers for 1956."

"Good idea," Patsy agreed.

An hour later Meredith and Patsy had searched the entire set of ledgers for the year 1956 and turned up nothing. Meredith looked at her friend and said quietly, "This is a wild-goose chase. Her death is just not listed."

"Do you want to try some other years?"

"No, there's no point," Meredith answered. "Maybe I have made a mistake about the date, but we can't stay here all day, searching through endless ledgers. Come on, let's go."

"No, wait a minute," Patsy said. "What if she died abroad?"

"My mother was never abroad."

"Humor me, let's go and talk to one of the clerks. Just for a minute. Please, Meredith."

"All right."

When they got back to the inquiry desk, Patsy zeroed in on the young woman who had helped them earlier. "We're looking for the record of a death, and we haven't been able to find it. Now, what if the person died abroad, that would mean it isn't listed, correct?"

The young woman shook her head. "No, it would be listed. Wherever a British subject dies, the death is eventually recorded here. The information

comes through all of the British embassies and con-
sulates around the world."

"I see."

"It's really quite simple," the clerk went on, looking from Patsy to Meredith. "If a person's name is
not in one of the registers, then that person is not
dead. He or she is still alive."

Meredith gaped at the clerk.

Patsy said, "Thank you very much for your
help," and with a slight nod she turned away. She
took hold of Meredith's arm, led her down the short
flight of steps and along one of the aisles.

They stood in front of the glass doors opening
onto the street, staring at each other.

Meredith looked stunned and she was slightly
trembling.

Patsy, who was nobody's fool, understood all of
the implications inherent in this unexpected knowledge, and she said, "I know what you're thinking,
darling."

"I'm sure you do," Meredith answered, her voice
so low it was almost inaudible. "If my mother's not
dead, which according to those ledgers she isn't,
then she's alive. Somewhere. In England probably."
Meredith paused, took a deep breath, and clutched
Patsy's arm. "Why did she send me away when I
was a little girl? Why in God's name was I sent to
an orphanage in *Sydney*, of all places? The other
side of the world. Why? *Why*, Patsy?"

Meredith's eyes were filled with misery and her
face was so bleak, Patsy's heart went out to her

friend. For a moment she was speechless. She swallowed hard and replied in a gentle voice, "I don't know, Meredith, it doesn't make any sense to me."

*"She sent me away because she didn't want me."* After she had said these words Meredith was so shaken she went and leaned against the wall, biting her lip. For a moment she was floundering; her senses were swimming.

Noticing her distress, Patsy took charge. "Listen to me, if your mother's alive, which she must be since there's no death certificate, then we are going to *find* her. Whatever it takes, we're going to do it. Come on, let's go back and look for your birth certificate."

"Why?" Meredith asked miserably. "What for?"

"We're going to get a copy of your birth certificate. If you *were* born in this country, as you think you were, and not Australia, then your birth will be registered in one of those red books."

"How will my birth certificate help us to find my mother?"

"There's a lot of information given on a birth certificate, Meredith. I know from my own and my children's. The name of the father, his occupation. The married name of the mother, and her maiden name. Place of birth of the child, residence of the parents, date and year of birth, obviously. We'll have enough to start with. Besides, I would have thought you'd like to have a copy of it . . . just for yourself, your own edification. And peace of mind."

Meredith nodded but said nothing. She was reluctant to start a search for her birth certificate.

What if it wasn't there? She would feel even worse than she already did.

Patsy coaxed her a little more, drew her slowly back to the aisles of ledgers. This time they went down the one on the right-hand side, where all the red-bound books were stored. Fifteen minutes later she discovered that she *had* been born in Great Britain. Her birth *was* registered.

"You see, I knew you'd find your name in one of those lovely red books," Patsy exclaimed, smiling at her, wanting to cheer her up. "Now let's order a copy of the birth certificate. Maybe they will be able to have it ready for us later today." Patsy pulled an order form out of the Lucite pocket attached to the end of the reading stand, handed it to Meredith, and said, "Fill this in, and then we'll take it over there to one of those windows, to order the copy."

Meredith nodded and pulled out a pen. After completing the form they went to a window. She was able to get priority service for twenty pounds. The copy of her birth certificate would be ready at the same time the following day.

On Friday afternoon, promptly at four, Meredith and Patsy returned to St. Catherine's House. Within minutes she was holding a copy of her birth certificate in her hands.

The two women went out into the street, got into the waiting taxi, and headed back to Claridge's.

Settling back against the seat, they pored over the

certificate. Meredith saw that her mother's full name was Katharine Spence Sanderson. Her father's name was Daniel Sanderson and his occupation was listed as accountant. Was it from him that she got her head for figures? she wondered. The address given for her place of birth was 3 Green Hill Road, Armley. Her parents' residence was listed as Hawthorne Cottage, Beck Lane, Armley, Leeds. Her date of birth was shown as the ninth of May, 1951, and her birth had been registered on the nineteenth of June by her mother. Her name *was* Marigold Sanderson.

"You know quite a lot about yourself now," Patsy said, turning to Meredith, squeezing her arm affectionately.

"More than I've ever known, Patsy." Meredith cleared her throat, and went on, "I never had any sense of identity when I was young. Not knowing who you are and where you come from is very frightening. It's almost like being a non-person. Since I didn't have an identity, I invented myself."

"Getting your birth certificate must mean a great deal to you."

"It does. It's . . . well, it's a kind of validation of who I really am." Meredith forced a small smile. "At least I've been celebrating my birthday on the correct date. The orphanage did get that part right."

"What are you going to do next? Oh, stupid, stupid question, Patsy Canton." Patsy looked at her intently. "You're going to Leeds, of course."

"Tomorrow, Patsy. We were going to Ripon on Sunday anyway, so I'm going to make it a day earlier."

"I'll drive you."

"But—"

"No buts," Patsy exclaimed. "For one thing, you need my help, my expertise. I know Leeds very well, and the rest of Yorkshire, and you're going to require a guide. Besides that, I care about you, Meredith. I wouldn't let you embark on a search like this alone. The whole situation is too emotionally fraught. You're going to look for a long-lost mother, and who knows what you're going to unearth in the process. You really do need a friend with you."

"Especially a good and dear friend like you, Patsy. Thank you. Thank you for helping me."

"We'll set off at the crack of dawn tomorrow, and get to Leeds in about two and a half hours. Maybe three. The motorway is pretty fast moving. I think our first stop should be Hawthorne Cottage in Armley."

"Do you know this place?"

"Oddly enough, I do. I had an uncle who owned a woolen mill there, and he lived in Farnley, which is nearby. Farnley Lee House, lovely old manor it was. Well, anyway, I used to go there with my parents, and we usually drove through Upper Armley to get to Farnley. Do you have any recollection of Hawthorne Cottage?"

"Vaguely. The cottage was near a river. There was wildlife on it . . . ducks, I think."

"The more we talk, the more you'll remember, I'm sure of that," Patsy said. "Isn't this what your psychiatrist said?"

"Yes, it is."

As they got out of the cab in front of Claridge's, Patsy linked her arm in Meredith's. "Let's go and have a drink. Celebrate."

"Celebrate what?"

Patsy laughed. "I always said I'd make a Yorkshirewoman of you. Now I don't even have to try, because you actually are one by birth. I'd like to drink a toast to that."

The phone was ringing as Meredith came into her suite at Claridge's. As she picked it up and said "Hello?" she heard Luc's voice saying, *"Chérie, comment tu vas?"*

"I'm fine, darling. I was just going to call you in Paris. Guess what happened today? I found out that my mother is still alive."

*"Mon Dieu."* There was a moment's silence, and then he asked, "But how did you find out?"

She proceeded to tell him in great detail, then added, "We're leaving for Yorkshire tomorrow instead of on Sunday as planned . . . to begin the search."

"Do you want me to fly over and go with you?"

"No, no, that's not necessary. I'd love to see you, darling, but I've got Patsy to help me. She knows Yorkshire like the back of her hand."

"All right, I understand. You want to concentrate. But I will be thinking about you. Call me tomorrow, *chèrie*. I'll be anxious. I love you."

# Chapter Twenty-Two

They left for Yorkshire very early on Saturday morning and arrived in Leeds in record time. Patsy circumvented the busy city center and took Stanningley Road to Armley. After asking directions a few times, she soon found Beck Lane.

As she pointed the Aston-Martin down the lane, she glanced at Meredith and asked, "Does anything seem familiar to you?"

"Not really, not even Beck Lane. It looks so short, so ordinary. But then again, when you're a small child things always appear to be so much bigger, more impressive. And also more frightening, of course."

"That's quite true," Patsy agreed. "We're almost at the bottom of the lane, and it looks to me as if it ends in a cul-de-sac."

Meredith peered out of the car window, her eyes scanning the scenery. "What I don't understand is why we're not seeing the river."

"I'm sure we will in a minute. When I looked up this area on a map of Leeds last night, I noticed that the River Aire and the Leeds and Liverpool Canal are adjacent to each other, run parallel. We learned that at school, but I'd forgotten. Those two waterways *are* ahead of us, Meredith, you'll see."

Beck Lane came to an abrupt end at a partially demolished brick wall, which cut the lane off from a large field beyond. It was here that Patsy stopped, turned off the ignition and parked.

"Let's go investigate," she said, opening the car door, and getting out.

Meredith followed suit.

The two women glanced around. They were standing in a deserted area; there were no houses, no buildings of any kind in sight. But back down the lane a few yards there was an old gate set in a ramshackle wooden fence, and Meredith suddenly noticed this.

"I didn't see that gate as we drove past," she said, "and it must lead somewhere." As she was speaking she began to walk down the lane toward it.

Patsy followed her.

The gate was open, hanging off its rusted hinges; Meredith went through it and realized that there had once been a pathway there. Now it was overgrown with weeds and grass, barely visible. The partially obscured path led toward a tumbledown building, in reality several large piles of bricks, stones, wood, and other rubble.

"Could *that* be Hawthorne Cottage?" Patsy asked, catching up with her.

"Possibly," Meredith replied quietly. Suddenly, she felt deflated, sad. During the drive from London she had begun to believe that Hawthorne Cottage was still standing, that her mother still lived there. But this had been wishful thinking on her part, she accepted that now. How foolish I am, she thought, expecting things to be the way they were almost forty years go. Everything changes.

Arriving at the demolished building, Meredith circled it several times, then she turned to face the River Aire, which was visible from this vantage point. She could see it gleaming in the pale spring sunshine, and, just behind it, flowed the canal. She wondered why she had never noticed the two waterways running parallel when she was a child.

Turning to Patsy, she voiced this thought.

Patsy said, "But you were so little, darling, only five or six. You wouldn't have paid any attention to something like that. Or maybe you've simply forgotten."

"I guess you're right." Meredith half smiled. "Also, I was much shorter then, I might not have been able to see that far."

Patsy laughed. "True enough."

Meredith remained standing in front of the mounds of stone and rubble, still gazing thoughtfully toward the River Aire. She was endeavoring to move backward in time, concentrating hard on the past, in the way Hilary Benson had told her to do.

Unexpectedly, in her mind's eye she saw a neat little lawn and flower beds, and, beyond the garden, a white gate set in an old brick wall, rambling roses growing all over it.

Hurrying forward, she walked through the desolate garden, heading for the river, and as she approached the bank she saw, behind a clump of overgrown bushes, the wall and the remnants of the gate. The wall had been reduced to a crumbling pile of brick, but the rambling rose bushes still spread themselves over it, and she supposed that in summer the roses would be in full bloom.

Her heart gave a small leap. She recognized this place, knew it well. Then she saw the rock and she stood perfectly still. A memory came rushing back, almost knocking the breath out of her with its clarity and vividness.

She saw herself as she had been as a small girl, sitting on that rock, always sitting there daydreaming. It was her favorite place, that rock high up on the river's bank. It was her view of the world.

She went and sat down on the rock; her eyes were moist as she gazed out at the water flowing past, splashing and tinkling as it fell down over the dappled stones of the river's bed. There was wildlife on this river, and she remembered how she had loved to watch the antics of the ducks, the plovers, and the other birds on the water.

Hugging her knees with her arms, she rested her

head on them and closed her eyes . . . memories . . . memories . . . they were coming back.

The mother was there. The mother with the red-gold curls and very blue eyes. Eyes so supernaturally blue, they were almost blinding. The mother loved the child on the rock, loved her to distraction. The child was the mother's whole world.

Then why did she send me so far away from her? *Why?*

Meredith had no answer for herself. Only Kate Sanderson could answer that question. If she and Patsy ever found her, which was most unlikely in her view.

The pain came back all of a sudden, the pain of her childhood, the constant she had lived with as a little girl. "Mam, Mam, where are you?" she heard the small girl cry, and Meredith's heart tightened. How she had dreamed of that face, the mother's pretty face. How she had longed for her, longed for those soft arms around her, longed for the warmth of her love, the soothing voice, the comfort of her presence. Meredith's heart held the memories intact, held them inviolate . . . the pretty face, the sparkling eyes of blue, the love, the tenderness, the scent of her . . . the mother she had never stopped loving or longing for . . . *her* mother. Kate Sanderson.

Meredith squeezed the tears back and swallowed. Her throat ached.

"Are you all right?" Patsy asked softly, sounding worried.

Unable to speak for a moment, Meredith did not answer. She sat up straighter and flicked the tears away from her eyes with her fingertips.

"I just don't know why she did it," she said to Patsy at last. "A moment ago I thought we'd never find her, but now I know we *must*. Just to ask her that question. *Why?*"

Patsy was silent; she simply nodded, affected by Meredith's emotion, the pain reflected on her face.

Finally, Meredith got up and looked at her friend, met her steady gaze. "You see, Patsy, my mother loved me very much. The way I love Cat and Jon . . . and that's why I can't fathom why she did what she did. It's a mystery."

Patsy put her arm around Meredith's shoulder. "We'll find her, I promise you that."

Together they walked back through the weed-filled garden, heading for the car. As they passed the mounds of rubble, Patsy asked, "Do you think that is Hawthorne Cottage?"

For a moment Meredith did not answer. She stood staring at the mass of old stones, but she did not really see them. Instead, she saw Hawthorne Cottage as it had been thirty-eight years earlier. She saw the sparkling windows, the fresh white-lace curtains, the copper pots gleaming in the kitchen. She saw her neat little bedroom with the rose-patterned quilt. And she heard that mellifluous voice. *"A wizard sells magical things at this stall, astonishing gifts you can see if you call . . . "* The voice faded away.

"Yes," Meredith said softly, "that's Hawthorne Cottage. What's left of it."

"This is 3 Green Hill Road," Patsy said, slowing the car, indicating the big Victorian building set behind wrought iron gates. "You were born there, Meredith. For years it was a maternity hospital. Now that I see it, I recall coming here with my aunt, when my cousin Jane had her first child. They used to live at Hill Top. I'll show you where on our way into town."

Meredith stared at the building with interest, and then asked, "You said *used* to be a maternity hospital. Isn't it anymore?"

"I don't think so," Patsy replied. "I vaguely remember that it became a general hospital, or perhaps a home for the elderly, I'm not quite sure." Glancing at Meredith, she finished, "Do you want to get out, go over there and have a closer look?"

Meredith shook her head. "No, no, that's fine. But I can't help wondering where I was christened though."

Turning on the ignition, driving on, Patsy said, "Probably at Christ Church in Armley. Do you want me to take you there?"

"I don't think so, I'm sure I won't remember anything. But thanks, honey."

"What about Leeds Market? Would you like to stop off, see whether or not it triggers any other memories? It was rebuilt in the seventies, after it burned down in a fire. But fortunately it was rebuilt in the same Victorian style it had always been. So it's the same now as it was when you were five or six."

"I doubt I'll have any significant recollections there, Patsy. I think that we ought to go to Ripon. We've quite a lot of things to review, and to discuss with the Millers. By the way, that was good news that they're going to stay on as the managers."

"Isn't it just," Patsy exclaimed, a smile flashing on her face. "I was thrilled when they first told me last week. I hope you're not angry that I didn't pass it on then, but I wanted it to be a lovely surprise for you when you arrived."

"No, I wasn't angry, and it was a *marvelous* surprise. Now we don't have to search for a good management team or interview anyone."

"True, but we do have to interview the various chefs. The Millers have done a lot of weeding out, as I told you, and we're down to three."

"That's not too bad, but hiring a chef is always a tricky business; you know that, Patsy. They usually do a lovely meal to impress, but invariably that happens only once . . . disaster frequently follows."

"The Millers have tried out these three off and on for a couple of weeks. One's a man, Lloyd Bricker. The other two are women, a Mrs. Morgan and a Mrs. Jones. So we'll be eating well this weekend, that's a certainty. However, I tend to agree with you, hiring a chef is dicey."

"We should be able to open the inn in May," Meredith remarked. "You don't foresee any problems, do you?"

"No, and I told you that when you arrived. It's just this chef business that nags at me. It's going to be fine, let's not worry." Patsy threw her a quick glance, then focused on the road again. "By the way, when are you planning to leave for Paris?"

"I had hoped to go next Wednesday. Now I'm not so sure. Agnes and I are supposed to visit Montfort-L'Amaury on Thursday so that I can see the progress they've made with the remodeling. And then I was going to Talcy with Luc. For the weekend. However, now that we're looking for my mother, I don't know what to tell you."

"Let's just take it day by day," Patsy suggested.


That afternoon, after they had eaten a delicious lunch prepared by the male chef, Lloyd Bricker, Meredith and Patsy did a tour of Skell Garth House. Each of them made copious notes, and once they had reviewed every room in the inn they found a corner in the empty dining room and went over their punch lists together.

"There're still a lot of things missing in many of the rooms," Patsy said. "Claudia's only partially understood me, I think. I explained to her several times that we're upgrading the inn, creating much higher standards, both in accommodation and service. She seems to have missed the point that real comfort and luxury are absolutely mandatory." She glanced at her pad, and added, "I'm sure you've listed the same things as I, Meredith. Hot water bottles in covers, oodles of towels in every room, bowls of potpourri and scented candles, wool throws, hair dryers, et cetera, et cetera, et cetera."

"Yes, I've noted all those things, Patsy, and they're easy items to add. We just have to ship them up from London."

"They've already been shipped," Patsy replied, making a moue with her mouth. "Well, perhaps she just didn't put them out yet. I'll talk to her about it. What do you think about the refurbishment in general?"

"It's good, Patsy, we picked some lovely fabrics and carpets. I noticed the draperies and bedcovers have been extremely well made, and the sofas and chairs beautifully reupholstered. Thanks to you. And the wallpapering and painting is excellent. But I am going to have to rearrange all of the furniture—and in most of the rooms."

"I knew you'd say that. When I came up two weeks ago to oversee the installation of the carpets and the draperies, I gave them your floor plans for the furniture arrangements. They seem to have ignored them completely."

Meredith nodded. "They certainly did." A faint smile flickered. "The Millers simply put everything back where it was before, and those old groupings were not the best. Or the most comfortable."

"I hope we haven't made a mistake, keeping them on," Patsy murmured, throwing her an apprehensive glance. "Do you think they're too set in their ways?"

"Perhaps. But I'm sure we can overcome that. I'll

have a long talk with them over the weekend. They've simply got to understand that we're raising our prices. Therefore our standards have to be higher, too. They're both bright, so I'm sure we can re-educate them, help them to operate the inn the Havens way."

Patsy grinned. "I'm glad you're such an optimist, Meredith. I was getting really concerned about them when we were upstairs."

"If I hadn't been an optimist, I don't think I would have survived that orphanage in Sydney."

"No, you wouldn't." Patsy glanced down at her pad, and went on, "The rest of the stuff on the punch list is all minor, to do with electrical outlets, the wattage of the lightbulbs and such, so we don't have to worry now. It can wait."

"I don't have a lot of other things either," Meredith said, and pushing back her chair, she stood up. "I'm going to take that walk, Patsy."

"Are you sure you don't want me to drive you to Fountains Abbey?"

"No, thanks anyway for offering. I really do want to walk, I need the exercise and the fresh air. See you later."

Patsy smiled at her and nodded.

Returning the smile, Meredith left the dining room, crossed the foyer, and headed out of Skell Garth House.

It was a fine afternoon, not too cold even though it was still April. The sky was clear, a soft pale blue filled with scudding white clouds. Wherever she looked, Meredith saw that spring was truly here. The trees were in bud, the grass already thick and verdant, and, here and there, patches of wildflowers grew in the hedges. She noticed primroses and irises, and then, as she came to the avenue of limes leading to Studley Church, she caught her breath. Daffodils were blooming everywhere, on the banks by the side of the road and under the limes.

As she walked past them, the Wordsworth poem Patsy had recited to her in January ran through her mind. It had seemed familiar then, and now she realized that she knew the last verse:

> *For oft when on my couch I lie*
> *in vacant or in pensive mood,*
> *they flash upon that inward eye*
> *which is the bliss of solitude;*
> *And then my heart with pleasure fills,*
> *and dances with the daffodils.*

She knew it by heart because her mother had taught it to her all those years earlier. And it had stayed in her mind, dormant perhaps, but nevertheless there.

Her mind focused on Kate Sanderson. The shock of discovering that her mother was not dead had partially receded, but she was still upset, troubled that Kate had apparently abandoned her, and so callously, when she was a little girl.

Meredith knew herself extremely well, and she had begun to realize earlier in the day, as they had driven from Leeds to Ripon, that anger and resentment were beginning to simmer deep down inside her. As she walked on, heading up to the church on the hill, she resolved yet again to find Kate, no matter what it took.

Upon reaching the top of the hill she stood looking down at Fountains Abbey, and just as it had in January, it seemed to beckon to her, pull her forward.

A magnet, she thought, it's like a magnet for me. She hurried down the steep path, almost running, and within a few minutes she was entering the ancient ruins.

On this clear bright April day she was more stunned than before by the dramatic beauty of the soaring ruined monolith.

Dark and imposing, it was silhouetted against the pale sky as if flung there by a mighty hand. But, the blackened stones were softened by the greenness of the trees surrounding them. Just a few feet away from where she stood the Skell flowed toward Ripon. Yet another river, Meredith thought, no wonder I love to live near water. I grew up with it.

Seating herself on a piece of ruined wall, she cast her mind back in time, trying to envision herself visiting this place with Kate Sanderson, but no memory came to her, even though she sat there for half an hour. Her mind was totally blank. Still, again she had the strongest sense that she knew Fountains, had been here before, and that something momentous, and tragic, had happened to her in this ancient spot. But what?

Only her mother had the answer.

Always, in the past, Meredith had used work to subjugate heartache, bring it to heel. Working hard until she dropped had enabled her to keep her mind off her troubles, to function properly.

And so for the rest of the weekend she threw herself wholeheartedly into creating a new look, her look, in most of the rooms in the hotel. It kept worry about her mother at bay.

With the help of Patsy, Bill and Claudia Miller and three handymen, she had furniture moved around until every arrangement pleased her, and each room had the look she was striving for. Beds, chairs, sofas, antique tables, and chests were repositioned under her direction; once this had been accomplished, she set about rearranging lamps and accessories and rehanging pictures.

The Millers were astounded by her, taken aback. As Bill put it to Patsy: "We couldn't believe it when she took off her jacket, rolled up her sleeves, and got down to it herself."

Claudia Miller was particularly impressed with Meredith's energy, stamina, and sheer doggedness. At one point, late on Sunday afternoon, a weary and exhausted Claudia said to Patsy, "I've never seen anyone work like this before. She doesn't stop, she's a whirlwind."

"I know. Meredith's never ceased to amaze *me*. She's a real workhorse. And also very talented," Patsy pointed out. "She has terrific style."

Claudia merely nodded.

Patsy added, "Meredith has really fine taste in decorating. She was born with it. And she has a great eye."

"So I've noticed. The rooms do look better the way she has arranged everything. I suppose Bill and I were a bit slow on the uptake. We really should have followed the plans you gave us more precisely." Claudia's expression was suddenly worried as she asked, "Are you and Meredith upset with us?"

"No, of course not. It's all right, don't worry," Patsy reassured her. "But do try and follow our instructions *exactly* in the future, Claudia, please. It'll save a lot of heartache for everyone. Tomorrow I'll help you to unpack all of the items I shipped from London last week, and Meredith will finish the public rooms down here. She expects to be done by lunchtime."

"You will interview the chefs tomorrow, won't you?" Claudia said. "Monday *is* the deadline."

"That doesn't present a problem. By the way, I enjoyed lunch today. Mrs. Morgan cooked it, didn't she?"

"Yes. She also is going to make dinner tonight."

"Not Mrs. Jones?"

"I'm afraid not. She burned her hand cooking dinner for us last night and she begged off today."

"I see. Do you have a favorite, Claudia?"

"Yes. Mrs. Morgan. She's the best in my opinion, and besides, she's the most adaptable, more easy going in a way, not quite so temperamental as Lloyd."

"And Mrs. Jones? Aren't you impressed with her?"

"She's a good cook, but I don't think she's right for the inn . . . at least, not the way it's going to be in the future."

"Do you mean she's not sophisticated enough?"

"No, I don't mean that, not really. You and Meredith said you wanted high-style English cooking, and country-type cooking to a certain extent. In my opinion Mrs. Morgan's the winner. She's the most all-round cook of the three of them."

Mrs. Morgan turned out to be a woman in her middle fifties, with rosy cheeks, bright brown eyes, and a cheerful smile.

Meredith noticed at once that she had a pleasant demeanor, and within moments of being in her company she felt quite at ease. The woman exuded calm self-confidence, and Meredith could tell from Patsy's expression that her partner had also taken an immediate liking to the chef.

"I understand from Claudia Miller that you are used to cooking for relatively large numbers of people, Mrs. Morgan," Meredith began.

"Oh yes, I am. Until a few months ago I was chef

at a hotel in the Scottish border country. It was an old house turned into an inn like this, but a bit bigger. And we also got a lot of local trade in the restaurant. So numbers don't faze me, oh no, they don't at all, Mrs. Stratton. Of course, I'm used to having a couple of sous chefs."

"Yes, I understand, Mrs. Morgan. That's not a problem," Patsy interjected.

"I gave Mrs. Miller all of my references, so I expect you've seen them." She looked from Patsy to Meredith.

"We have indeed." Meredith smiled at her. "And they're excellent. We also enjoyed the meals you've cooked this weekend."

"Thank you very much, Mrs. Stratton, and please call me Eunice. I prefer it. Much friendlier, isn't it?"

Meredith said, "Yes, it is, Eunice." She paused for a moment, shook her head, then said, "I've known only one other person called Eunice. And that was my baby-sitter when I was a child."

Eunice laughed. "What a coincidence. You had a baby-sitter called Eunice in America, and I was a baby-sitter here in Yorkshire."

Meredith stared at her. After a split second she said, "Where in Yorkshire?"

"Leeds. That's where I come from originally. My husband's from Ripon, and he's been nagging me to come back here for years."

"Whom did you baby-sit for?" Meredith said, continuing to stare at the chef.

"A lovely little girl. Her name was Mari."

"What was her last name?" Meredith asked in a strangled voice.

"Sanderson," Eunice answered, and threw Meredith a swift glance. "Are you all right, Mrs. Stratton? You look a bit odd."

"I'm the little girl, Eunice. I'm Mari Sanderson."

"Get away with you, then, you can't be Mari!" Eunice exclaimed, her astonishment only too apparent.

"But I am."

"Well, I'll be blowed, this is one for the books, I can tell you that." Eunice chuckled. "Can you imagine me, of all people, being a chef, Mari? Do you remember how I always used to burn your lunch? I drove your poor mother crazy."

"I'd like to talk to you about my mother," Meredith said.

# Chapter Twenty-Three

"My mother and I got separated when I was little," Meredith explained. "I don't know how this happened, but it did."

"She was poorly. In hospital, I do know that," Eunice told her.

"Who was looking after me?"

Eunice brought her hand up to her mouth, frowning slightly, looking thoughtful. Finally, pursing her lips, shaking her head, she murmured, "I don't know, to be right truthful with you. I suppose at the time I thought you'd been taken in by relatives."

"*Relatives,*" Meredith said slowly, "I don't ever remember relatives, Eunice, there was only my mother and me. Just the two of us."

"Yes . . ." Eunice sat back in the chair, her face troubled. Hesitatingly, she asked in a quiet voice, "So what exactly happened to you?"

"I don't exactly know. But I did eventually go to live abroad."

Patsy glanced from Meredith to Eunice, and addressed the chef: "When did you last see Mrs. Sanderson? Can you remember that?"

"Let me think. . . . Well, it must've been the summer she got ill. I've got to think back . . . yes . . . yes, it was then. The summer of 1956. I went to Hawthorne Cottage to baby-sit one day and there was no one there. So I went back home. We lived in the Greenocks, just off Town Street, in those days. Anyway, a few days later I ran into Constable O'Shea, he lived near us in the Greenocks. He told me Mrs. Sanderson was in hospital. When I asked about Mari he said she was fine, being taken care of very well. And that was that. A few weeks after this we moved away from Armley. My mother found a house near her sister in Wortley, so off we all went."

Meredith had listened carefully; leaning forward intently, she said to Eunice, "The name Constable O'Shea rings a bell, but I can't quite place him in my mind."

"Can't you? Well, he was very fond of *you*, Mari. Very fond. He was the local bobby, walking the beat in Armley. He used to be stationed at that police box on Canal Road. Are you sure you don't remember him?"

"No, I don't."

Patsy said, "Constable O'Shea might be able to throw some light on what happened to you."

"Yes, that's true," Meredith agreed, and turned to Eunice again. "Do you think he still lives in Armley?"

"Oh, I don't know, I mean, I lost touch donkey's years ago. And he'll be retired. He was about thirty in those days, so he'd be sixty-eight, thereabouts, by now. Mmmm. Now, who do I know who still lives in the Greenocks? Let me just think."

Patsy stood up. "I'll go and get the Leeds telephone directory from the office." She hurried across the dining room and out into the small foyer.

Left alone, Meredith and Eunice looked at each other carefully without speaking. It was Eunice who finally said at last, "You've grown up to be a wonderful-looking woman, and you've certainly made a go of it, you really have. Living in America, owning all these inns."

Meredith half smiled, made no comment. She was looking back into the past again, trying to remember Constable O'Shea, but she was having no success at all. She couldn't even picture his face.

Eunice went on. "Are you married, then?"

"I was. I'm divorced now. I have two children. And what about you, Eunice, do you have children?"

"Two, like you. Malcolm and Dawn. They're both married, and I have five grandchildren. Are your children married?"

"My daughter's engaged. My son's still at college, he's only twenty-one."

Patsy came back into the dining room carrying the Leeds telephone book. Placing it on the table in front of Eunice, she sat down next to her and said, "Now, let's look at all the O'Sheas who live in

Armley. There can't be that many. Perhaps we'll find one living in the Greenocks. What was Constable O'Shea's first name, Eunice?"

"Peter. No, wait a minute, it wasn't Peter. It was an Irish name. Let me see . . . *Patrick!* Yes, it was Patrick O'Shea."

Patsy was running her finger down the O'Sheas listed, then she looked up and said, "There are two living in Armley and one in Bramley with the initial P. But none in the Greenocks. Well, I might as well go and phone all three numbers, that's the only way we'll find out anything. I'll use the phone over there." Carrying the directory, she hurried over to the phone on the table at the entrance to the dining room.

Meredith got up and walked over to the window, stood looking out at the garden, her mind on her mother. Turning around, she gave Eunice a penetrating look and asked, "Did you ever run into my mother in the ensuing years?"

"No, I didn't." The chef's eyebrows drew together in a frown. "She didn't die, then?"

"I don't think so, Eunice. We're trying to find her."

"Oh."

A moment later Patsy rushed across the dining room, still clutching the telephone book in her arms. She was beaming. "I've found him! He now lives at Hill Top. That's near St. Mary's Hospital, Meredith. He's out at the moment, I didn't actually speak to him in person. But I talked with his wife, and he's definitely the right Patrick O'Shea. He's a retired police sergeant, she told me, and she vaguely remembers Mari and her mother. Anyway, she said he would be home around two o'clock this afternoon. I asked if we could go and see him at that time, and she said we could."

Meredith sat facing Patrick O'Shea in the sitting room of his house at Hill Top in Armley. She did not remember him at all; she realized that she had probably so blocked him out, it was almost impossible to recover the memory. He was a tall man, well built, with graying dark hair and a pleasant manner.

"You were such a bonny little girl," he said to her, smiling. "Marigold. I always thought it was such a lovely name for a child. Anyway, to continue, that morning you came looking for me you were so upset. Crying. You thought your mother was dead—"

"But she wasn't was she?" Meredith cut in swiftly.

"No, but she wasn't well. You'd come to the police box on Canal Road. I carried you home, it was quicker. And anyway, you were weeping, so upset you were. We found your mother sitting in a chair in the kitchen. She was white, white as a sheet, and obviously very sick. At least that's what I thought. She said she'd fainted earlier that morning. I'd put in a call for an ambulance, and it came within fifteen minutes. They took her to Leeds Infirmary."

"And what happened to me?" Meredith's eyes were riveted on Patrick O'Shea.

"The last thing she said to me, as the ambulance

doors closed, was 'Look after my Mari for me, Constable O'Shea.' And I did. I spoke to my sergeant at the station, and we decided the best thing to do was take you to Dr. Barnardo's Home in Leeds, the children's home, until your mother was well."

"And what happened when my mother got better?"

"You went back to live with her at Hawthorne Cottage, as I recall. But I don't believe things were good with her, she was struggling, you know, trying to find a job."

"What happened to . . . my father?"

"I don't rightly know. At least, I don't have a lot of details. Kate told me once that he'd left her, gone off to Canada. That's all I knew. I suppose he didn't come back."

"I don't remember him. He must have left when I was very little."

Patrick O'Shea nodded. "I believe he did."

"Do you think my mother became ill again, Mr. O'Shea?"

"She did indeed. She was in the infirmary a second time . . . oh, it must have been the following year . . . about 1957, if my memory serves me well."

"Do you think I was put back into the children's home?"

"Possibly. Yes, that's very likely. There was no one to look after you. And I sort of lost track of your mother after that. In fact, I never really knew what happened to you both. Suddenly you'd left Hawthorne Cottage, another family was living there. I never saw you or your mother again, Mari. I mean, Mrs. Stratton. A few years later I did hear she was working in Leeds."

"Do you know where?"

"Yes, just let me think for a moment . . . it was a dress shop, I do know that. A posh one, too, in Commercial Street . . . Paris Modes, that was the name of it."

"Is it still there?"

"Oh yes, I think so."

"As I explained, Constable O'Shea, my mother and I got separated. I was sent abroad. I thought she was dead. But I've just discovered she's probably still alive. I must find her."

"I understand. She's not listed in the phone book, then?"

"No, she's not."

"Perhaps there's someone at Paris Modes who can help you, give you more information about her whereabouts."

"Well, he was certainly nice enough," Patsy said as she and Meredith drove away from Constable O'Shea's house at Hill Top, heading for the city. "But you don't remember him, do you?"

"Not really, Patsy. I wish I did." Meredith sighed. "I suppose I truly blocked everything out. If only I could recall those early days more fully, but I can't. I have flashes of memory like an amnesiac sometimes does, but that's it."

"Try not to worry, I'm sure we'll get more information at the dress shop."

"I'm not sure at all. Very frankly, Patsy, we're on a wild-goose chase, in my opinion. All of this happened thirty-eight years ago, and my mother's not going to be *still* working at Paris Modes. And I'm certain there's no one there who will remember her."

"You don't know that for sure, Meredith. So let's just go to the shop, ask a few questions. Somebody might remember Kate Sanderson, and give us a lead."

"Yes, we can go, but hasn't it occurred to you that my mother might not live in Yorkshire anymore? She could have moved away. Moved anywhere, in fact. There's a very big world out there."

"I know what you're saying, darling, but I think you're wrong. I have this feeling inside, call it intuition if you like, that your mother is very close by. You'll see, we're going to find her."

When Meredith was silent, Patsy sneaked a look at her. Her heart sank. Meredith's face was bleak.

Patsy drove on in silence, but after a while she said, "I'm not too sure about parking in Leeds. I think the best thing to do is to go to the Queens Hotel and park the car there, near the railway station. It's only a few minutes' walk to Commercial Street from City Square."

"Whatever you say. I don't remember Commercial Street. Only Leeds Market."

But, twenty minutes later, as they walked down

that particular street, Meredith suddenly stopped and clutched Patsy's arm. "Marks and Spencer is somewhere near here. I remember that now. My mother liked to go there; she bought my underwear at Marks." Meredith had an instant vision of herself walking down this street, clinging to her mother's hand. She said to Patsy, "Almost always my mother bought me an ice cream. Once I tripped and dropped my cone. I was so upset, I started to cry. And I remember how she comforted me . . . and gave me her ice cream. . . ."

"You see, more and more memories are coming back," Patsy exclaimed, looking pleased. "And here we are at Paris Modes."

Patsy pushed open the door, and the two of them walked into the elegant dress shop. Immediately a young woman in a neat black dress came gliding forward.

"Can I help you?" she asked politely, smiling at them. "We have some wonderful new lines in from Paris."

"Oh, yes," Patsy said, "we know you have lovely clothes, very smart indeed. But we don't want to buy anything. Actually, we came to see the manager."

"We don't have a manager," the young woman replied. "Mrs. Cohen owns the business, and she runs it herself."

"I see. Is she here? Can we see her?" Meredith asked.

The young woman nodded. "I'll go and get her, she's in the office."

A few seconds later a woman of about fifty, elegantly dressed and well put together, walked out into the shop from the office behind a Coromandel screen.

"I'm Gilda Cohen," she said, extending her hand to Patsy.

"Pleased to meet you, Mrs. Cohen. I'm Patsy Canton, and this is my friend, Mrs. Stratton."

"A pleasure, Mrs. Stratton," Gilda Cohen said, shaking her hand.

Meredith smiled at her. "I'm looking for someone, Mrs. Cohen. A woman who used to work here. But many years ago. I'm afraid it was long before your time."

"Whom are you looking for?" Gilda Cohen asked curiously.

"My mother. She worked here in the late fifties, or perhaps the early sixties. Her name was, or rather is, Kate Sanderson. We were separated when I was small and I always believed she had died when I was a child. But lately I've been given reason to believe she's still alive. I want to find my mother."

"I'm sure you do, Mrs. Stratton, that's quite understandable, and you're correct, Kate did work here, when my mother was running the shop. I inherited it from her. I was at college in those days, but I knew Kate slightly. A lovely woman. My mother was very fond of her indeed, and sorry to see her leave."

"When was that, Mrs. Cohen?" Meredith asked.

"I think it must've been in the middle or late sixties. But don't let's stand here in the middle of the shop. Come into my office and sit down. Can I offer you a cup of tea?"

"No, but thank you anyway," Meredith said.

Patsy also declined, and the two of them followed Gilda Cohen into her office. They sat down together on the sofa and looked at Gilda, who had positioned herself behind her desk. "As I said, my mother was rather fond of Kate, took her under her wing a bit, and she stayed in touch with her after she left."

"Do you know where she went to work?"

"Yes, she returned to the town she came from, Harrogate, and took a job with Jaeger. My mother once told me Kate hadn't been happy in Leeds, and she always referred to her as 'my wounded bird,' although I'm not certain why. I married young and had a child, so I wasn't working in the shop in those days. I didn't know her all that well. But she certainly made an impression on my mother, and on other people too. Everyone spoke nicely about Kate."

Meredith sighed. "I don't suppose she could still be working at Jaeger. What do you think, Mrs. Cohen?"

"Oh, I know she's not, Mrs. Stratton. She didn't stay at Jaeger for longer than a couple of years, then she moved on. The last time I heard about her from my mother, Kate was running Place Vendôme in Harrogate, a really fine boutique selling couture clothes." Gilda Cohen leaned back in her chair. "If only my mother were still alive, she would be able to tell you so much more about Kate."

Meredith gave Mrs. Cohen a sympathetic look. "I'm sorry you lost your mother."

"Yes, it was sad for us all. However, she had a really grand life and lived to be ninety. Never had a day's ill health as long as she lived."

There was a small silence and then Patsy said, "Is Kate Sanderson working at Place Vendôme now?"

"I don't believe she is, Mrs. Canton. The last I heard she had left there. She'd moved away from Harrogate, actually."

"Another dead end," Meredith said in a miserable voice.

Gilda Cohen said, "I can ring Annette Alexander, the owner of the boutique. She just might have an address for Kate."

"Oh, would you? Are you sure you don't mind?" Meredith asked. "Otherwise, we can just drive over to Harrogate." She glanced at her watch. "It's only four-thirty."

"Yes," Patsy said. "We can pop in to see her on our way to Ripon. We have to pass through Harrogate."

"No, no, that's all right, I'll call her for you right away. I don't mind at all." So saying, Gilda Cohen picked up the phone and dialed the boutique.

"Hello, this is Gilda Cohen, is Mrs. Alexander there?"

There was a small silence as Mrs. Cohen listened.

Then she covered the mouthpiece and explained: "They've gone to get her, she's just saying good-bye to a client. Hello, oh, there you are, Annette, how are you?"

Gilda listened once more, and then said, "I have two ladies here who are looking for Kate Sanderson. I know she left you a few years ago, but you wouldn't happen to have an address or a telephone number for her, would you?" The next short silence was followed by an exclamation. "Oh really!" Gilda cried. "Just a minute, let me ask."

Again covering the mouthpiece with her hand, Mrs. Cohen said, "According to Mrs. Alexander, your mother left to marry someone. But she can't remember his name. She wants to know where she can contact you if she does remember?"

"Skell Garth House in Ripon, Mrs. Cohen," Patsy said. "The number is Ripon 42900."

Gilda Cohen repeated this to Annette Alexander. After thanking her and saying good-bye, she hung up. Looking directly at Meredith, she said, "If my mother were alive, she'd be very pleased to know Kate got married finally. Mother always thought Kate was so sad, and she used to tell me Kate had had a tragic life."

"You've been very helpful, Mrs. Cohen," Meredith murmured softly, standing up. "Thank you so much."

"Yes, thank you," Patsy added, also standing.

"It's been my pleasure, I just wish I could have done more to reunite you with your mother, Mrs.

Stratton. Annette is very dependable, and I can guarantee she'll ring you if she remembers who it was your mother married."

"I hope so."

Gilda Cohen escorted them to the door, shook their hands. As they stepped out into Commercial Street, she said, "I'd love to know if you do find Kate, Mrs. Stratton, she was such a favorite of my mother's."

"I'll be in touch," Meredith promised.

"Why didn't we think of that," Patsy muttered as they walked along Commercial Street. "It's the most obvious thing. She was a young woman, and pretty, you said."

"*Very* pretty. Beautiful really." Meredith linked her arm in Patsy's and continued. "We'll never find her. This is yet another dead end, you know."

"No, it isn't!" Patsy cried. "Quite the contrary. I'll call Valerie at the office first thing in the morning and she can go to St. Catherine's House. They keep marriage certificates there. I'm quite sure they do. We'll find out who your mother married."

Meredith instantly brightened. "What a great idea! Let's call her now."

"She's not in the office today. Don't you remember, she went to Milan for the weekend. She won't be back until late tonight."

"Are you certain they keep marriage records?" Meredith asked in a quiet voice as they walked down into City Square.

"I'm positive. It's a general register office of

births, deaths, and marriages." Patsy paused before adding: "I've been thinking . . . perhaps we ought to go to Dr. Barnardo's Home, make inquiries there. They may be able to throw some light on what happened to you. And to your mother."

Meredith looked at her askance. "No way. I know those places. They never tell you anything, they're cloaked in secrecy. I'd go to see them only as a last resort." Her mouth settled in a grim line.

Glancing at her, Patsy decided to say no more for the moment. On the drive back to Ripon she talked about a variety of other things, wanting to take Meredith's mind off her mother. And orphanages.

Laughing suddenly, all at once she said, "You know, Meredith, we're really quite awful."

"What do you mean?"

"Once we'd discovered who Eunice Morgan was, we put her through an interrogation and then fled, raced off to find your mother. The poor woman must think we're crazy. We didn't even finish our interview with her."

"I realized that myself a short while ago. Anyway, how do you feel about hiring Eunice?"

"I'm all for it. I think she's the best of the lot. I found Lloyd Bricker a bit of a snob and too arrogant by far, and Mrs. Jones didn't really impress me that much."

"In my opinion she's a goldbricker," Meredith said. "I agree with you about Lloyd. So let's hire Eunice, shall we? She's certainly a good chef. We've sampled her fare." Meredith gave Patsy a small smile. "And obviously she no longer burns the food as she did when I was a child."

Patsy laughed, glad to see a flash of Meredith's old humor.

The telephone call came the next morning.

Meredith and Patsy were sitting in the dining room, having breakfast and going over their notes about the inn, when Claudia Miller came hurrying over to their table.

"Excuse me. You have a phone call, Meredith. It's a Mrs. Alexander."

Meredith and Patsy exchanged startled glances, and Meredith immediately got up. "Thanks, Claudia. I'll take it over there on the phone by the door."

"All right. I'll just go and put it through."

A few seconds later Meredith was saying, "Hello, this is Mrs. Stratton."

"Mrs. Stratton, good morning. Annette Alexander here, I hope I haven't called too early."

"No, not at all, Mrs. Alexander."

"I thought I'd better ring you immediately. I just received a bit of information that might help you. Do you know, I racked my brains last night, trying to remember the name of the man Kate married, but to no avail. And then it occurred to me that my sister might know who he was. She used to work for me at Place Vendôme at the same time as Kate Sanderson. In any case, I rang her up last night, but she was out. She just got my message and phoned me ten minutes ago. Apparently Kate married a man called Nigel. My sister thinks his last name was Grange or Grainger, and that he was a veterinarian. In Middleham. I know it's a trifle sketchy, but I do hope it helps."

"It does, thank you very much, Mrs. Alexander. While I have you on the phone, perhaps you can tell me something else. Do you recall when Kate Sanderson left Place Vendôme?"

"She left my employ in the early seventies."

"I see. Well, thanks again, Mrs. Alexander."

"I was happy to be of help, and give Kate my best, if you find her."

"I will. Good-bye, Mrs. Alexander." Meredith hung up and returned to the table.

Patsy looked at her questioningly, raising a brow. "Well?"

Meredith took a deep breath, exhaled, then said, "According to Annette Alexander, my mother married a man called Nigel, and his last name was either Grange or Grainger. He is, or was, a vet. And in the early seventies, when my mother left her employment, he was living in Middleham. Or, rather, *they* were."

"Middleham! Good heavens, Meredith, that's right next door practically. It's a small village on the moors, about half an hour from Ripon. You see, I told you I had a sense that your mother was close by."

"We don't know that she is. We don't know what

happened really. And they could have divorced or moved away."

"I'll soon find out if he's still around," Patsy cried assertively, and jumped to her feet. "I'm going to look him up in the local telephone directory. He's bound to be listed if he's the vet in Middleham."

Meredith sat back in her chair and watched Patsy walking across the floor with great determination. Whatever it took, her friend was hell-bent on finding Kate Sanderson. And what a *good* friend Patsy had turned out to be. Meredith knew that she would have been lost without her in the last few days.

Patsy was suddenly back at the table, looking pleased with herself. She sat down, glanced at the paper she was holding, and said, "His name's Grainger, not Grange, and he lives in Middleham. At Tan Beck House. And there's the phone number."

Meredith took the paper and glanced at it, then raised her eyes to meet Patsy's. "Thank you," she said, and looked down at the paper again. "Now that I know she could be only a few miles away, I feel rather strange."

"Do you mean about seeing her?" Patsy asked, her brow furrowing.

"Yes."

"Perhaps you're afraid."

"Do you know, I think I am."

"I'll go with you to Tan Beck House."

"Thank you, but perhaps I should go alone, Patsy."

"Shouldn't you phone her first?"

"I'm not sure. In a way I prefer to see her face-to-face before she knows anything about me. If I phone first, I'll have to start explaining myself."

"You're right. So do it your way."

# CHAPTER TWENTY-FOUR

It was with some trepidation that Meredith walked up the path to the front door of Tan Beck House.

For the past thirty minutes she had been sitting in Patsy's Aston-Martin, trying to gather her courage to go there in search of Kate Sanderson.

Since her apprehension had seemed only to increase the longer she sat, she had, in the end, turned on the ignition and driven back down the road.

As she had alighted from her car a moment earlier she had seen that the lovely old stone house was substantial but not overly large, the kind of house a vet or a doctor or lawyer would live in. It was well kept, with a freshly painted white door, sparkling windows, and pretty lace curtains; an array of spring flowers brought color and life to the beds in the garden on either side of the flagged path.

Now she stood at the front door, her hand on the brass knocker. Her nerves almost failed her. Taking a deep breath, she banged it hard several times and then stood back to wait.

The door was opened almost instantly by a youngish woman with dark hair who was dressed in a gray sweater and matching slacks under a green-striped pinafore.

"Yes, can I help you?" she asked.

"I'm looking for Mrs. Grainger. Mrs. Nigel Grainger. Is she at home?"

The young woman nodded. "Is she expecting you?"

"No, she's not."

"Whom shall I say is calling?"

"I'm Mrs. Stratton. Meredith Stratton. She doesn't know me. I'm a friend of a friend. I was hoping she could help me with something."

"Just a minute," the young woman said, and leaving the door ajar, she hurried across the highly polished floor of the small entrance foyer.

She returned within seconds, opened the door wider, and said, "Mrs. Grainger would like you to come in. She won't be a minute, she's on the phone. She told me to take you to the sitting room."

"Thank you," Meredith said, stepping into the foyer and following the young woman, at the same time glancing around quickly, wanting to see everything.

She noticed a handsome grandfather clock standing in a corner and a collection of blue and white porcelain effectively arranged on an oak console table.

Showing her into the sitting room, the young woman said, "Make yourself at home," and disappeared.

Meredith stood in the middle of the room, thinking how welcoming it was, struck by its warmth and charm. It was of medium size, tastefully decorated, the walls painted red, with bookshelves running floor to ceiling on two of them. The woodwork was a dark cream, hand-painted to resemble faux marble, and there was a dark red and blue Oriental rug in front of the stone fireplace. Between two tall windows an antique desk faced out toward the back garden and a small lawn. Beyond were rolling moors and an endless expanse of blue sky filled with scudding white clouds.

Meredith turned away from the window at the sound of footsteps. She held her breath as she waited for Mrs. Nigel Grainger to open the door.

At the first sight of her Meredith's heart dropped. This was not the beautiful young mother of the red-gold curls and bright blue eyes whom she had worshipped in her childhood dreams.

Mrs. Grainger was a woman in her early sixties, Meredith guessed. She wore beige corduroy pants and a white shirt with a navy-blue blazer, and she looked like a typical country matron.

The woman hesitated in the doorway, looking at Meredith questioningly. "Mrs. Stratton?"

"Yes. And hello, Mrs. Grainger . . . hello. I hope you'll forgive this intrusion, but I came to see you because I'm hoping you can help me."

"I'm not sure how, but I'll try," Mrs. Grainger said, still poised in the doorway. "You're American, aren't you?"

Meredith nodded. "Mrs. Grainger, I'll come straight to the point. I'm looking for a woman called Kate Sanderson. Annette Alexander of Place Vendôme in Harrogate gave me reason to believe that you and she are the same person. Is that so?"

"Why, yes, it is. I'm Katharine Sanderson Grainger, and I used to work at Place Vendôme, years ago, before I was married." Kate frowned, the quizzical expression reflected in her eyes again. "But why are you looking for me?"

Meredith was extremely nervous. She had no idea how to tell Kate who she was and, momentarily, she was at a loss for the right words. Finally she said in a tremulous voice, "It's about . . . about . . . it's about Mari."

Kate Grainger looked as if she had been slapped in the face, and slapped hard. She recoiled, gaped at Meredith, and took hold of the door to steady herself.

Then quickly recovering her equilibrium to some extent, she asked in a tense voice, "What about Mari? What is it you want with me? What do you want to tell me about Mari?"

"I . . . I knew her, Mrs. Grainger."

"You knew my Mari?" Kate cried eagerly, sounding breathless. She took a step forward.

Meredith could see her better now. She noted the vividness of the blue eyes, suddenly filled with tears, the reddish-gold hair, paler than it once was and shot through with silver, recognized that well-loved, familiar face, touched by time but still quite lovely. And she knew with absolute certainty that this *was* her mother. Her heart tightened imperceptibly, and she was seized by an internal shaking. She wanted to go to Kate, put her arms around her, but she did not dare. She was afraid . . . of rejection . . . of not being wanted.

"You knew my Mari," Kate said again. "Tell me about her, oh, please tell me . . . "

Choked up, unable to speak, Meredith simply inclined her head.

"Where? Where did you know my little Mari? Oh please, please tell me, Mrs. Stratton. *Please,*" Kate pleaded.

"In Australia," Meredith answered at last in a strangled voice.

"*Australia.*" Kate sounded outraged, and she drew back, her eyes wide.

"Sydney." Meredith's eyes were riveted on Kate, who was shocked and also puzzled.

"She loved you so much," Meredith said, her voice a whisper.

Kate reached out, grabbed the back of a wing chair. She gripped it tightly to support herself. "You speak of her as if she's . . . you speak of her in the past tense. She's no . . . *dead,* is she?"

"No, she's not."

"Oh, thank God for that," Kate exclaimed, sounding relieved. She went on. "I've prayed for her every day for years and years. Prayed that she was all right, that she was safe. Please, Mrs. Stratton, tell me something. Did she send you to me? Send you to find me?"

"Yes."

"Where is my Mari? Oh, do please tell me." Kate's emotions were very near the surface, her feelings visible on her strained face. Who was this woman bringing news of Mari? News of her beloved child, lost to her for so many years? She began to tremble.

Meredith took a step forward, drew closer to Kate. Kate's heartache was written on her face, and Meredith realized how distraught she was. And also how sincere.

Groping around in her mind, she sought appropriate words to explain to Kate who she was.

Stepping closer to Kate, she looked into her face, and before she could stop herself, she said, "Mam . . . it's me . . . Mari . . ."

Kate could not speak for a moment, and then she exclaimed, "Oh my God! Oh my God, Mari, is it really you?" Kate took hold of Meredith's hand and drew her to the window. "Let me look at you. Is it you, Mari, after all these years?" Reaching out, she touched Meredith's face tenderly with one hand. "Is it really you, love?"

Tears were spilling out of Kate's eyes, trickling down her face. "Oh Mari, Mari, you've come back to me at last. My prayers have been answered."

Meredith was also crying. And the two women, separated for almost forty years, automatically moved into each other's arms, held on to each other tightly.

Kate was sobbing as if her heart would break. "I've waited for this day for over thirty-eight years, prayed for it, begged God for it. I'd given up hope of ever seeing you again."

Mother and daughter stood holding each other for a long time, drawing comfort from each other as they shed their tears of sorrow and joy . . . sorrow for the past, for all those years they had missed together . . . joy that they had been reunited at last, before it was too late.

They sat together on the small sofa in the library, a tray of tea and sandwiches on the coffee table in front of them. But neither of them had touched the sandwiches which the young housekeeper, Nellie, had prepared.

They held hands, kept staring at each other, searching for similarities. And there was a kind of wonderment on their faces. It was the special wonder a mother feels when she sees her newly born child. And in a way, Mari was newly born for Kate that day.

"I never came to terms with my loss," Kate said, her voice soft, echoing with sadness as she remembered all those grim years she had endured without her only child by her side. "I thought of you every day, Mari, wondered about you, yearned for you, longed to hold you in my arms."

Meredith stared deeply into those marvelous eyes. "I know, Mam, I know. It was the same for me always, and when I was very little, especially. I was always wondering about you, wondering why you'd sent me away from you, why you didn't want me. I never did understand that." Meredith brushed the tears away from her eyes. "How did you ... lose me? How did we get separated?"

"It was a terrible thing and it really started with Dr. Barnardo's Home ... do you remember that day when you were five, when you found me passed out on the kitchen floor?"

"Oh yes, I went to fetch Constable O'Shea."

"He'd arranged for an ambulance. I was put in Leeds Infirmary and he took you to the children's home. I never blamed him, he didn't know what else to do, since I didn't have any family. Anyway, I was in hospital for about six weeks. As soon as I was on my feet again, I went and got you, and we were together at Hawthorne Cottage, the way we'd always been. But about a year later, in the spring of 1957, I became ill once more. I took you to Dr. Barnardo's myself this time. I'd nowhere else to put you. Dr. Robertson was worried about me, he wanted me to go into the infirmary for some tests. It was there that they discovered I had tuberculosis. Seemingly it had been dormant for several years. Suddenly it had flared up, fanned no doubt by undernourishment, worry, stress, fatigue, and a run-down condition in general. Tuberculosis is very contagious, it's airborne, and I couldn't be near you, Mari, for your own sake. The doctors at Leeds Infirmary sent me to Seacroft Hospital, near Killingbeck, where I was treated. I was in quarantine for six months." Kate paused, took hold of Meredith's hand, held it tightly, and looked into her eyes. "I sent you messages all the time, Mari. Didn't you get any of them?"

"No." Meredith returned her mother's intense look. "Why didn't you come and get me when you were better?" she asked, a hint of resentment flaring. She pushed it down inside her.

"But I did! As soon as I was released from Seacroft Hospital. I was on the mend, no longer contagious, taking antibiotics. Streptomycin, actually. But you weren't there anymore. The people at Dr. Barnardo's told me you had been adopted. I was in shock. Distraught and angry. And heartbroken. I didn't know how to find you. I had no one to help me, no family, not much money. It was like battering my head against a brick wall. They just wouldn't tell me anything, and there was no way I could get you back."

Kate shook her head sorrowfully, found her handkerchief, and wiped her streaming eyes. "I was utterly powerless, helpless, Mari, and so frustrated. I've never really dispelled my anger, it's still there inside. It's gnawed at me for years. What happened ruined my life. I have never recovered from the loss of you, never really been happy, or had any peace of mind. I've always been haunted, worried about you. My only hope was that one day, when you were grown-up, you might want to meet your biological mother, and that *you'd* try to find *me*."

Meredith, who had again been moved to tears by Kate's words, exclaimed, "But no one adopted me! They lied to you at Dr. Barnardo's. They put me on a boat with a lot of other children and shipped us all to Australia. I was in an orphanage in Sydney."

"An orphanage!" Kate was stunned. She stared at Meredith in horror as the terrible truth dawned on her. "What kind of thinking is that? It was stupidity to send you from an orphanage in England to another one at the far side of the world. And why?" She closed her eyes for a moment, then snapped them open. "They said you'd been adopted by a nice family, that you were living in another city in Britain. It was my only consolation . . . that you were growing up with people who cared about you, loved you, and were good to you. Now you're telling me you were never adopted."

Kate was shaking.

Meredith soothed her, tried to calm her, then explained. "Well, I was adopted, but in Sydney, of course, not in England. When I was eight. But it was only for two years. The Strattons were killed in a car crash when I was ten. They weren't very nice people. Mr. Stratton's sister put me back in the orphanage."

Stiffening on the sofa, grasping Meredith's hand

tighter, Kate said in a fearful voice, "The Strattons didn't hurt you in any way, did they? Abuse you?"

"No, they didn't. But they weren't very loving or kind." Now, staring at Kate in bafflement, Meredith went on. "If you didn't give them permission to send me to Australia, then how could Dr. Barnardo's do that? I mean, they did it without your consent."

"Yes, they did." Kate drew away slightly, and now it was her turn to give Meredith a piercing stare. "All of a sudden you sound as if you think I'm not telling you the truth. But I am, Mari. You must believe that."

"It's not that I doubt you. I just don't understand this whole thing."

"Neither do I. I've never been able to understand it. All these years it's been like living a nightmare." Kate extricated her hand from Meredith's and stood up.

Slowly, she walked across to the desk, opened a drawer, and took out a large envelope. Tapping it, she said, "A few years ago in the late eighties, I read some articles in the *Observer*. And what I read truly frightened me, filled me with horror, not to mention sorrow. The articles were about child migrants being sent alone to Australia and put in homes and institutions. At the time I prayed that you hadn't been one of those children. I suppose I clung to the belief you were living somewhere in England with your adoptive family. Now my worst nightmare has come true." Kate's voice faltered and she was close to tears again. "You *were* one of those children, Mari."

Fighting her tears, Kate paused, and then after a moment she asked in a low voice, "You are telling me the truth, aren't you, Mari? You weren't abused, were you?"

"I promise you I wasn't . . . I *wasn't*, Mam. I was in mental anguish, and I cried myself to sleep for years, missing you so much. It was such a loveless upbringing. And, of course, I had to work hard, we all did, scrubbing floors, doing mountains of washing. And we weren't very well fed. But no, I wasn't physically or sexually abused."

"Just mentally and emotionally," Kate said, anger surfacing again. "Imagine, sending you and other little children twelve thousand miles, all the way across the world just to put you in another institution. It was ludicrous."

Kate walked back to the sofa and sat down, still clutching the envelope. Finally she gave it to Meredith. "The articles were entitled 'Lost Children of the Empire.' I kept them. You can read them later. They'll make your hair stand on end." She shook her head. "No, of course they won't . . . you lived through it . . . lived what the journalist wrote about."

"Why did you keep the articles?"

"I don't know. Later, Granada Television made a documentary about the child migrants. I watched it with growing horror. It left its terrible imprint on me, I've never been free of it."

"So Dr. Barnardo's sent a lot of children to Australia. Hundreds. Is that what you're saying?"

"No, Mari, thousands. Over a hundred and fifty thousand, actually. Probably even more, but it wasn't just Dr. Barnardo's. Many other worthy charities were involved in the child migration schemes."

"Such as?" Meredith asked, staring at Kate questioningly.

"The Salvation Army, the National Children's Home, the Children's Society, the Fairbridge Society, and a variety of other social and welfare agencies operating under the aegis of the Catholic Church, the Church of England, the Presbyterian Church and the Church of Scotland."

"Good God!" Meredith exclaimed, aghast. "It was enormous."

"I'm afraid so," Kate answered. "And a lot of those children, especially the boys, were made to work outside in the blistering sun, doing all manner of chores, bricklaying, building dormitories. And they were often horribly abused—sodomized by the priests. It was a horrendous life for them."

"But *how* could it happen? I mean, why didn't the government intervene?"

"The British government weren't going to do that. They were part of it. And what *they* did to us, to mothers and fathers and children, was unconscionable."

"It was also illegal," Meredith pointed out. "Hasn't anyone thought of suing the British government? I certainly feel like it . . . all those wasted years, all those years of grief."

"I don't know whether anybody sued or not. There

was a huge public outcry after the documentary aired. It revealed a horrendous scandal and pricked the conscience of the nation. People were outraged. The government tried to deny its complicity, but everyone understood there had been collusion."

"But why did the government do it?"

Kate said in a voice of scorn, "What an easy way it was to populate the colonies, sending children to the far-flung corners of the empire. It's been going on for hundreds of years, and small children were still being shipped off as late as 1967."

"How appalling. It's contemptible."

Kate nodded and said, "You'll see a clipping from the *TV Times* in the envelope, announcing the documentary. The magazine listed telephone numbers, helplines. I rang them up, Mari. I was so worried you might be one of those children. I wanted to know how a mother could find a child that had been sent as a migrant. The helpline people told me that wasn't possible, that a mother couldn't find a child. Apparently a parent and child could be reunited only if the child set out to find the long-lost mother or father."

Kate leaned back against the sofa, closed her eyes for a moment. Then, looking at Meredith at last, she said, "You grew up to be a beautiful woman, Mari. You look like my mother. You have her face, her eyes."

Meredith was thrilled to hear this, and a vivid smile flooded her face with radiance. "I don't remember having a grandmother."

"She was already dead when you were born. She was killed in a bombing raid in the Second World War. It was my father who brought me up after he got out of the army. He died when I was seventeen."

"What about my father? Where is he?"

"He's dead too, Mari. He left us when you were about eighteen months old. He went off to Canada with another woman, deserted us. I finally divorced him when Nigel wanted me to marry him."

"Has he made you happy?"

"He's tried very hard, very hard indeed, Mari. But I haven't been easy to live with over the years. My grief for you has always consumed me to a certain extent . . . it's so hard to lose a child, especially the way I lost you. It's not as if you died. I knew you were out there somewhere. I yearned for you . . . yearned to see you, to touch you. My heart was broken. Poor Nigel, he's had a lot to contend with. But he's patient. Long-suffering. He's a good man."

"And you never had another child?"

"Oh no. I was thirty-eight when I married Nigel. Perhaps I should have, maybe it would have helped me, I don't know . . . Nigel was a widower, his wife had been a friend of mine. Veronica. A lovely woman. She died of a brain tumor, and I helped Nigel through that very bad period in his life. Comforted him as best I could. Five years after her death he proposed. I brought up his two sons, Michael and Andrew. And it's been a good marriage in so many ways."

"I'm glad you've had someone nice like Nigel.

I've often wondered . . . how old were you when I was born?"

"Nineteen. I'll be sixty-three this summer, Mari." Kate let out a deep sigh. "All those years without you. How did you find me? Did it take you a long time?"

"No, not really, once I'd started looking. Before I tell you how I *did* locate you, I have another question for you."

"Anything, Mari, ask me anything."

"Did you ever take me to Fountains Abbey?"

"Yes, several times. It's a favorite spot of mine, and it always has been. Coming from Harrogate as I do, I've spent a lot of time in Ripon over the years. But why do you ask?"

"Did anything terrible or upsetting ever happen to me or to us at Fountains?"

"Yes. I started to feel unwell there in the spring of 1957. I'd taken you on a picnic, and I passed out for a while. I know you were very frightened because we were alone. Eventually I came around, and somehow we made it into Ripon and caught the bus back to Harrogate, then another one to Leeds. It was a Sunday. Later that week I was diagnosed as having TB, and I was packed off to Seacroft."

"I never saw you again, did I?"

"No, you didn't."

"That explains it." Meredith recounted her experiences at Fountains, told her about her sense of déjà vu. "No wonder I felt a tragic thing had happened there, had such a sense of loss. Anyway, what that experience did was create something called psychogenic fatigue in me. My physician sent me to a psychiatrist and she and I began to dig into my past. She was convinced I was suffering from repressed memory."

"You mean you repressed your memories of me?"

"No, not exactly. I did remember certain things. But being torn away from you so cruelly, wrenched away from your love and care as a child was so painful to me, I'd blocked everything out. Dr. Benson managed to get me on the right track, but it was my daughter, Catherine, who triggered the most important memory, at least so *I* think."

"You have a daughter and you named her for me?" Kate exclaimed, her face lighting up.

"She's twenty-five and beautiful. She has your eyes. And I think your disposition. I didn't actually know I was naming her after you . . . I spelled her name with a C. But obviously I'd remembered your name was Kate . . . Katharine. It was buried in my subconscious."

"What was the memory she triggered?"

"Just before I left for London last week I went to see her, to discuss plans for her marriage. She made tea, later brought out a dish of strawberries, and she said something to me that brought a memory rushing back. I saw your face very clearly, that face I'd loved all of my life and longed for. And I just knew it was my mother's face I was seeing in my mind." Meredith had begun to weep; she searched for her handkerchief, blew her nose.

Kate's eyes were moist when she asked, "What was it Catherine said?"

"Just a few simple words actually . . . 'I have a treat for you, Mom. *Strawberries.*' Instantly your face was before my eyes and *you* were serving me strawberries. At that moment a variety of other memories came back to me, and I had many more on the plane coming over to London that same night."

Meredith paused, blew her nose again, and continued. "There's something I should explain to you. I'd always believed you were dead. That's what they told me at Dr. Barnardo's. So when the memory of you had fully returned, I confided in my English partner, Patsy Canton. She took me to the General Register Office in London to look for your death certificate. You see, I wanted, *needed,* to visit your grave. I wanted closure for myself at long last. But of course there was no certificate; we knew you must be alive. It was Patsy's idea to look for my birth certificate, since we were seeking as much information as we could. My birth certificate led us to Armley and Hawthorne Cottage. Although it's now a pile of rubble, I did discover how well I knew that spot, and more lovely recollections of you surfaced."

"I'm glad you found me before it was too late," Kate murmured.

"So am I."

Now Kate glanced at Meredith curiously and said softly, "You don't wear a wedding ring. Are you divorced?"

"Yes, I am. You have a grandson, by the way. His

name is Jon and he's twenty-one. He's studying at Yale. I can't wait for you to meet him and Catherine."

*"Grandchildren,"* Kate said wonderingly. "I have grandchildren. How wonderful."

"I'm very proud of them. They've turned out well."

"The one thing you haven't told me is how you got from Australia to America."

"That's a very long story," Meredith responded. "I'll explain everything later. After all, we've got the rest of our lives."

There was the sound of footsteps in the hall, and Meredith swung her head. She saw a tall, distinguished-looking man standing in the doorway observing them.

Kate had also turned around. She jumped up, exclaiming, "Nigel, she's found me. As I always prayed she would. My Mari's found me. She's home to me at last."

"Thank God," he said, walking into the library to join them, a look of immense relief spreading across his face.

Meredith rose, stretched out her hand to him.

He took it. And without any kind of preamble he pulled her into his arms and embraced her. "Now, at last, Kate will have peace of mind," he said.

As they drew apart, Meredith found herself looking into one of the kindest faces she had ever seen.

Nigel Grainger's smile was warm as he gazed at her.

"Thank you," she said. "Thank you for keeping my mother safe for me."

# Epilogue

## *TIME FUTURE*

"Now, ladies, look right at me and smile," Jon said, picking up his camera, peering into the lens. "Not quite right," he muttered. "Mom, move in closer to Grandma. And, Cat, you do the same thing. I want to get a really tight shot."

"Oh, do hurry up, Jon, I want to go and find my lovely new husband!" Cat exclaimed.

After a few minor adjustments, Jon finally began to shoot the roll of film. Within minutes he was exclaiming, "There, all finished, and it wasn't so bad, Cat, was it? Now I have a lovely set of shots for Grandma's album, and for you if you want them. *Three generations of women.* I never dreamed I'd see that day."

Cat offered him a loving smile. "I just know I'm going to like yours better than the professional photographer's pictures."

Grinning, he said, "Go on, scoot. Find that new husband of yours. In a few minutes there's going to be chaos here, once the Pearson clan start swarming all over like locusts."

"Hey, watch what you say," Cat cried, waving her hand at him, displaying her wedding ring. *"I just became a Pearson, remember."* She walked over to kiss him on the cheek and said affectionately, "Thank you for giving me away, Jon."

"Did I do okay, sis?"

"You were terrific." She laughed again and floated off on a cloud of white silk and tulle, heading toward Keith, who stood talking to his father in the entrance hall of the inn.

Jon strolled over to Kate and Meredith. He said, "It was a great ceremony, Mom, and the old barn was really effective as a church. I guess it was the way you decorated it with all that white silk and the banks of white flowers."

"Thanks, darling, and I was pleased myself with the way it turned out."

Kate murmured, "I found the ceremony very moving." She smiled at her daughter and grandson. "I must admit, I cried."

"Most women do cry at weddings, Grandma." Jon squeezed her arm. "And you're the icing on the cake. I'm so glad Mom found you."

"Oh, so am I," Kate answered.

"Well, I'm off to have a drink with the guys," Jon announced, edging away.

"Guys?" Meredith repeated, raising a brow. "Who do you mean?"

"Luc and Nigel. They just came in."

He strolled off, leaving Meredith and Kate near the entrance to the inn's dining room.

Both women looked elegant; Kate was dressed in a dark rose-pink wool suit and Meredith in a smoky-blue dress and coat; standing close together as they were, it was easy to see they were mother and daughter. They bore a strong resemblance to each other, although Meredith was taller.

It was the second Saturday in October, a lovely Indian summer day. The sky was cerulean blue, clear and cloudless, filled with brilliant sunshine, and the foliage at Silver Lake was spectacular. The trees had just turned, were a riotous mass of reds and pinks, russets and golds.

"We couldn't have asked for a better day," Kate said, glancing out of the window, looking down toward the lake. "It's perfect for the wedding."

"We've been lucky, although Connecticut usually is lovely in October." Taking hold of Kate's arm, Meredith ushered her into the dining room, recently enlarged to accommodate the many guests attending the wedding. "Just come in here for a moment, Mother, I want to say something to you."

Kate threw Meredith a concerned look. "Is there something wrong? You sound so serious."

Meredith shook her head. "No, I just wanted to

thank you for being here with me these past two weeks, and for doing so much to help with Cat's wedding. You've been wonderful."

"I should be thanking you, Mari," Kate replied, and made a moue with her mouth. "I'll never be able to call you anything else but Mari, you know."

"That's all right . . . I understand."

"I never thought this would happen," Kate suddenly volunteered. "That I'd be able to spend this precious time with you. You'll never know what it's meant to me."

"Oh, but I think I *do* . . ."

"You've spoilt me, Mari, and Nigel. The trips to Paris and the Loire, as well as New York. All this wonderful traveling, why, we'd hardly been out of Yorkshire until you came back into my life."

Meredith made no comment, she simply touched her mother's arm affectionately. There were moments when she couldn't quite believe that she had found her mother after all these years.

Kate glanced out of the window again, her face thoughtful when she finally turned back to Meredith. "I'm glad you found your way here to Silver Lake those many years ago. It's such a beautiful spot, so like Yorkshire. You must have had a guardian angel watching over you."

"Perhaps I did."

"Yes, you were lucky to find Amelia and Jack, to have them in your life, if only for those few brief years. They made up for your earlier heartbreak, Mari, that loveless upbringing at the orphanage in

Australia. You had love and kindness and caring from them, and I will be forever thankful for that. They helped to make you what you are today."

"Who knows what I would have been like if I hadn't met them. A terrible mess, probably."

"Maybe not, we'll never know. But I think there's something special in *you* . . . a will to endure, to succeed no matter what."

Meredith leaned into Kate, kissed her on the cheek. "I love you, Mother."

"And I love you too, Mari."

The two women walked back through the dining room, their arms linked. Just before they reached the door, Kate said, "It's going to be wrenching, leaving you. I wish I didn't live so far away."

Meredith was silent.

Kate looked at her swiftly and added, "I know you said I can visit anytime. But I can't very well keep leaving Nigel alone. And he can't always come with me, Mari, because of his practice."

Meredith said, "As it turns out, I'm not going to be so far away after all."

*"Oh?"*

Meredith peered across the entrance hall of the inn, now crowded with people. The reception was in full swing. A small smile flitted across her mouth.

Kate noticed this, followed the direction of her daughter's gaze, then swiveled her eyes back to Meredith.

"I'm going to marry him, Mother," Meredith said,

her gaze still resting on Luc. "And so I'll be living in Paris. Only a couple of hours from Yorkshire."

"Oh darling, I'm so happy for you. Congratulations!" Kate exclaimed. There was a brief pause before she said worriedly, "But what about your business here? It means so much to you."

"There's only Silver Lake Inn left, now that I've sold the one in Vermont. Blanche and Pete have been running this place for years, and doing such a good job of it. They'll continue. I've enough to keep me busy with the inns in England and France."

"It's good that you've been able to work it out. Luc's such a wonderful man."

"He's had his share of heartbreak too. I think we both deserve a break, a bit of happiness—" Meredith broke off as Luc walked over to join them.

Putting his arm around Kate, he looked down at her and said, "Ever since we met in June, I had a feeling I knew you, Kate. Suddenly, a moment ago, I realized why. You remind me of the woman who brought me up, my grandmother."

Grandma Rose, of course, Meredith thought, recalling the painting at Talcy. They had the same coloring, the same blue eyes, the same heart-shaped face.

"How lovely," Kate murmured, then continued. "I understand congratulations are in order. I'm so happy the two of you are getting married."

Luc beamed at her. "Ah, so Meredith told you the good news."

Kate nodded, excused herself, wanting to leave

them alone. She walked across the room lightly, as if floating on air, went in search of her husband. She was so happy, so proud. Who would have thought that her little Mari would turn out to be such a remarkable woman.

Luc took hold of Meredith's hand, stared deeply into her smoky-green eyes. "You know, *chérie,* you look so very serene today. It lifts my heart to see you so happy. From the moment I met you, I wanted to erase the sadness from your eyes, dispel the pain I knew lurked deep within you. But now I don't have to . . . I believe finding your mother has done that."

Meredith did not answer for a moment or two. She simply returned his penetrating gaze; then finally she said, "It was finding *both* of you, Luc. You and she make me feel complete, whole."

Luc smiled at her. "That's because we love you."

He tucked her arm through his, and together they moved forward into the throng of wedding guests.

# HarperAudio
# BOOKS ON TAPE

**Why not listen to a Barbara Taylor Bradford novel on cassette?**

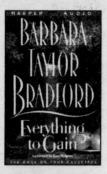

**EVERYTHING
TO GAIN**
–
**Read by Kate Mulgrew**

**LOVE IN
ANOTHER TOWN**
–
**Read By Lisa Banes**

**DANGEROUS
TO KNOW**
–
**Read by Patricia Clarkson**

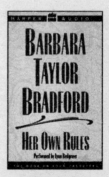

**HER OWN
RULES**
–
**Read by Lynn Redgrave**